D1681007

◇

Chaton Coin Press

◇

STATE OF HORROR

LOUISIANA

VOLUME II

State of Horror Anthology Series

State of Horror: New Jersey

State of Horror: Illinois

State of Horror: North Carolina

State of Horror: Louisiana Volume I

State of Horror: Louisiana Volume II

STATE OF HORROR

LOUISIANA

VOLUME II

-Edited by-
Jerry E. Benns

CHARON COIN
PRESS

PO Box 478 High Ridge, Missouri 63049

Published by Charon Coin Press

Charon Coin Press
PO Box 478
High Ridge, MO 63049
www.charoncoinpress.com

Library of Congress Control Number: 2015935628
ISBN-13: 978-0692406724
ISBN-10: 0692406727

Printed in the United States of America

◇
Charon Coin Press
◇

"Laissez les bons temps rouler!"

◊
Charon Coin Press
◊

TABLE OF CONTENTS

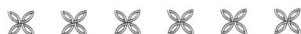

◇
Charon Coin Press
◇

ACKNOWLEDGMENTS

State of Horror: Louisiana has become such a forceful gathering, almost a force of nature in itself, rivaling even the best hurricane parties. What started out as a re-release received so much support from the authors who submitted, it was difficult to contain it in one book. What does one do with an overflow of great tales? This is what contributed to the book in your hands as *State of Horror: Louisiana Volume II*. As we put the book together, I reflected on the importance of the authors' support and talents. I hope you join us in thanking the authors from the previous release who had enough faith to continue with the series and the new authors whose appearances added greatly to the collection of stories. Our thanks go out to all the authors for submitting and making the project enjoyable.

When asked how I do everything, my answer is simple—I don't. Putting the books together is not an individual effort, but that of a team who comes together to create the product you now hold in your hands. I would like to take a moment to thank those who make this all possible. From the amazing cover illustration created once again by Natasha Alterici to the additional promotion assistance by Susan R., we are building a process to bring these projects to life. Thanks to Laura W. for doing what she loves to do, reading and lending her insight into the process.

I have mentioned before how important my dear friend and colleague, Margie C. is to me and this project, but it bears mentioning again how these books would not be possible without her help. Her enthusiasm is a driving force and her efforts can be seen throughout.

I asked myself how I could truly put in words how

much I appreciate all that the next person does to make things happen. Words cannot express fully the level of gratitude I have for my wife, Christine. I would like to thank her for her help with the book and with life in general. As we put this project together, her help kept my world moving forward throughout all the challenges. Thank you for all you do.

Last, but not least, all of us at Charon Coin Press, and the authors from this book, would like to thank you, the reader. Without your love for reading and choice of this book to read, we would not be able to make this happen. It is with our warmest gratitude that we present to you *State of Horror: Louisiana Volume II.*

Jerry E. Benns

◇

Charon Coin Press

◇

◇

Charon Coin Press

◇

INTRODUCTION

The corner of my mouth turns up as I watch a couple looking around in amazement at the lights up ahead. This must be their first time visiting. The rain earlier today washed some of the dust off the sidewalk, leaving puddles in the cobblestones. Caution is required to keep shoes from getting wet. It is early and walking around with soggy socks is no way to spend the evening. Zydeco music can be heard from the corner on the left, and a blues tune from a doorway on the right. The sounds blend with the voices from the pedestrians wandering down the middle of the street. Up ahead, a group of twenty-something men lean over one of the many galleries, calling out to a passing group of like-aged women. The smell of seafood floats from a window in passing as the cook steps out to get some air—a nod and smile is met with the like as eye contact is made. Taking the final steps to the corner, a sense of familiarity embraces me as the sounds of Rue de Bourbon herald me back. The question becomes where to explore today? With a smile, a glance to my right, I step onto the street and head down river toward Café Lafitte's. Welcome to New Orleans and welcome to Louisiana.

Before we explore this stop on the tour, let's look at the history which brought us here. *State of Horror: Louisiana* was originally released in April 2011, and included eight stories. The overwhelming response by authors, as well as the quality stories submitted, left me at in a dilemma—how to decide which to keep. The answer became simple—expand the books into two volumes. I went back through the stories with a new goal to seek out the stories that captured the culture, the history, and the feeling I so enjoy from Louisiana. This book is just half of the journey on our tour of *State of Horror: Louisiana* with the updated stories from previous authors of the initial 2011 release: Teresa Bergen, B.A. Sans, Edward Moore, and Jonathan S. Pembroke. Joining them are eight authors with new tales to tell and another visit to the *Dying Days* world by Armand Rosamilia. Overall, these thirteen stories are a great way to continue our Louisiana tour.

As I have mentioned, I enjoy visiting the state of Louisiana. I may have lost count the number of times I travelled down river from my home in St. Louis to the streets of New Orleans. Recently, I explored a little culture outside the city streets, venturing out into the delta. My explorations took me to the traditional plantation homes as I learned more about the history and culture of centuries past. I spent some hours hearing stories of the bayou from our guide, and exploring the Cajun culture and history. The bayous are full of mysteries, folklore, and danger.

While reading the stories selected for this book, I could feel some of the history and lore I had discovered, resonating throughout. This is what we seek on our tours with *State of Horror*. The stories will visit the bayou, the small towns, major cities, and the streets of New Orleans. Historical figures make appearances as well as historical sites. The stories are each unique in their tales, but connected through the pulse of the state of Louisiana. You can feel the culture and geography throughout. If you have not visited Louisiana, I suggest you do. Until then, explore it with us in these pages. It is time for you begin the tour, it is time to explore *State of Horror: Louisiana Volume II*.

Laissez les bons temps roulez, my friend.

Jerry Benns
State of Horror; Editor

◇
Charon Coin Press
◇

GATOR BAIT

by Stuart Conover

"Why are we going on this boat again?" Frank asked for the fifth time while slapping his big meaty hand against his arm, trying to kill one of the swarms of flies which seemed to be circling him.

"No one twisted your arm to come buddy," Cliff said through the smile plastered on his face as Beth's hand kept caressing his leg and sneaking up his inner thigh.

"'Sides," Beth slurred out, "It's not like you were trying to take any of the girls at that bar back to our room while we were gone."

She laughed at Frank's annoyance, too buzzed to care if she was teasing him too much before leaning back into Cliff, her dyed black hair just shading her eyes from the sun.

"It's going to be dark in a little bit is all and I just don't see the point of this touristy crap," he muttered, "None of them were my type anyway."

"The point is that you fine folks left the CBD for adventures in the bayou with Big Amos," their tour guide cut in, "and I plan to show you some sights. You'll see voodoo shacks, gators, and so much more before darkness falls. We'll end things with what will be the closest thing to a homemade meal you folks have probably had in years."

Every time Amos, spoke Beth couldn't help but giggle at his overly thick accent which Frank was pretty sure was more for show than how anyone in the area actually spoke. Another thing he was sure about was Amos didn't mind the laughter as his eyes were firmly attached to the curves that were just exposed from the low-cut tank top Beth was wearing. Whenever she moved, Amos' eyes moved with her.

If she had been slightly more sober, Beth would probably be uncomfortable with the attention, but right now she hadn't seemed to notice it. Either that or she just didn't care.

The boat lazily drifted down the bayou, the current barely moving them. It was all part of the experience according to their guide. Cynically, Frank just assumed there wasn't enough to see for them to be going faster. With his two friends getting a little overly cozy, all Frank wanted to experience was some cell phone reception as he checked his phone again for signal.

Even with his woman teasing the hell out of him, Cliff wasn't selfish enough to not notice that his best friend hated every minute of being here. Caring might not be at the top of his list at the moment but he couldn't just ignore it.

"Hold on a min babe," he whispered as he gave her hand a quick squeeze so she'd stop with her own squeezing.

Reaching into his backpack, Cliff pulled out three bottles.

"We've got to drink em while they're cold Franky," he said as he passed the first bottle to his friend who gave him a grateful look.

"I'm okay lover," Beth lazily slurred out while seemingly half asleep against him.

"I'll happily take that extra brew off your hands," interrupted Amos who for the first time wasn't staring at the water or Beth's exposed flesh. There was a look of hunger in his eyes as he continued, "I'd like to have a sip of something before the bend ahead and this water isn't cutting it."

"What's around the bend?" Cliff asked and sighed while untangling himself from the half-asleep, horny girl at his side.

"Hey!" she protested, playfully slapping his ass while he leaned forward to pass the beer to their guide.

The men all casually sipped their brews while Beth tried to sit up straight and actually look around for the first time as Cliff lowered himself back into the seat next to her.

"Well I'll tell you what's around the bend in just a moment here," Amos paused to chug down most of his drink.

Cliff grunted as he sat and briefly wondered if this excursion had been a bad idea. Not that he would say it out loud because to do that would be to admit that Frank was right. He'd be hearing about that the rest of the trip if not longer, if he admitted that.

They came to the bend and the boat seemed to shake to its very core as it made the turn.

"Now you fine folks might not believe in voodoo or the Gods they believe in, but these folk here do and they worship a mean fellah named Bacalou." Big Amos made the sign of the cross as he said the name. "You don't want to play around with those who pray to that one. It doesn't matter if you believe in their voodoo, they do."

As they approached the small outcropping made up of little more than shacks, they could see 15 to 20 people around a large fire with a giant alligator being cooked on a spit."

"It's like a pig roast!" Beth explained excitedly, "Do they wrap gator meat around everything like we use bacon?"

As the boat neared the group of people on the shore, it sped up because those people furthest from the flames noticed the boat and started running after them shouting something. As the engine sped up it got louder and no one could make out what they were yelling, though Frank thought he heard one of them say "attakapa".

Whatever that meant.

"No mon'cher" Amos said nervously, never taking his eyes off the crowd who were still staring at the boat from the shore behind them. "We use bacon too, only out here ours is a little wilder, as we use hogs."

"What was their deal?" Frank asked as the crowd faded into the distance behind them.

"Voodoo might be accepted here but anyone not a believer still looks on with a laugh. Look at the backwards folk," there was a hint of annoyance in Big Amos' voice, "Those people though, follow the dark path. The evil path. Even the other voodoo priests spit in their direction. Power ain't worth the price of your soul and they've all sold theirs. They hate everyone as much as they are hated."

"Power?" Cliff snorted, "They live in shacks in a swamp, that's not power."

Amos didn't respond to that and stared ahead of them.

Cliff finished his bottle and Beth took it from him and threw it over the side.

"Don't you folks be messing up the bayou like that." Amos snapped angrily.

"I bet our guide lives in one of those voodoo shacks," Beth whispered far too loudly.

They sped forward for another ten minutes in quiet before Amos cut the engine. As they slowly drifted forward, he pointed off of the boat's front left side.

"Do you see that big upturned tree?" he asked.

They did. It was the only thing that stood out from the shoreline since they left the supposed voodoo worshippers behind.

"On the other side of it will be an inland area which usually harbors a family of gators."

For all of his complaints, Frank suddenly had his phone out and was preparing to take a picture with it. Cliff smirked as he dug out his own camera from his backpack before pausing and pulling out another beer for himself. Who didn't want to post a few pics of alligators online?

As they came around the tree Beth let out a whine. There was nothing there.

"Sorry folks," Amos said almost sheepishly, "I guess they must be out hunting."

"Or being turned into voodoo dinner" said Frank.

"That was a much larger gator, boy," Amos sucked in a breath, "Ones that size live alone."

"What a great tour guide," Beth whispered before breaking into a fit of giggles.

"You clearly don't need a personality test to become a licensed tour guide here," he whispered back.

The boat kicked its engines back on and they rode in silence for a few minutes before Amos spoke up again.

"OK I know there were no gators at the last spot but there are always a few in the area coming up," he said with a fake, far-too-friendly tone to his voice, "also there are no licensed tour guides on this boat ma'am."

"I kind of want to see some alligators," Frank responded while Beth had the decency to blush from having been overheard.

Cliff just laughed.

"When the engine is off, whispers can carry on the

water," Big Amos went on, "It might be best to remember your manners when other people can hear you."

That fake friendliness was still in his voice but Cliff suddenly felt uncomfortable as a shiver somehow ran up his spine, even with the heat.

Feeling apprehensive, he cracked open the second beer he had taken out and took a long swig. The sooner this tour was over the better as far as he was concerned. Nothing quite like pissing off the only person who could get you home while in the middle of nowhere.

"Wait, what did he mean when he said he wasn't licensed?" Beth asked.

"They revoked everyone's licenses running tours in this bayou," Amos grunted out.

"I knew we could get a cheap tour here without other boats obstructing our view since it was technically off limits" said Cliff nonchalantly.

"Can we get in trouble for this?" She paused and stared at their guide, "Wait, why were they revoked?"

A bellow of a laugh followed as Big Amos cut the throttle and the entire area quieted as if the bayou itself waited for his response.

"Well girly," he said in what was now a very lecherous southern drawl, "The official report says a group of college tourists about your age got drunk, took a tour, and fell into the water to become gator chow."

He paused, enjoying the shock on their faces and didn't care if it was from the story or the venom oozing out of his voice.

"It was a group of three uppity young children about your age who were so self-absorbed they didn't even realize what was happening to them until it was too late. Too busy with their snide little comments thinking no one would realize that they were being made fun of until..." Big Amos suddenly stopped and trailed off starting the boat forward again.

"Until?" Beth whispered.

"Until they fell into the water with the gators," he quickly responded, "Just like I told you."

Beth took what was left of Cliff's beer and drained it before pushing herself under his arm. Careful not to throw the empty beer bottle out of the boat, she lowered it to the floor by her feet.

A few minutes later they started slowing down again and Big Amos spoke with the fake enthusiasm having dropped from his voice.

"On your left you'll actually see some gators this time." He brought the boat to a stop. "I wouldn't get too close to the edge—you wouldn't want to fall in."

All three of the friends wearily looked up at the guide then started looking at the gators trying to get a shot of them with their cameras. The excitement in the air which buzzing around them at the first stop was not drained away. The two gators seemed to be lazily laying in the sun in shallow water without a care in the world.

"These should look good online," Frank muttered, "Once we get signal again to post them that is."

"You won't be getting any reception until about five minutes from where we launched," interrupted Amos.

"We were trying to have a conversation here" Beth spat out, the beer giving her anger a brief round of liquid courage.

"Well Girly, your mouth is being lippy while I'm just trying to help your friend," he snapped back.

"Beth, quit provoking our guide," Cliff yelled and before she could respond turned to Amos, "And you. Do your goddamn job and guide us. Drop the holier-than-thou attitude too if you want to get paid when we're done here."

Everyone quieted down; they were all taken aback by Cliff's outburst. His friends from barely ever seeing him angry and Amos because he didn't think the young man had it in him.

"There's another one," Frank said, breaking the silence and pointing to where another alligator had surfaced near the boat. "They seem pretty used to being near people."

The third alligator seemed to appear out of nowhere and was sluggishly moving toward the boat. As the sun was starting to set, only the top of its head was visible and the rest just a shadow below the water.

"I come by here often and they usually get a free meal when I do" replied Amos. "You folks want to watch them a bit more or head out? I could toss them some food if you want to see them really move, right now is usually their quiet time unless they get to eating on something."

"Hun?" Cliff asked, the anger having drained from his voice.

"Whatever." Beth responded, still staring at the gators but crossing her arms, refusing to acknowledge him.

"Yeah man, let's see how they eat," Frank responded with a huge grin on his face, "This is going to be so awesome."

Amos popped open the seat behind him and pulled out a cooler. Inside looked to be various slabs of meat.

"So when these guys start getting fed you're gonna want to watch out, they get a might bit vicious."

He threw a piece in and the closest gator leapt toward it with a speed that would be hard to imagine possible just a moment before.

The other two who had been sunning themselves suddenly perked up and one of them pushed off into the water.

"Now those two over there are probably a family with

how close they were to one another," Amos continued, "But this first one I fed is a bit too large to play well with others so I imagine they won't want to get too close to him."

He threw a chunk of meat between the two slightly closer to the smaller one that had just jumped in. The larger gator watched as the smaller one immediately put on a burst of speed and snapped its jaws around the prize.

"But I can change that; if they get too close together things can get real interesting."

Another piece of meat tossed in, this one closer to the first gator he had fed and it pushed up above the water and for the first time they had a chance to see how big it really was as its entire body surfaced for a moment.

The smallest of the three now joined its family and they watched as the larger gator took the meat it had just been given. The movement could only be described as graceful after the last piece that had been thrown in. They were slowly getting closer.

"Now if I were to drop the food directly in between them it would start all kinds of a ruckus" Amos said as he went to throw another piece of meat.

"I don't want to see them fight" squealed Beth as he hurled what was in his hands through the air.

Instead of looking away though, she watched as it landed, unable to tear her eyes away. Fortunately for her it was directly in front of the smallest who grabbed at and wolfed it down.

"Now now children. I wouldn't set the gators on one another. That's just unsportsmanlike. Beside, there's plenty of meat for them to enjoy right here."

Frank looked back at their guide and saw that the man was once again staring directly at Beth and not really paying attention to anyone else there. Frank was disgusted the man was so clearly just drooling over her and neither she nor Cliff was seeing it. He felt as if he should say something when suddenly Amos looked up at him and his eyebrows rose as a smile slowly spread across his face.

"Would any of you want to feed the gators? That's a treat you won't get on any of the licensed tours you mentioned earlier."

Beth quickly lost the attention she had so heavily focused on the gators just a moment before and remembered to look angry while Cliff shrugged. Frank though, he was all over that idea.

"If we're here anyway we might as well get our money's worth guys." Not really caring what his friends thought, he reached back to grab some of the meat. "Hey what am I feeding them anyway?"

"Oh, just a little special treat I like to mix up for them." Amos handed a big chunk over to him, "Just be sure to throw it to the far side of either one of them, they're all too close together already."

Frank looked down at the slab of meat in his hands, still not sure what it was and brought his gaze up to the creatures before him. These were some of the coolest things on the planet and he was going to get to feed one. He brought his arm back and tried to decide who should get the food before throwing it in the air.

It looked to land directly in front of the largest of the beasts, but at the last moment the gator curled its body and caught it midair.

"Oh my God, did any of you get that?" He looked over to his friends who seemed to be intently ignoring one another and everything else about them, "Oh come on guys, tell me one of you two were recording that."

He quickly turned back to Amos, all of his annoyance replaced with the excitement of what he'd just done.

"Can I throw another piece in?"

"Frank" Beth said, exasperated and clearly wanting to leave.

"Are you sure neither of your friends would like to do the honors?" Amos asked, hissing out the word friends.

"Cliff?"

"No buddy, you go ahead and do it."

"Can you film it man? If that happens again I'd love to have it on video!"

"Sure thing, but I'll need your camera, the video on mine sucks."

"Yeah sure!" Frank started to reach into his pocket before he realized his hands were covered in gore from the meat. "Um, do you have a towel or anything?"

Amos looked on amused, "You're wearing jeans. Use 'em."

Sighing, Frank reached down with the cleaner of his two hands slowly wiping it off on his jeans, which cost far too much, and he wasn't even sure if he would be able to clean the stain out. Still, his hand was clean now and he took out his cell and passed it over to Cliff.

"Maybe you could stand behind a little and get an action shot?"

Cliff groaned but went to humor his friend.

As he threw the meat out the gator again did a partial roll to get the food and Frank was clearly ecstatic.

"Did you get it? That was awesome!"

"Oh yeah I got it. I also got you doing a happy dance right after which is so getting shared to all of our friends."

Frank reached for his phone, "Not funny dude."

"OK folks, playtime is over. There's one more stop I like to make before we head back."

"You mean we're not going back yet?" Beth whined.

"I suppose we can if everyone really wants to."

"What's the last stop?" Cliff asked, agreeing with Frank's earlier statement that they really had not gotten even a fraction of their money's worth.

"It's an old abandoned shotgun house the voodoo priests used to live in a little further into the swamp."

"Why did they move?" Frank asked.

"Guys, who cares? It's just an empty house. How is that going to matter from the boat? Let's just go back to the city, get some real food, and go back to drinking." Beth clearly wasn't having any of it.

"What do you two say?" completely ignoring Beth's plea to leave, "I usually dock there and let everyone get a good look around before I show them where they used to perform their rites."

"Do they have any old voodoo stuff there still?" asked Frank, while watching the video of the gator being fed.

"Well they've got symbols on the walls and there's a huge fire-pit full of ash they used like the one they were cooking that gator with earlier," Amos paused, "It's where they supposedly performed their sacrifices. Human sacrifices."

"Yup. We're not going. Let's go home." Beth turned toward Cliff for the first time since he yelled at her, "Back me up here."

"I don't know; I kind of want to see what's over there. Just a few gators and some crazy people yelling at us doesn't seem like enough for what we're paying for it. Let's go see where the crazy people used to live."

"They aren't crazy, they just don't…" Their guide was angry again, "Why do you people have to call what you don't understand crazy?"

He turned to look directly at Beth and for the first time without an ounce of hunger in his eyes, "Looks like your boyfriend and friend want to go, why don't you be a lady and suck it up for them. It'll only take a couple of minutes to get there."

"Amos." The warning tone in Cliff's voice was making it obvious he was stepping over a line.

"Fine." Amos barked out, "Sorry. It's just down a little ways and they want to see it. We can go back though if that's what you want."

Beth was tense and took a deep breath before responding.

"No. We can go. Everyone else clearly wants to, but right after, we're going back."

"Sure, I'll put you right where you belong once we're done in the house."

He hadn't exaggerated that they were only a few minutes away. It was hidden in the trees and without a guide knowing where to look, it could have quite easily been missed. They pulled onto land and everyone jumped out of the boat with Amos tossing an anchor over the side before following them.

"So imagine this whole area crawling with those voodoo worshippers I showed you earlier. They had over twice as many back in the days they lived here and had to eventually leave."

"What made them leave?" interrupted Frank.

"Well, I was getting to that." Sighing, "They had a plague come through, a pox on their people. The other believers said it was sent by their Gods, but the people in town claimed it was from malnutrition. Whatever the reason, it wiped a good amount of them out and they mostly relocated."

"Mostly?" asked Frank.

"A few of them stayed behind but," he waved to the rooms around them, "clearly no one made it."

The four went inside and slowly started looking

through the house. The rooms were small but there were a lot of them. Some of them still had the remnants of what their former owners had left, however most had been pretty cleared out.

"As you can tell they didn't have much. No electricity, no running water, these people lived right off the land." Amos walked them through the various rooms as the waning light filtered through holes in the walls. "They had a living area, the rooms each housed a family, and then a few makeshift one-room buildings out back, but we won't be going through those."

"Why not?" asked Cliff

"Well those sometimes have animals and who knows what is in them, so I prefer to avoid them. Why don't you three look around and I'm going to go grab some water from the boat."

The second he was gone, Beth spoke up.

"Let's go check out the shacks out back."

"Are you crazy? He just said there could be wild animals in them" said Frank.

"I don't care, you guys wanted to come here in the first place and I want to check out the back so let's go."

She turned to leave with or without them so Frank and Cliff looked at one another, shrugged, and set out after her. They hurried to try to check them out before Amos was any the wiser.

There was a grouping of six of the shacks in the back. They opened the door to the first one and it looked completely empty. When they opened the door to the second though, they all stopped.

Someone had been living here.

When it was clear whoever it was, wasn't home, Beth quickly walked in.

"There is a picture of Amos in here guys, he's younger

but it's him." She laughed, "I told you earlier he lived in a shack!"

"You shouldn't have come back here!" Amos yelled from behind them.

As they turned, they could see he had bottled water in one hand and a machete in the other. "You should have stayed in the house." He raised the machete above his head, "I told you not to come back here!"

Frank put up his arms in a sign of surrender, "Whoa man, we didn't mean anything by it, no one knew that you liv…"

He stopped mid-sentence and jumped back to avoid the blade suddenly being swung at his face.

"You have no respect for other people's privacy. No respect for listening to your elders!"

He swung again and Cliff went to tackle Amos while Frank stood frozen.

The blade was coming down full force as Cliff pushed the psycho to the ground. This was not what he had bargained for.

"Guys help me hold him down." Cliff yelled but at that moment Beth screamed. Turning back it was quickly obvious the blade wasn't still in Amos' hand.

"No." He cried. "Oh no. No no no. Frank. No."

He stood up and ran toward his friend but there was nothing he could do. Frank fell to his knees and before Cliff could get to him he fell, face forward as the machete embedded in his forehead pushed him to the side.

Full of rage, he turned back just in time to get sucker punched and the world went black around him.

When Beth saw Cliff fall she stopped screaming and ran toward the boat. She didn't know what else to do but run. Frank was down and probably dead, she had to run. Cliff was down on the ground unconscious, she had to run.

There wasn't anything she could do but run and Big Amos was right on her heals.

She jumped into the boat and tried to hit the gas like she'd seen in the movies and nothing happened. She looked around and Amos who was standing on the shore right next to the boat and held up his hand.

"Looking for this, Girly?" he asked, as the key for the boat dangled from his fingers. "You know I've been watching you all day."

Slowly he walked toward the boat. As she watched him approach, she inched backward, each step taking her closer toward the front where they had been all day.

"You're a special kind of lean meat. When you aren't drinking you probably spend all day working out don't you? Yeah. I know your type."

"Why are you doing this?" she begged as he boarded the boat.

"Why am I doing this? Why are you doing this? I told you to behave. I told you to watch that mouth of yours. I told you to not go by the huts. All day long I told you what to do and you wouldn't listen would you? Why am I doing this? This is your fault."

He was moving closer and when he was just a foot away she dropped down and reached behind her. The beer bottle she hadn't thrown over was still there and as he leaped toward her she brought it up against the side of his face.

He screamed and just as quickly as it had begun it was all over.

Later that night the boat slowly made its way back the way it had come. Left in its wake were three dead and one wounded. As it slowly came to the downed log where the gators were supposed to be, the boat came to a stop. Barely visible in the middle of the night they lay against the log and waited. A minute later two splashes could be heard, one in front of each of the majestic creatures.

"I've got something special for you tonight," called out Amos, "Some real tender meat, freshly cooked and right off the bone."

COUSEUSE
by Herika R. Raymer

Karyl Barton found what she was looking for.

She pulled into the gated self-storage area, quickly found a parking spot, and exited the van—glad for the respite. Normally she loved shopping during these storage sales, especially when it was for her job, but when on assignment with PJ and Ruth what should've been a joy had become a chore. PJ's nagging, in her unnecessarily loud voice, coupled with Ruth's nauseating sycophancy had soured the usually pleasant drive. Escaping from the harpies who refused to join a 'scavenger hunt' rather than 'shopping at a proper store', she quickly lost herself amidst the various items offered at the storage auction. She wanted to find something good enough to impress Mrs. Barber, owner of The Fashion Factory where she worked. It was a unique specialty dress shop which provided costumes in addition to the usual fare of cocktail dresses, formal dresses, ball gowns, and evening gowns. Now, with Mardi Gras drawing near, it was time to decorate the shop and Mrs. Barber preferred to have different displays every year. She was a fan of anything seamstress-oriented, and the employee who could bring something not only aesthetically appealing, but also was able to help with the annual costume work load, received a bonus. Unfortunately, nothing looked appealing. Dreading returning to the car where her annoying co-workers waited, she continued her search. She became disheartened when it looked as though she wasn't going to find anything suitable.

Then she saw it.

It was a storage unit just being opened for the event. The auctioneers were emptying out an older unit, judging from the dust and rust spots on the doors. They were struggling with something in the back. She took a peek in to see, and gasped.

It was a dusty, cobweb-covered Victorian Couseuse. She recognized it from photos kept on the walls at work. From the moldy smell of the unit, it had probably been in storage for some time. A shame, but maybe she could clean it up. The sides were closed, so she had no idea what the metal inside looked like—probably rusted like the walls here. Still, it didn't have to be open. If she were able to get it to look presentable, she was sure Mrs. Barber would be pleased.

"How much?" she asked.

The men looked over at her, a little incredulous. "For this?" one asked.

She nodded.

As another rubbed his chin, she noticed a faint odor. It was something burning, or burnt. She was about to mention it when the man hurriedly gave a quote. "$50."

She opened her mouth to haggle, and then realized what the man had said. Did he even know what he had? Best to not mention anything. "Sold."

Astonished at her luck, Karyl guided the men to the van. She noticed they handled the machine as though it were fragile and was grateful she didn't have to ask them to be careful. Once at the van, they were called back to the storage unit. They hesitated since the machine still had to be loaded. When she assured them she could get the

Couseuse in the van with the help of her coworkers, they left in a hurry. PJ and Ruth heard her just as she was opening up the back.

"Girl! What're you doing?!" PJ exploded as the two women exited the vehicle, slamming the door behind her.

"Just help me get this into the van. The men got it here and all we have to do is..."

"You can't be serious!" PJ went on. "We were given perfectly good money to spend on shopping, not salvaging!"

She bit back a snide remark. "This is a good place to find great floor items without breaking the budget," Karyl pointed out in a strained voice. "I just need to..."

"This is ridiculous!" PJ raged on. "You had us sweltering out here while you found some trash to dress up? Take that back immediately and get us to a proper store!"

"Look!" Karyl finally snapped. As she saw the sneer on the other's face, she quickly regained control. "We're all hot and want to be back in the store, where it's cool. So I'll make a deal, I will pay for this. I will reimburse the money in the shop fund and you can use it to find something you like. Okay?"

PJ seemed to be in a bind. As assistant manager, she had obviously hoped Karyl would be insubordinate and then she could complain to the store manager, Carmen, with Ruth as a witness. Instead, Karyl was tempting her. The opportunity to get something flashy and expensive proved too much and PJ acquiesced.

"Great!" she smiled. "Can you lend me a hand?"

"Do I look like a furniture mover?" the other snarled. That was a short truce.

Ruth, at least, grabbed the other end of the vintage sewing machine and helped her heft the machine up. They managed to get the lip into the van when Ruth yelped and almost dropped her end. Quickly, PJ moved forward to catch it and pushed it into the van. As it settled she hollered as well. Karyl looked at them to see what was wrong, but could swear she smelled something burning again. She turned her attention to her coworkers, who were cradling their hands.

"Bitch!" PJ yelled. "You did that on purpose! If I get an infection you're gonna pay my bills!"

Sighing, she reached into the van, pulled out her travel first aid kit, and tended to the wounds. Expecting to see burns, she was relieved to find splinters. "I seriously doubt you are going to get an infection from a splinter."

"You don't know that!" the other snarled. "Look how old that thing is!"

"Time to go," she went on after tending to the injuries and ignoring PJ. "You still have your selection to make."

Distracted, the two women got back in the van and they were off. The smell of smoke lingered. Karyl kept expecting someone to mention it, but no one did.

◊ ◊ ◊ ◊

They returned to The Fashion Factory late that afternoon. The Fashion Factory was located a few blocks from the Pecanland Mall and prided itself on being the specialty dress store in Monroe, Louisiana whose main attraction was the employees were certified seamstresses. In general, it was a great place to work, with three exceptions.

Her overbearing coworkers could not wait to show Carmen their purchase and practically flew out of the van. After yanking their purchase from the back, they left Karyl to tend to the Couseuse alone. Thankfully, Maggie came out to help. She saw the vintage sewing machine in the rear and gaped.

"Beautiful," was all her coworker said as she grabbed the dolly and joined her.

Karyl had to agree, though she could have sworn it looked more worn at the auction. Now, the metal only looked grimy and the wood looked like all it needed was a wet cloth rubbed across it. With Maggie's aide, they rolled it into the store.

"I thought all of these burned up." Maggie said as they carted it to Karyl's work area.

"What?"

"Back in the 1800's. A factory full of these burned to the ground."

She looked at the delicate girl with interest. "How do you know this?"

Maggie grinned. "I come from a long line of seamstresses. One of the reasons Mrs. Barber hired me. I probably know almost as much as her."

"Well you definitely know more than me."

They laughed and selected a spot on the platform close to her work station. The pair moved things around and set it in place, sweating and panting by the time they were done. While they did so, she got more information about the Couseuse from her friend.

"Well," she began, "the Couseuses were originally designed and built by Barthelemy Thimonnier. To make a long story short, there were people who were afraid the machines would steal their jobs, so they..."

"Burned down the factory?"

Maggie nodded.

"That's intense."

She shrugged. "Fear of industry. Then, like now, the idea of machines taking work from people caused desperate acts. Can't say I don't share the concern, but I definitely would not do anything so extreme."

"Me either."

Karyl looked at the sewing machine with new eyes. She imagined she could see the scorch marks, but the structure was sound and, she was sure, cleverly built for the time. It must have been awful for the inventor to watch a building full of his creations burn. At the thought, the smell returned, and with it a feeling of loss. It was so intense, it actually made her ache. It prompted her to begin cleaning it, her touch careful and respectful. Eventually, under the soot, the machine stood as solid as it did when it came off the assembly line.

The whole time they could hear PJ proclaiming how wonderful her addition, an expensive piece of canvas art, was. When she saw the sewing machine she began to complain loudly about how the salvage hunt ended in her being 'injured on the job'. Of course, that combination of words brought Carmen over in a hurry. Not surprised, Karyl steeled herself for what was coming while Maggie stepped away to make a phone call.

There was a reason why Karyl privately termed PJ, Ruth, and Carmen 'harpies'. PJ was a venomous woman who constantly sniped about others. Ruth was nice to everyone to their faces, but stabbed them in the back at the first opportunity. Worse, Carmen, as assistant manager of the store, did nothing about it because they also served as her spies. For now, the duo were her favorites. It made working at The Fashion Factory uncomfortable, if not hostile. The only peace was when Mrs. Barber visited two or three times a week, days on which PJ was conveniently scheduled off.

"What happened?" the stout woman demanded.

Karyl shrugged and kept her voice carefully neutral. "We were moving this piece and she and Ruth got a splinter. I can write out an incident report if you like."

"That might be a good idea," the older woman agreed, her eyes drifting over to the machine. As if compelled, she reached out to run a finger over the wood.

The younger woman held her breath, waiting for a yelp. The smoky smell returned and when Carmen ran her palm over the exposed metal there was a hiss of pain. She pulled away and looked at her palm, where a reddish mark was fading. One of the other coworkers went to get a first aid kit while the woman regarded her with hostile eyes. Aware of the woman's vindictive tendencies, she knew the next few days were going to be hell. No wonder Carmen and the other two got along so well.

"Go fill out the paperwork now." She growled. "You are lucky I don't throw this damn thing out now…"

"Mrs. Barber is looking forward to seeing it," Maggie interrupted as she ended her call. From the glint in her eyes, it did not take a detective to figure out who she had been talking to. Like Karyl, she knew her coworkers' habits, better still she knew the owner would want to see the Couseuse. So she wasted no time in calling the head honcho to advise her of the treasure in her store.

The woman turned red with frustration. "Just don't be surprised if it disappears after she leaves."

Thankfully, Karyl's vindication came the next day with the owner's immediate attraction to the Couseuse. As a fan of sewing, she was immediately enchanted with the antique machine. It stood proud on its platform: the wood was pristine, the metal shone, and the gold-inlay etchings glittered teasingly. It looked so different than it had on the storage lot. Mrs. Barber cooed over it, touching it with the respect her loathsome employees had not. She whispered adoringly to it, telling it how beautiful it was. Karyl rarely saw the owner so enthralled and was glad her efforts hadn't been in vain. Carmen would not dare throw out the owner's favorite piece.

◊ ◊ ◊ ◊

She discovered how delightful the Couseuse could be a few days later.

The annual Mardi Gras parade was approaching, and it was scheduled to take place along the Frenchman's Bend. Though it would not be as grand as the New Orleans' showcases, the krewes of Monroe's parade took great pride in their displays. The doublooms being made for the float sponsored by The Fashion Factory were specially designed to help attract attention for any out-of-towners who would be attending.

Working diligently to meet a deadline for upcoming Mardi Gras, she nearly cursed when she was called into the assistant manager's office. Upon seeing a familiar gleam in Carmen's eye, she knew she was in trouble.

"You need to pick up PJ's work load," the older woman ordered. "She had a family emergency and is on leave."

Karyl stared at her. The woman knew she had a backlog already, and adding to it meant that she was not going to meet her own deadline. Despite the welcome quiet, PJ was known to cry illness when she just wanted personal time. Karyl sincerely doubted there was any 'family emergency', but Carmen would never doubt her precious PJ's claim. There was always an open employee to dump the work on. She knew nothing about PJ's workload—the designs, the measurements, or even how many were needed. Not to mention she still had to do the shop's monthly request for designs for new outfits. She had some sketches done, but nothing concrete. A missed deadline meant possible loss of business. Was the woman intentionally trying to get her fired?

Perhaps not, maybe she was just trying to flex her administrative muscles again. She was not pleased Mrs. Barber made a point to stopping by the vintage sewing machine at every visit. It annoyed her immediate boss an employee, moreover not one of her favorites, possibly had favor in the owner's eyes. It looked as though Carmen was determined to 'bring her down' a few notches by overloading her with work. As her immediate boss filled her in on the parameters of PJ's workload, Karyl could feel her temper mounting. This was impossible!

She chewed on her frustration for a few minutes before managing a civil tone. "Can I get help?"

"Everyone is already on assignment," the older woman answered without looking up from her paperwork.

How in the world was she going to do this?

"I'll need help." She insisted.

Carmen stopped for a moment to look at Karyl with disdain. "Get to work."

She wanted to make a case to Mrs. Barber; except Carmen made sure the owner was distracted. The best she could manage was a written request for an extension on both jobs, which she handed directly to the owner while she complimented the Couseuse during a visit. This way she got the time she needed. Carmen was not pleased, but it eased the pressure a bit. The matter settled, she finished her work order first. Happy to get it done early, she turned her attention to PJ's order.

When she finally got a look at it, there was no feasible way to get it done in time—even with the extension. The only thing PJ had done was take the order. No patterns were pinned, no material selected or ordered, nothing was cut—in short, nothing had been prepared. The stress was mounting. She wanted to ask Maggie for help, but Carmen was keeping her busy.

Karyl sat at her desk, first trying to decipher PJ's bad penmanship and then attempting to decode her pattern orders, which took the first two days alone. Now all she had to do was to get the patterns drawn, material selected (hoping they had plenty in stock and did not need to order more) and cut, and then sewn together to a multitude of measurements; this was incredible. There was no other word for it.

She was pinning patterns when Ruth walked up.

"Carmen really has you working, huh?"

Karyl nodded mutely, her lips holding several pins. She gestured to the work pile. Stacks of materials with a paper pinned to it outlining color schemes and measurements for each design.

"Guess you could use a hand."

She grunted but was glad her mouth was full. Anything she said would undoubtedly have been reported to the head crone. She wondered what the spy wanted.

Unexpectedly, Ruth picked up one of the patterns and began helping. She watched her coworker in disbelief for a few moments, and then continued her work. She had to admit, this was one of those moments where she appreciated Ruth's niceness in public. The minion was always earning brownie points with the others by being so helpful. If she had her guess, it was also probably why PJ's workload was so heavy, because Ruth always helped her with it.

Then it hit her—good grief she was being used to make Ruth look good! All the while making Karyl look bad for falling behind. It was insulting! If she didn't love sewing so much and didn't like the owner so well, she would quit.

Her anger grew as she worked, but the stitches

remained in line and flawless. Ruth had helped with half the work, but it was still not enough. From the other's expression, she realized that even with the two of them working, the order was not going to get finished. The other girl shrugged and continued working—she would still look good for offering to help.

Silently screaming, Karyl worked.

On impulse, the other girl put some material on the Couseuse for an extra surface to work on. Her hand touched the wood as she steadied herself to stand. She paused for a moment with a strange expression on her face, and then sat down at the machine to continue working. By the end of the day, she was still there. Karyl finished her shift and got ready to leave.

"Time to go."

"Yeah, see ya." Ruth responded distractedly, still stitching.

She noticed the smoky smell had returned. She looked around. "Do you smell that?"

"Smell what?"

"The smoke?"

"No." Ruth answered and began to hum softly, blatantly dismissing her.

Confused, Karyl left.

◊ ◊ ◊ ◊

Ruth was still there the next morning, using the Couseuse.

Karyl was amazed it still worked. The soft clicking of the machine accompanied her coworker moving the material along the needle, expertly using it. As she approached, she saw an array of costumes already done. There were flourishes added which were not in the original design. Looking closer, she saw it was an addition the other was doing with the vintage sewing machine.

"Nice work."

Ruth didn't answer; she just kept working and humming.

Shrugging, Karyl joined her. They worked with silent efficiency, accompanied by that smoky smell. It had to be her imagination, but it seemed more intense now that the sewing machine was in use. Ruth didn't talk, only hummed that strange tune. She kept expecting the girl to mention the smoky smell. After a while, she was able to tune out both the tune and smell. Though she found herself hoping the other woman would ask for a break so she could have a chance on the vintage machine. Only it never happened. Each afternoon, she would bid her goodbye. She found herself waiting to see if her help was needed, but it never was. She left each night wondering what it was like to use it and hoping she might find out the next day. Each morning, during the day, and each night Ruth was there, working and humming; reluctant to leave the Couseuse. Everyone was concerned, trying to get her away for a break. They would attempt to lure her away with food, only to watch her nibble at the food while sitting and working. Even Carmen noticed and tried to get the girl away from the machine, but eventually the spy would return.

With Ruth working almost non-stop, it was no surprise when they met the deadline. The customers especially liked the added flourish to their Mardi Gras costumes. Ruth was complimented on her initiative and Mrs. Barber was delighted the Victorian sewing machine was still functional.

The day would have ended well if Ruth had not collapsed. One moment she was sitting, working, and humming. The next there was a sick thud as she hit the floor.

There was an uproar as she was taken to the hospital.

Mardi Gras came and went, but the employees of The Fashion Factory barely noticed.

◊ ◊ ◊ ◊

Ruth was hospitalized, for how long no one knew. After Carmen returned to her desk, there was speculation as to what happened. A sudden disease maybe?

A booming voice announced PJ's return. She asked about Ruth and the resulting tirade was even louder. When she learned how her order was filled, care of the vintage sewing machine, she stormed over. No word of thanks, just a narrow-eyed examination of Karyl and her addition to The Fashion Factory. It was as though PJ blamed them for Ruth's condition.

More orders arrived, all requesting stitching from the now operational Couseuse. Mrs. Barber was elated. Carmen wanted to assign one person to handle the machine. Naturally, PJ volunteered. The designs were preset, the sewing machine had a set pace, and all she had to do was guide the material. True, the original sewing machine was most likely meant for more, but Mrs. Barber did not want to overtax the machine. So when PJ volunteered, Carmen immediately accepted.

She had bought it and cleaned it up, she and Maggie had set it up, and Ruth had somehow gotten it to work, yet PJ wanted to hog all the glory. Karyl should have been offered the chance. After all she had been waiting patiently as Ruth worked for her turn, yet she was being denied. It rankled her. At least business was picking up. They were all busy, even PJ. Karyl took some savage joy in the fact that what the wretch had undoubtedly thought would be an easy job ended up being very demanding.

It was not long before PJ assumed Ruth's routine. Contrary to her usual pattern of cutting out of work early or showing up late, the harpy now seemed dedicated to her work. She was at the Couseuse all day, working. Sometimes into the night, and she was always found at it in the morning. The smoky smell, which had been absent while Ruth was gone, had returned. Karyl had become so accustomed to it that it no longer bothered her; in fact, she found it comforting. Nothing was burning, so she reasoned it must be a residual scent on the Victorian sewing machine from the factory fire, probably being released when it got too warm from continual use. The smoky smell was enchanting somehow, like an old perfume.

What did bother her was that the woman had taken to humming. The tune sounded oddly familiar. She wanted to say something about it, but given that PJ had finally become serious about her work, meeting deadlines and producing great stitch work. Karyl was reluctant to complain in case she brought back the loud-mouthed monster. Carmen, concerned at the change in behavior and looking out for her remaining favorite, made sure PJ ate, drank, and went home to sleep. It was odd how the woman was mothering the girl. They were always seen together— PJ becoming more withdrawn and Carmen looking more worried and scared. Karyl noticed it, but she thought it was the result of the duo talking about Ruth. Only Carmen and PJ were allowed to visit her in the hospital, and whatever they saw was distressing them.

A few weeks later PJ collapsed.

Karyl came in that morning, and saw PJ at her station as usual—working at the stitching and humming as she moved rhythmically. It was the first time she had gotten a real chance to look at PJ. She did not look good. Her skin was pale, her cheeks sunken in, and she seemed to be unnaturally focused on the machine. In fact, now that she thought about it, the shop had been very quiet these past few weeks. Karyl had been so busy she had noticed and appreciated the quiet, but had not connected it to the fact that PJ was no longer talking, only humming. Karyl went over to see if she was alright.

When she touched her forehead, PJ was cool to the touch.

"Hey, you ok?" she asked as she took hold of her shoulder and shook her gently.

PJ did not answer. She just fell over. Carmen was practically screaming as she ran over. Karyl stood there, paralyzed, as Maggie called 911.

◇ ◇ ◇ ◇

"Did she eat or drink something she was allergic to?" the doctor asked Carmen.

They were still in the hospital. PJ had been admitted and put in the same room as Ruth. The seamstresses had not been allowed in the room, but had been called away by the supervising doctor. They had not waited long, almost immediately after their arrival the doctor called Carmen into his office. Karyl was not permitted in the room with them, but Carmen had neglected to close the office door completely when she went in. The boss was listed as an emergency contact on both women's medical information. She also had permission to learn about their conditions, which was why the doctor spoke with her. So Karyl was able to eavesdrop slightly, and she could see her boss from where she sat. The assistant manager shook her head.

"Curious. Her condition is the same as Ruth when she was admitted to the hospital."

"But she..."

"Is in a comatose state now, yes," the doctor supplied. "But if the pattern holds they will both be alive but not conscious. There is evidence of brain activity, but it is like they are in a dream state."

"Do something!" the older woman sounded scared.

He gave her a sympathetic look. "We don't know where to start. Ruth's family has authorized experimental treatments, but so far there has been no change."

They talked for a bit longer, but Karyl was not paying attention. Ruth? PJ? Both struck by a strange illness? It was frightening. Was it something in the shop?

She could hear Carmen asking about possible contagions, but the doctor seemed even more befuddled at the lack of virulent evidence. Taking a chance, she left the office and snuck into Ruth and PJ's room. They had been put together per Carmen's request. What she saw was a shock.

Ruth was no longer the youthful looking young woman she remembered. Her skin was sickly, her cheeks sunken as if malnourished, and her fingers seemed to be continually twitching. And she was still vaguely humming that tune! PJ was not much better. She looked a little healthier, but her eyes were vacant as she also hummed those haunting notes and twitched her fingers. It was like she was there, but not. Even more disturbing was their humming was synchronized, as were their finger movements.

Unnerved, Karyl joined Carmen in the hall and escorted her to the car.

"… no reason…" she was whispering.

Karyl was shaken up as well. They had lost two coworkers with no real cause.

They returned to the shop and updated everyone. Carmen went back to her desk and simply sat, obviously distressed. No one really knew what to say, so they left her be. The woman was a shell of her previous self, as though losing her two favorites had taken the spirit out of her.

Karyl guessed she should have expected it when, the next morning, she saw Carmen sitting at the Couseuse. The woman was humming as she stitched. She approached slowly, an intense feeling of jealousy surprising her. She controlled herself as she spoke.

"Carmen?"

The older woman looked up with a kind of crazed gleam in her eye. "Customers want the stitching done with the Couseuse." she said in a placid voice, so different from her usual coarse tone. "Ruth and PJ are sick. They were my responsibility, and you girls are very busy, which makes this my responsibility... so I should pitch in. Right?"

There was something pathetic in the way she said it.

Karyl had no answer for her. Tamping down her inexplicable feeling of envy, she just sat down next to her and began to work. Since Carmen was by Karyl's workstation, she ended up becoming the older woman's caretaker, much in the way Carmen had been PJ and Ruth's. She made sure the assistant manager ate, drank, and drove her home so she could get some sleep. She even took her once a week to check on 'her girls', Ruth and PJ.

"It makes a beautiful noise," she said one day on the way back to the shop.

Karyl looked at her oddly.

"The Couseuse."

She nodded, not sure what to say.

"The hum as it works, it is like a song."

"I'm sure it is nice."

"You should hear it," she went on.

"I do," she reassured the other. "You hum it."

"I don't do it justice." Carmen said softly. "You should hear the real tune."

It sounded like Carmen was getting ready to have her own break down. Even though the three women had made the shop a hostile place, she could not help but feel for the woman sitting in the seat beside her. As she continued to take care of Carmen, she realized she was feeling responsible for her. With every meal she made sure the woman ate, with each drive to and from her house to the shop, Karyl's attachment to her grew stronger. Yet despite her efforts the assistant manager continued to deteriorate, and Karyl felt frustrated and worried at her inability to stop it. No amount of sleep, food, or drink was helping.

And she would not stop working!

Karyl tried repeatedly to get Carmen away from the Couseuse, but she could not. It did not help that orders kept coming in. Each design Carmen made was different and beautiful, some alternative flourish to the set pattern that she was working with. The old woman was oblivious to the compliments showered on her by Mrs. Barber and the customers, and she was still wasting away. Everyone could see it, and were worried. She offered, more than once, to take over the work for Carmen, but the other refused to leave her station except to go home to sleep.

"Karyl," she finally said at one point.

"Yeah?"

"Come here and try this."

"Really?" she asked dubiously. After all the rebuffed offers to help, it seemed odd Carmen would allow her to get near the Couseuse now.

Carmen smiled through her sunken cheeks and rose from her chair to make room for her younger companion. She patted the seat invitingly.

Karyl hesitated, and then approached. The young woman was curious. This was a machine from the 1800's in pristine condition. Granted, it was slow moving in comparison to modern machines, but customers who were versed with the history of sewing were more than willing to be patient. She had been inexplicably jealous when Ruth and PJ worked on the machine; she wanted to see how it worked. Now was her chance to finally sit with the machine and be part of its magic. She sat down carefully and breathed in the smoky perfume.

As she lay her fingers on the wood, it felt warm—like a living thing. She shook off the thought, reasoning it was body warmth left over from Carmen working there. The older woman guided her hands and feet, and showed her how to work the machine. She even hummed a bit, as if providing Karyl with a rhythm to follow. It helped. As the assistant manager hummed the song, Karyl moved in time with her.

Then she heard it.

The song of the Couseuse.

Low, beautiful, and alluring.

She began to hum as she worked, feeling complete. As she continued, an image formed in her mind. It flowed before her mind's eye like an old movie.

The fire raged despite the efforts to put it out. Tended by medics, Barthelemy Thimonnier watched his garment factory burn. Inside, his Couseuses were reduced to ash. The enormity of the injustice weighed heavily on him. It wasn't just his machines being destroyed; it was his dreams.

Yet amid the rubble, this one survived. A miasma of the hate and fear which had fueled the desperation permeated the air and enveloped the lone machine. Caressing the scorched outside, the haze seeped into the ruined surface. The zeal of Thimonnier's devotion warred with the malignant energies of its persecutors, leaving their imprint in the wood and metal.

It was almost painful when Carmen pulled her off so that she could finish the work. Karyl did not fight though.

The feeling of loss explained, and the intense desire to complete the task for which the machine was built replaced it. She knew sooner or later she would get her chance.

When Carmen collapsed a few days later, her eyes vacant, her hands twitching as they followed the patterns, and her body pale and sickly—Karyl immediately took her place on the Couseuse.

BINKY
by Teresa Bergen

G loria always thought she wanted children, but now that she was left alone with her new husband's daughter, she wasn't so sure. It didn't help that Eva, skinny and eleven, with sullen, downcast eyes and rubbed raw elbows, was just hitting puberty. Or that Eva's mother was in Texas, being treated for about ten different mental problems. Or that Gloria and Eva had known each other for one week before Eva's father, Alan, had to leave for Plaquemines to deal with family business. And neither Eva's nor Gloria's already bad dreams were improved by the fact that family business included rounding up Alan's parents' bones and transporting them to new grave sites further inland from the Gulf.

In better times, a new wife might have complained, but welcome to post-hurricane New Orleans, where "sacrifice" was on everybody's to do list.

Eva had surely sacrificed. One of her friends had died, and others had moved away. The girl and her mother had seen the worst of the storm, spending a night in the attic, until water swirled around their ankles and they hacked their way to the roof with an axe. There they clung together for two more nights in the open air and wind, and two days while their possessions and the mother's already long compromised sanity floated away.

"No, ma'am," had been the extent of Eva's

conversation on this particular August day. As in, "No, ma'am," she wouldn't like any breakfast, and "No, ma'am," she didn't want to go to the movies, and "No, ma'am," she didn't want to talk about what was bothering her. All these "ma'ams" were not delivered with real respect, but with sly sidelong glances to see if Gloria was getting the point, that theirs was a formal relationship, not of the girl's choosing.

Gloria was a young looking thirty-six, though not as youthful as before the storm. She was from California and still didn't like being called ma'am, even by cashiers and bank tellers. By her own stepdaughter, it could break her heart if she let it.

Wind whistled outside. In the six years Gloria had lived in Louisiana, this was the first hurricane season to make her nervous. The news people said a tropical storm might or might not be coming their way. Maybe the storm would turn, as they usually had, until last year. Gloria stood in the kitchen, staring at the refrigerator and wondering whether eating another peanut butter sandwich would fall into the category of nervous eating, which she was trying to curtail. She preferred nervous drinking, but now she had the girl to think about.

Then she thought she heard scratching. It sounded like how her dog, Bellocq, had scratched at the kitchen door of her old house, the one she lost in the hurricane. The house where her best friend, her dear, dear dog, had waited fruitlessly for her to come back and save him.

The scratching came again. Her neck prickled. The backs of her thighs went numb.

Everything had been crazy when the mayor announced the mandatory evacuation, and she still hadn't really believed. How many times had she evacuated in the last six years? At least twice, maybe three times. The storms always turned. The city was charmed.

Scritch. Scritch.

There was no place to stay for hundreds of miles around. Motels were booked, planes were full. She had turned to her ex-husband in Baton Rouge, whose new wife very reluctantly said she could stay for a night or maybe two. But no dogs—she was a cat person.

Scritch. Scritch.

Bellocq would be okay if she left him lots of food and water. Evacuations never lasted more than a couple of days. But Bellocq was a dachshund, his short legs not made for swimming. Gloria had never expected her small house to be covered by flood water, right up to the ceiling, plus a few extra feet.

Scritch. Scritch.

Gloria's fingers tightened around the refrigerator handle. She heard Eva's footsteps padding down the hall toward the kitchen.

SCRITCH. SCRITCH.

Eva's face was bright with anticipation. Gloria had never seen the girl excited about anything.

"Don't open the door," Gloria said, her voice hoarse.

"It's probably some lost little animal, ma'am," Eva said, her voice sweet and Southern.

SCRITCH. SCRITCH. SCRITCH.

Gloria couldn't move. "Honey, please. No," she whispered.

Eva just smiled. She looked confident, a whole different person. She slid the deadbolt and turned the knob.

Gloria expected to see Bellocq, bloated and decomposed, come for revenge. Instead, when Eva flung open the door, a shiny black pit bull leaped at her. Gloria screamed. But Eva opened her arms and caught the dog in a huge hug. The dog had a chest like a barrel. It must weigh almost as much as Eva, who whirled around like she was dancing with the dog, while the frightful thing licked her face.

"Do you know this dog?" asked Gloria.

The dog stopped licking. Girl and dog turned as one to look at Gloria as if she were interrupting a private reunion. The dog's eyes were almost as dark as its fur. And Eva's own eyes were dark, like her hair, though her skin was pale. The girl and the dog looked related somehow, alike as siblings, intimate as lovers. The dog's muscles rippled with strength, its fur glistened, its head was as big as a bowling ball. Gloria saw Eva's strength for the first time. This girl who effortlessly hugged a pit bull to her chest was the girl who had survived on a roof for days. This was the girl who endured separation from her mother and friends, and the sudden, unexpected remarriage of the father she barely knew. This was the girl who endured Gloria.

Gloria retreated to her art studio. It was a good thing her husband's number was on speed dial, because her shaky fingers could barely press one button.

He picked up on the fourth ring. "Gloria," he said, in a way which let her know he was in the middle of something.

"Alan," she breathed, not knowing where to begin.

"What's wrong?"

"It's Eva."

"What happened?" he asked, instantly alarmed. His ex-wife had hardly let him see the girl. Now he lived in fear of losing her again.

"This weird dog showed up," Gloria began.

"Did it bite her?"

"No. No. She loves it. They seem to know each other already. They were dancing in the kitchen," she stumbled on.

"So she found a new pet?" he asked, confused. "That's

wonderful. Eva's lost so much."

"But there's something weird about it. It's...unnatural."

"Unnatural," he repeated, obviously not impressed. Alan was a man whose first wife had broken down mentally, slowly, over the years, then quickly, at the end. He was out of patience.

"The way it showed up. Scratching at the door. The way it seemed to know her already."

"It's probably been stray since the hurricane. It's probably so happy someone opened the door, it was ready to be anybody's instant best friend."

She imagined him talking his ex-wife down hundreds of times, probably just like this. "But it's a pit bull, Alan. She picked it up like it weighed nothing. I don't think I could pick that dog up!"

"A pit bull, eh?" Alan laughed. "My tough little girl."

"Alan, I'm telling you, something is wrong with that dog!"

He stopped laughing abruptly. "You want to hear something wrong, Gloria? I'm standing here in a storeroom at a cemetery, over what is alleged to be the skeletal remains of my mother and father. I know my mother had more than one arm and one leg when I buried her. And I damn well know my father had a head. But one hurricane later, Gloria, two of my mother's limbs and my father's head are...I don't fucking know where!" His voice exploded at the end. Gloria heard him breathing, trying to get his temper under control. "I think it will do Eva a world of good to have a pet of her own. I have to take care of business now. I'll talk to you later." He hung up before she could plague him with one more word.

She sat on the floor, crying, feeling ridiculous. She should be calm and support Alan, and not drive him crazy with her imagination. But guilt about Bellocq possessed her. He was the most precious creature, eight years old, a long-haired, spotted dachshund, the smartest dog she ever knew. How could she have betrayed him, leaving him alone to drown? How could she help but freak out with the scratching at the door, and the wind howled, and Alan was away looking at bones during the storm season?

The walls of her studio were almost bare. She specialized in painting New Orleans scenes, especially the cottages and shotgun houses in her own neighborhood, the Bywater, and in the Lower Ninth Ward. She and Alan had found a new house in her neighborhood, but the whole area had been hit hard. Only one other house on their block was now occupied, the rest awaiting repairs or demolition. Everywhere, the post-hurricane rescue graffiti remained on front walls. Dates, name of emergency service, numbers of bodies found inside, spray painted on every house. She had taken all her work down from the walls, because she could not stand to be surrounded by ghost houses or portraits of Bellocq, her ghost dog.

At first, Gloria had told herself that maybe Bellocq had been rescued. But how would he have gotten out of the house, and how would his little legs be able to swim through the floodwater? Still, she had visited the Lamar-Dixon shelter, completely stuffed with animals, overcrowded and turning additional dogs away. She combed the makeshift LSU dog barn, hot, humid, stinking of shit and deafening with the barks of hundreds of dogs. She was there the day the dogs arrived from an evacuated New Orleans veterinary hospital, their owners waiting expectantly, only to find that the air conditioning in the truck had failed, and the delivery consisted of 73 dead and two dying dogs.

She called Noah's Wish and the SPCA and every shelter in Mississippi, just in case.

But no spotted dachshund.

Her house was a total loss. She was never able to go back inside, because it had collapsed to the point that there really was nothing to go into. She spent an afternoon digging through the rubble, a month after the fact. However, if there were any dachshund bones, they were as lost as Alan's father's head.

After talking to Alan, Gloria collected herself enough to remember her ordinary duties. Dinner. The girl would need to eat, and the new pet would need to eat, and Gloria could use some dinner, too.

The girl was hard to feed. She preferred candy to vegetables. She would pick at a ham sandwich, taking a few bites out of the middle, nibbling on a crust, scrapping the rest.

In the kitchen, Gloria molded hamburger patties, the raw meat cool between her hands. She heard laughter down the hall, behind Eva's closed door. Alan would have taken this as a good sign, but Gloria felt her neck prickle. Who laughs so hard in the company of a stray pit bull?

The girl and dog emerged when the hamburgers were almost done. They entered the kitchen side by side, Eva standing straighter than usual, the dog with pit bull friendliness, that look of easygoing fun on the surface, but always an undercurrent of watchfulness, seeing what it could put over on you, especially if you were scared.

"Are you hungry, dear?" Gloria asked, striving for normalcy and falling flat. The unearned "dear" made her sound like an old lady, ill at ease with children but trying to win them over. A flicker of amusement crossed Eva's face.

"Yes, ma'am," the girl said, meeting Gloria's eye for a moment before returning to her usual dropped gaze. Not only did Gloria mistrust and dislike this stepdaughter, she realized she was a bit afraid of her. But why should Gloria be frightened of a child? Or maybe it was the fear of what this would do to her marriage, if Alan ever suspected.

The dog didn't miss her fear. She saw the excited flicker in its eyes, the happy shake of its stumpy tail.

"Binky and I could eat three hamburgers each," Eva said. "We're starving."

"Who?" Gloria asked weakly. "What did you call it?"

"His name is Binky," the girl said. Again the lifting of the girl's eyes, the wag of almost tailless tail.

"But he doesn't look like a..." Gloria trailed off, not wanting to say the name.

"You try calling him," Eva said, her eyes flashing with mirth.

"No, I have to cook," Gloria stammered.

"Just call him. He'll come to you."

"No," Gloria said more sharply.

The girl giggled. "Binky! Binky!" The dog stood on its hind legs, extending its front paws, which Eva took in her hands. When Eva smiled, she transformed into a much prettier creature. They stood, holding hands. Beauty and the beast. Or maybe beast and the beast. "See, he likes it."

Gloria's stomach cramped. It would be a long time before Eva left for college. Gloria would never make it. And why did Eva choose that name? How could she know?

"Uh, I think that hamburger's done," Eva smirked as a wisp of smoke curled from the pan. Gloria wordlessly spatulaed it onto a plate.

The girl looked sideways and half smiled at the dog, who was also smiling.

◊ ◊ ◊

Usually Gloria left her bedroom door open at night, in case Eva needed anything, but tonight she shut it. She didn't like the idea of that dog roaming around, nosing into her bedroom, its eyes staring at her sleeping face, waiting.

Binky. Had Gloria imagined the knowing look on Eva's face, on the dog's, when the girl announced its name? But nobody in the world knew she dared not speak that name aloud.

Gloria's parents had dabbled in Eastern religions since before she was born. Pictures of Sai Baba had hung on their walls, his intense eyes staring out from beneath his massive afro. There had been early morning yoga sessions in the living room, where Gloria dutifully folded herself into preposterous shapes. They had spent long evenings chanting with Hare Krishnas before being served spicy yellow gruel that burned Gloria's tongue. Mostly it was boring and annoying, but her parents' transcendental meditation phase had terrified the young Gloria.

In all their other Eastern dabbling, Gloria had been a kid, an innocent bystander, encouraged to participate but not expected to get much out of it.

When she turned twelve, her parents came to her, beaming, and announced it was time for an initiation of her own.

"Uh, that's okay," she had told them. "I'm fine." She already couldn't bring other kids home because of the embarrassing religious photos everywhere. And now she'd have to spend her afternoons in some freakish temple getting initiated?

But her parents were determined. "This is something you'll use all your life," her father had said.

"We really want to do this for you, honey," Mom said. "And believe me, it's not cheap."

How Gloria would have loved a few new clothes instead of an initiation!

The TM place was in a Gothic house, painted purple,

with pointy spires. There were only two other students in the two-week course: an old man, and a thirtyish guy with Jesus hair and beard. Their teacher had clear blue eyes and dressed in a long white tunic and white pants. Gloria could never remember much about the content of those classes, except a large dry erase board covered with diagrams about the conscious and unconscious mind, which were of no interest nor made any sense. During their third session, the older student had a spectacular heart attack, spluttering and staggering before falling dead on Gloria's feet, his eyes bulging up at her. Gloria had screamed and screamed, yet her parents forced her to go back the next day, to finish her preparation for initiation.

Before her classmate fell dead on her feet, she had mostly alternated between being bored, confused, and pissed at her parents, but afterwards, she feared and hated the place. She couldn't sit in the room without remembering the thud of his body, the feeling of a person's life draining out, in an instant, on her feet. She absolutely would not wear those shoes again.

The initiation itself took place in a tiny room where her teacher conferred the secret Sanskrit mantra upon her. It could never be written down, only whispered in her ear. "Binh Kee," her teacher said. Or maybe "Bin Ki." How was Gloria supposed to know? It sounded for all the world like "Binky," a name for a cartoon character or a pet lizard, not the awesomely powerful mantra her teacher swore it was.

"You must never tell anyone this mantra," he said. "You must never say it aloud." He stared at her with unnaturally clear blue eyes, like a hyper-perfect sky. "Do you understand?" he asked. "You must never say it aloud."

"Got it," she said, picking a scab on her elbow so she wouldn't have to look at him.

"Never," he repeated.

"Yeah. Okay," she agreed. "Never."

And she hadn't.

And it turned out she had used that mantra all her life. It had lodged in her head during the week following initiation, when she was brought every afternoon into that little room in the TM center, to silently think her mantra for thirty minutes at a time. She would open her eyes and peek, and always her teacher would be staring back with blue, unblinking eyes.

"Binky," he whispered in her ear. "Binky."

Her parents had moved on to study their doshas at an ayurvedic school, but Gloria's mantra had taken hold. She used it at night when she couldn't sleep. It consoled her when boys hurt her feelings, and, later, men. She thought it for an hour straight when she had a root canal.

So how had Eva decided to name that hellhound Binky?

She must have dozed, because it was 3:40 when she opened her eyes. She lay awake for a few bleary moments, wondering what had brought her out of sleep. She thought she heard something over the air conditioner, and reached up to flip the switch off.

Scritch. Scritch.

Her heart pounded. She held her breath. She had to pee very badly, but there was no way she was walking down the hall to the bathroom.

Scritch. Scritch.

She automatically began to think her mantra, as she did in times of fear. Binky, Binky, Binky. Now it conjured the sly, laughing face of the black pit bull. She heard it whine, a flirtatious little sound, like it was pretending to be a damsel in distress, but with glittering, devious eyes.

She could hear the wind outside, thumping the shutters,

and she thought about how empty the block was, how deserted was the whole neighborhood.

Scritch. Scritch.

She could call Alan from the bedside phone. But what would she say? The dog is scratching at my door? He would think she was as crazy as his first wife.

Maybe she could call her first husband, who was more imaginative and might have been sympathetic, at one point. But he had remarried. Even if his new wife didn't answer the phone, he would be expected to explain a 3:42 AM call.

Scritch. Whine. A low, moaning little whine, and then she heard the doorknob moving. That thing must be on its hind legs, trying to turn her doorknob.

Her hand shot to the phone. Police? SPCA? National Guard?

Then she heard Eva's sleepy voice. "Binky! What are you doing? Come back to bed!"

There was a pause. Eva's bedroom door closed. Had the dog retreated? Or was it still outside?

Gloria put a chair in front of her door. She drank the half glass of water on her bedside table, then peed in the empty cup. There was no way she was leaving this room until the sun came up.

She turned on the lights and, with shaking hands, took a book out of her nightstand drawer. *The Blended Family: Bonding with Your Stepchildren.* She tried to concentrate on chapter one, which was total crap. At least the scratching had stopped.

◊ ◊ ◊ ◊

The day was boiling and sticky as Gloria woke tangled in her sheets. She had fallen back asleep for an hour or two, after first light. She'd left the A/C off so she could hear better, and now it was about 90 degrees in her bedroom. The wind had dropped. Maybe the storm was turning. She pulled on shorts and a T-shirt, then hesitated before opening the door.

The hallway was empty.

She felt gritty and hallucinatory as she trudged toward the kitchen, which smelled of bacon. Eva was crouched on the floor, facing the pit bull, their mouths joined by a crisp strip of bacon. They ate toward the middle, Eva giggling.

"What the fuck are you doing?!" Gloria burst out, talking the way she normally would, forgetting Alan's cautions against profanity. Eva and the dog's eyes slid sideways at her, the bacon a bridge connecting them. "That's a pit bull! You don't want to put your face so close to it!"

Girl and dog turned back toward each other and finished the strip. Eva let the dog have the last nub. She kissed its nose. "I love you, Binky," she said with great sweetness and sincerity. Then she turned to Gloria. "I think Binky would like to ride in your convertible, ma'am," she said.

"What?" Gloria asked. The pale girl hadn't wanted to leave the house for days. Was she using the dog to express her own wishes? "Do you want to go for a ride, Eva?"

"Well, if Binky does, I'd ride along," she said.

The girl might be crazy, like her mother. The convertible was Gloria's last vestige of her single life in New Orleans, between the first and second husband. She didn't relish the idea of this big, brutish dog in her Miata.

Or the girl, either, if she was going to be honest about it.

"Where do you want to go?" Gloria asked.

"Just for a drive, ma'am."

"Okay," she said, thinking of Alan, of how cheered up

he would be to hear Eva wanted to leave the house. Alan couldn't find his father's head! Of course she could squire the girl and her dog in the car, no matter how creepy the dog was, nor how ridiculous they would look in her two-seater. The dog would have to sit on the girl's lap, which might be illegal, but lots of things were overlooked these days.

Outside, the dog lingered by a bush, sniffing and leg lifting, as Gloria and Eva eased into the low seats of the Miata. "Call him, ma'am," Eva said.

"What?"

"Call Binky, see if he comes to you," she said excitedly.

"Come on, boy!" Gloria called, her voice false, as it was obvious she didn't really want the dog in her car.

The dog ignored Gloria. Eva laughed. "No, you have to call him by name."

"You call him," Gloria said. "He's your dog."

"I want to see if he obeys you, ma'am."

"He hardly knows me. Now are we going or not?"

The girl laughed. "Binky! Binky!" The dog bounded toward them and hopped onto her lap, as lightly and easily as a cat. It sat facing out the passenger side, its front feet propped up on the door. Gloria tried not to think about what its toenails were doing to her green paint.

They drove aimlessly up Elysian Fields, in the direction of Lake Pontchartrain. Gloria never got used to the spray-painted shorthand on the houses, the record of which emergency group had checked the house when, and how many bodies they had found. Plus the animal rescue groups who had come looking for trapped pets and spray painted their own notes. "Dog under porch." "Large dead python."

"Turn here!" Eva cried. "Turn here!"

Gloria turned, as she had no plan of her own. Too late, she realized she was driving in the direction of Eva's old house. "Oh, honey, I don't think we want to go over there."

"Yes! Binky wants to see my house!"

Gloria had never seen the house herself, and was curious. But Alan would kill her!

"Show Binky! Show Binky!" Eva chanted, clapping an accompaniment with her hands. The girl was in high spirits. The wind was coming back up.

"Which direction?"

"Keep going straight! Keep going!"

Binky let out an excited howl.

The street was in sorry shape. A couple of people might be in the early stages of rebuilding, their houses gutted, only the frames intact. Most of the houses were blown half off their foundations, or were entirely rubble, or the rubble had been hauled away and only concrete slabs remained. The whole street smelled hot and moldy and evil.

"There it is! My house!" Eva yelled excitedly, though Gloria couldn't understand the girl's enthusiasm. The yellow house had slid most of the way off its foundation, back side first, so that the rear third of the house had completely collapsed. The rescue graffiti beside the front door indicated the National Guard had found one dead body inside.

"Someone died in your house?" Gloria blurted out before she remembered sensitivity and all that.

But the girl looked nonchalant. She popped the door open before the car even stopped. "Come on, Binky!" she yelled. Then she and the dog were frolicking through the neglected, littered yard.

The wind blew harder now, so what was left of the house visibly swayed.

Gloria tried to think of who could have died in the house. It seemed like Alan would have mentioned that Eva had been stuck on top of a house with a dead body sloshing around inside. But, there it was, clearly noted, one dead body another horror the girl had endured. She peered at the marks on the house, confused. That wasn't the date of the hurricane. But she couldn't think about it now; Eva was getting too far ahead. Like it or not, the girl was her responsibility now.

"Wait up!" she called. Surely the dead body was long ago removed. Eva and the dog danced in the wind, the girl's black hair streaming behind her. "Stay away from the building!" Gloria yelled. Any more wind and the house was bound to slide further off its concrete slab.

"Whee!" Eva seemed to be yelling as she spun around. The dog leaped and landed, leaped and landed, circling the girl. The two edged closer to the leaning house.

"Stay back!" Gloria warned again the dog had caught an interesting scent. It nosed toward the collapsing house, tail stub wagging. Then the dog dove through a low opening and was inside the battered hulk.

Eva sobered. She and Gloria waited. The wind blew. They heard nothing.

Then a terrific crash from inside, followed by a whimper.

"Binky!" the girl yelled. "Binky!" In a flash, the girl had lowered herself toward the dark hole into the house.

"No!" Gloria grabbed the girl's arm with a bruising grip. "You can't go in there!"

But the girl was hysterical. She thrashed and tried to bite Gloria.

"Binky!" she screamed, her face collapsed in woe.

The rain started crashing down, like a thousand buckets heaved upon them.

Gloria desperately wanted to drag the girl to the car and drive off. But Eva was too strong. Something had to be done to save the dog.

"I'll go in," Gloria said.

"No! Me! I want to go!"

"Wait in the car. Put the top up," Gloria said, giving the girl the keys.

Gloria dropped down into the mud and crawled through the dark hole into what was left of Eva's house and then she had to call the dog. There was no way around it.

"Binky?" she said tentatively, the first time she had uttered that name aloud. The dark and the smells were like a tomb. She could smell death, and rot, and the horrible, toxic mold which had taken over all the neglected New Orleans houses. "Binky!" she called, her voice stronger. She had to do this quickly. "Come on, Binky! Come on!"

The wind howled now, and she could hear closer sounds, rustling, creaks, maybe things taking cover in the house. "Binky? Binky!"

Then the dog shot past her, panting exuberantly as it burst through the opening to the outside.

"Binky!" Eva yelled delightedly from outside. "Oh, Binky!" The girl was laughing, and so was the dog. Gloria had never heard a dog laugh, but she could think of no other word to describe the sound the pit bull was making. It made her neck hairs rise. Could a little girl and a dog be evil? And how could she make Alan understand?

Gloria turned toward the dark opening, just as the rain and wind joined forces to collapse that edge of the house. The circle of light disappeared.

The space around Gloria had become very small. "Eva!" she screamed in terror. "Eva! Get help! Eva! Help!"

Something whined, and in the darkness it sounded exactly like Bellocq.

"Bellocq?" she whispered, but the noise didn't come

again.

She remembered the mark on the door. One dead. And the error. It had been today's date.

The rain was worse, if that was possible. She could feel the water accumulating around her in puddles, and then she heard an engine. It sounded like her own car.

Did the girl know how to drive?

"Eva!" Gloria cried.

But who could hear her over the wind?

THE BELLS OF RUE LA BARRIERE
by J. Lamm

The empire that was the Terry Zilo Ministries started back in the early 1980s under the control of one Terrence Zilo, a prominent and charismatic figure who had the face of a Norman Rockwell boy but the oratory puff of a bull. His personable charm was an example of how someone could take a modest grassroots ministry program—one that could squeeze fifty people under a tent—and then build it into a burgeoning media realm. People seemed to flock to him, wanting to follow his lead and share in the example he set. His ministry campaign and local presence in the Baton Rouge area was only strengthened by a collection of landholdings—selected with scrupulous consideration—and amassed over time. And as the capital city grew and tax laws changed, more people migrated in and the property values increased exponentially. The brilliance of his holdings, coupled with his severe business acumen, had morphed Zilo from a pretentious preacher to a real estate magnate. And with over 200 acres of land dedicated to his ministry alone and people coming in from out-of-state just to watch his sermons for a single day, major hotel chains began popping up in the developing area just to accommodate the out-of-town guests. At the height of his prominence, Zilo was being broadcast on over 200 television stations covering more than two million households. This led to the founding of his own bible college program and dormitory building, all located on the same plot of land to the western end of Rue la Barriere.

But then it all fell away after Zilo was photographed with his arm around a prominent New Orleans escort, going in and out of a hotel, and chalking up the point made by Hebrews 13:4—a verse on adultery Zilo's wife would certainly agree with; a verse quoted once or twice in Zilo's own sermons.

The media chewed him up. And bit by bit it started to crumble away. This fall would dry up the large amount of money constantly flowing in. The traffic died down; the hotel rooms left unfilled; the collection plates tarnished in disuse; and the bells that tolled the start of every Sunday service fell into silence. Gone was the idea of the bible college; gone was the idea of ever completing the Terry Zilo Bible College Dormitories, the eventual home to the most significant paranormal event that would never be recorded in history.

And even though the bulk of the ministry buildings still operate in some way, the Zilo dormitory building stands as an unfinished relic and an eyesore to Baton Rouge. It is now primarily used for storage of the organization's unused religious items and it is home to stationary things like dusty pallets of bath tiles that will never be plastered—too heavy to lug back out once the project was kaput.

The pipes and metal have long since been scrapped and the majority of the walls have been coated in a fine amount of graffiti—celebrating a multi-cultural ideology and a diverse range of hate speech. And it is here—on this western end of the street—that over the years has become known as Louisiana State's most prominent breeding ground for disappearances and suicides: the delta region's bastard lovechild between The Golden Gate Bridge and the Bermuda Triangle.

Yet, surprisingly, it took years for someone to actually get around to fencing off the property to stave off the constant influx of transients and adventurous teens who wanted to use the dormitories as a hang-out joint. With its lonely state of neglect and its variety of unkempt rooms, it was a perfect place for squatters and transients; and, with its easy access to the roof, it had also become a popular place for a person to leap to their death.

Rumor has it that if you managed a way into the dormitories you weren't going to be seen again. This myth grew as time went on, resulting in only increasing the place's attraction for some of the youths of Louisiana. Visiting the interior was now a popular rite of passage for some and waving to your friends from one of the many open window holes was a double-dare game ender to others.

Ten years after the last construction worker left the fenced-in security of the site, The Haunted Café opened its doors to the public. Located across the street in a bland strip mall, which had everything a person would need if they were looking for Chinese food, a wedding dress, or a reliable tax service, it was the perfect place for the lesser of the brave to convene: those who were also inclined to imbibe large doses of over-priced hot water strained through ground-up coffee beans and diluted with steamed milk and cinnamon. Here, on Rue la Barriere, patrons would sip their coffee and try to catch a glimpse of suspicious (and possibly supernatural) activity on the famed eighth floor.

Why the eighth floor? No one knew for sure but everyone had their theory.

And it is this very topic Mark Surine is going to help

explore tonight, not out of his own choice, but as a favor to his girlfriend who has volunteered as part of some college extra credit study. Here, on the eighth floor, and despite his better judgment, Mark is helping set up a new lighting system designed to hopefully catch proof of the existence of ghosts. The operative word here is "helping" since Mark's main function revolves entirely around how he could put his strong back to good use; he had long since graduated from college and had, in his time, little to do with this field of study. In the process of moving the equipment he was keyed into the night's logistical breakdown. They were to set up shop on the first floor: a collection of PCs, radios, tables, and other assorted gadgets that would, apparently, help them determine whether or not there was an afterlife. Then they were to patch in to the testing equipment eight floors up. Lastly, and the most time consuming of all: sit, wait, watch. However, for the time being, they were still setting up the lighting devices.

"Alright, so we're going to test each room for several hours," Dr. Gatreau began after the heavy lifting and lugging were done. "I developed these lights myself but we don't have a lot of them. Actually, I only have two." He looked less like a professor than a surly, middle-aged, stand-up comic in his "alternative" stage of development.

"How's this supposed to catch ghosts?" Mark asked.

"Well, it's not going to catch a ghost, per se. I'm looking at a different type of capturing. What this does is measure for irregularities in the room's reflectivity."

Mark's silence and stare told the man he didn't understand what he was getting at.

"Alright, so how do we see things?" he asked Mark.

"With our eyes," he answered.

"No, we see things because light reflects off of them, and then we can see them with our eyes," said one of the assistants as he snapped cables into place. His name was Derrick, a young man, slight-of-frame, and the proud owner of glasses which looked to be made out of telescope lenses. "Everything we see is a result of light bouncing off of objects."

"Right. Color reflects light and black absorbs it," added Shawn, another assistant to the professor. He was a large, bearded man who was predisposed to speaking in condescension.

But the doctor had to finish the line of reasoning. "So what I've designed is a device that will send pulses of light out into a room at a very rapid rate. We'll receive data of any change in the room's reflectivity. Theoretically, there should be no change in how the light bounces back to the device. However...if it does," he said, trailing off.

"We're measuring the LRV," said Derrick.

"The Light Reflectivity Value," added Shawn.

"And how does this reveal if a ghost is present?"

"Because if we can see a ghost then that means light is bouncing off of something, be it an object or an entity" said Derrick as he attempted to beat Shawn to the explanation. "If there is any fluctuation of reflectivity in the room then that means that something may be crossing over from one plane and over into our own."

"In other words, something is there that wasn't there before. We just have to filter out interference like dust," said Shawn, chiming in over Derrick. "What we're really looking for here are human shapes or large masses of reflective fluctuations. Supposedly this area in here is the best place to be."

"So if something materializes in the room or plods into view. You're looking for some type of large atmospheric change. A difference in what was already registered. Alright, got it. Good luck, I guess."

Having finished their work, the boys headed downstairs to complete the first floor setup. Shawn lagged behind as he toyed with his phone—presumably the app he had been developing.

"Is that the app that Josh guy was telling me about," asked Mark as he looked over his shoulder at the cellphone-lit face of Shawn. Mark was referring to Josh, the barista from across the street at the Haunted Café whom he met as he waited for the crew to show up for the night.

"Yeah, I just got the prototype in the other day. It's a hardware attachment for the phone. It's an all-inclusive program which includes EVP recognition, measures thermal activity, and includes GPS and mapping to steer the user in the right direction to changes in the room's atmosphere. It seems to be pretty operational."

"Well, that's pretty cool."

"Actually," said Derrick a few steps ahead, "Electronic Voice Phenomena and thermal imaging is outdated. You can chalk up thermal imaging changes to something like a beehive behind a wall or some guy standing by a door for too long and leaving his heat signature. Beside, any findings in EVP are just auditory hallucinations anyway. It's like when you're playing music really loud in your house and you can swear you hear someone calling your name behind you. We have a natural tendency to want to make sense of nonsense in the things we see and hear."

"Well I think it's a good thing, Shawn," added Dr. Gatreau who was at the head of the line going down the steps back to the bottom floor. "If we find anything in the LRV data you can corroborate it with your own findings. It'll be a one-two punch of evidence."

◊ ◊ ◊ ◊

Once downstairs and back on the first floor, Derrick and Shawn argued over something wrong in the connection between the computers while Dr. Gatreau looked for a way to get into the basement—another rumored hotspot of suspicious activity. The stairwell had been blocked off and locked to keep people out. Even though it was part of the deal in the price they paid to do this study, the key to the basement access door was, unfortunately, not supplied. Bec, a frumpy college girl with a cheerful disposition and penchant for peppermint oil, stood between Derrick and Shawn offering up annoying bits of advice which were of no help to either and succeeded in only making the two rivals even more tense toward one another. Just behind them was Loraine, a professor with a Master's degree in Criminal Justice and whose presence here was due to a favor owed to Dr. Gatreau and to provide a critical eye on the details as they went along. She was chatting away with someone on her phone, trying to keep it quiet, and pouring over Dr. Bill Gatreau's manifest and notes. Everyone was busy doing their own thing, helping out, pouring over, or searching through. It was the perfect opportunity to get away for a bit.

They had set up shop in an emptied-out room on the first floor. The sound of the outside generator filled the space as it chugged along to power their PCs. They were a skeleton crew of people who on any normal day would never spend time with each other. Their personal effects were stashed away inside this space, piled up on a metal folding table: Loraine's attaché case, Dr. Gatreau's unpacked cases from the school, and a pair of book sacks that belonged to Bec and Liz, Mark's girlfriend. Bec's bookbag appeared to have been recently purchased down by the local mall and was plastered in buttons which displayed her school spirit; Liz's backpack was an old green canvas style bag her father had given her from back in his Army days. It had been through the ringer but held up nicely through the years. This bag had been with her all through high school and even though the left strap was broken, she still insisted on using it just about every single day.

"Hey," Mark whispered to Liz, slightly touching her elbow. "I was thinking about going across the street—freshen up my coffee a bit. Wanna come with?"

Liz mulled this over as she bounced her head back and forth indecisively. Her red hair and blue eyes looked especially attractive in the fading light which cut through the buildings non-windows. She was one of those girl-next-door cutie-pies who never had to wear make-up; the kind of girl who talked an endless amount of trash about sitcoms but loved "reality" television; the kind of girl who was always great in small doses. "I think I'll stick around here. If Bill gets back and I'm not here it might look bad. You know how it is. But, hey, look. Could you maybe get me a cup?"

"Yeah. Black, right?"

"You got it. You're the best. Thanks."

In all respects, Rue la Barriere is a swollen varicose vein spat out of the capital city's bottom end, i.e., its most interesting end. The bulk of the street stretches just outside of the mall district, just passed the boutiques, and just far enough away from the suburbs. It is an afterthought and an aside—in how thoroughfares go—with a fat overgrown median, an abundance of tree shade, and a quiet disposition. With all things considered, Rue la Barriere was the very place to be if you were a dog whose life culminated in being struck by a car. Leaving the dormitories and getting back to the Haunted Café was a welcome respite for Mark; just crossing the street was the difference between leaping from Sarajevo to Palm Springs. In the time he'd been away, the café had really become busy. All kinds of kids were there with their laptops and phones out, sipping their expensive drinks and sharing exaggerated stories about their own spectral experiences.

"There he is," said Josh from behind the counter. "Came for a refresher, huh? How's it going over there?" At this revelatory line some of the people in the café perked up to check out who was among them. Josh passed over a new cup of coffee for Mark and an added Grande Medium Roast for his girl, or, his "main squeeze" as he put it, then offered out his hand in a friendly gesture.

Mark shook his hand and caught a whiff from Josh's long sleeve sweater. It was the kind of sweater a guy gets from his mom on Christmas, and it smelled like the kind of detergent and fabric softener she would use as well. "So, everything on the up-and-up over there, so to speak? I have a good feeling about tonight. This isn't like those other investigations." he continued. "Some of my friends came out to check out the progress." He pointed out Chloe, a girl not old enough to drink but old enough for tattoos, and Kyle, a boy who had just grown into his coolness. Mark wasn't sure, but it seemed like Josh lingered his eyes on just how close the two were sitting at their table from across the room. "Yeah, they've got a real interest in this kinda stuff, too."

"Well, thanks. I really appreciate it," Mark said. "You guys will be here all night, huh?"

"Pretty much. Hey, any chance I could swing over?"

"I completely forgot to ask about it but it shouldn't be a problem. They seem cool enough. If anyone says anything I'll vouch for you. It's cool."

"You know what," Josh said, putting his finger to his lips as if he had just remembered something. "Chloe, my friend here, has a lot of cool stories about that place. Let me introduce you guys." Josh rounded the counter and pulled Mark over to the table with his friends, leaving an annoyed customer by the register who would eventually opt to give up and go back to his table. Mark exchanged pleasantries and Josh prodded Chloe to tell him about the person she knew who was a friend-of-a-friend who killed himself after going into the building alone.

"It was back when I was in high school," she began. "We knew of this guy from another school who was dating this girl at the time that went to our school. One day he just went right on up to the roof and jumped off. It was so far from the road that no one saw the body for a long time. They finally found it months later when someone went inside to see if they could steal some pipes or something. Real fucked up stuff. I heard it had been so long that some animals had gotten to him. They said his face was all gnarled and fucked up."

"Yep, and one night I was working here," Josh added, "and I could see these figures moving around the eighth floor. Just these shadowy people-shapes staring out the upper windows."

"It was probably just gutterpunks," said Kyle. He wore a hoodie and sported a pitiful attempt at facial hair. He had a meticulously crafted appearance—a failure if he was going for the geek-chic look; a success if he wanted to resemble Waldo after he'd been found drying out in a rehab. Kyle had, what some would consider to be, a very "punchable" face.

Mark thanked Josh again and went to join the crew across the street. *Back to the Dark Ages*, he thought.

When he rejoined the team he discovered Derrick had gone back upstairs to fix a problem with the connection. Bec sat in the glow of the computer monitor light while communicating with him via walkie-talkie.

"It looks like some of the wires got yanked free. Maybe we tripped over something when we came back downstairs," he said through the radio.

Bec radioed back up to Derrick. "Well, it seems to be working now. You can come on down now." She looked a little worried.

Loraine stood up and joined everyone over by the computers. "It's very possible we could have some squatters still up there." It was the first bit of conversation from the woman Mark had heard since she got on site. "Wires just don't unplug themselves." When she spoke over Mark's shoulder a heavy scent of cigarette smoke and stale coffee breath hit him. She looked dead serious in her belief there might be other people in the building mucking up the operation.

"Well, that's why we've got you here," said Dr. Gatreau. "You can go up there. Slap some cuffs on someone. Rough 'em up; take 'em down."

Loraine stood stone faced. "I'm not a cop, Bill. And you're not doing anything. Why don't you go up and give your boy a hand."

"I *am* doing something. I'm working on basement access as well as the most important job of all— supervising."

Loraine walked off in the middle of his sentence to retrieve her phone and pack of cigarettes.

"Ah relax," the doctor said to Loraine as Derrick came through the stairwell doors. On his way to rejoin the group, he gave an enthusiastic thumbs-up.

"That should do it. I think we're all good to go."

"I'm really glad you came tonight," Liz said to Mark. "It means a lot." The two walked down the first floor landing and chatted a bit while the crew waited by the computer monitors. There was a bit of downtime while everyone watched as the data streamed in from the LRV devices upstairs. They came to a part of the building where the walls weren't yet finished. If you looked up you could see rectangular holes in the floor above where the tubs would've been placed; the pipes inside the concrete walls had been cut away; there were recesses for windows or countertops. For almost 20 years the place remained virtually unchanged, collecting dust and spray-paint opinions. The building was an ominous thing to behold from inside: a ten-story, three-hundred-room vacant building that was a post-apocalyptic fetishist's wet dream.

Mark found a convenient place, picked up Liz, and sat her up on a waist high ledge. She put her hands on his shoulders and smiled at him. One of the first things she told him when they started dating was a memory she had from back when she was three or five-years-old—too early, he felt, to significantly judge the validity of a memory. It was about how she had been in the back of her parents' car, riding home one day, and passing by an old house. She said as they passed by the old house she swore she saw an old ghostly woman sitting in a rocking chair on the front porch. When she first told Mark this he laughed a bit. He said she was much too young to remember accurately and what she probably saw was just an old lady or maybe she was getting a dream and a real experience mixed together. It was quite possible she just imagined what she saw when she was a kid and now, through the passing of time, that imaginary thing had solidified into a memory. Because, really, what do you remember vividly at such an early age?

Back then, his reaction seemed to have really annoyed her. She was certain of what she saw and resented his casual dismissal of her claim. But ever since that initial experience she had held an interest in paranormal investigations.

"I can't wait to see what we get tonight," she said.

"Yeah, I think the coffee shop kids can't wait either. They seemed pretty pumped up about all this. They're amassing quite a crowd."

The way she looked at him; the way she rubbed her hands on his shoulders as she sat there in the darkness, silent, looking at him—it made him uneasy. Something was being unsaid and he knew what it was.

Mark had been out of college now for almost a year and still had yet to find a stable job—a real career path. He had also been quite content in allowing their relationship to putter along at the same slow pace. 'Spinning your wheels,' was how she put it. When she clapped her hands down on his shoulders and looked off into the distance he knew she was done and wanted to get down, head back to the team, and end the awkward silence. But then she spoke.

"What are we doing after this?"

"Breakfast, I hope."

"That's not what I mean—"

"FUCK!" It was Derrick from over by the computers. Liz looked over her shoulder and hopped down. Shawn was voicing something and sounded upset but they were unable to make out what he was saying.

By the time they got back to the team Derrick had stormed off with his flashlight & radio to head back upstairs.

"We were getting something pretty interesting," Bec began to explain. "But then we lost connection...again."

"What were you getting?" asked Liz.

"It started off small at first," the doctor began to answer; the echo of Derrick's stomping up the stairs faded away the higher he went. "We thought it was falling dust but it got larger and larger. It would come and go. Very interesting stuff."

"And then it just stopped all together. Nothing," Bec said as she looked over at Mrs. Boman, clearly afraid of the possibility they might not be alone and that someone was screwing around with them. However, she was reasonably certain Derrick would fix the problem without any problem and they'd be back online.

But five minutes turned into ten and all attempts to reach Derrick with the radio had come up silent.

"He took his radio with him, right?" Loraine asked.

"Yes, I watched him take it," replied Bec.

"Well, someone should go up and check on him."

"Don't worry. He's got it," assured the doctor.

But ten minutes turned into twenty, and as the time went on, an uneasy hush settled on the crew.

Liz walked over to the stairwell, stuck her head inside and looked up, listening for anything. She was soon joined by Mark, both listening with their shoulders at the entrance of the stairs. And indeed there came some sounds from up high—the sound of metal hitting floor, maybe a door closing. It was hard to tell if these little noisy occurrences were the result of a person milling about or just the associated sounds of an old building settling in the cooling night.

Each floor of the dormitory had several holes; it was quite possible to fall through these holes if you weren't paying attention to where you were going. Having a flashlight was imperative here. This also meant sound carried from floor to floor, that is, if the sound was loud enough.

"Did you hear that?" Liz asked.

Loraine came over and asked what the two were talking about. She suggested again that there might be people up top. "Alright, I'm going to take a flashlight and radio to check it out."

"I'll go with you, Mrs. Boman," said Mark. "If you're right then I don't want you going up alone," But as Mark volunteered he felt Liz's hand grip around his wrist, a nonverbal wish for him to stay with her. Luckily, Shawn offered up his assistance, stating that he knew the equipment and might need to lend Derrick a hand.

They agreed to make it quick.

And without further word, they headed off upstairs in search of Derrick and what might be holding him up.

Soon after their departure, Dr. Gatreau shuffled over to Liz and Mark. "This might be a good time for you to top off the gas in the generator outside, Mark. If you please. Since things seem to be down for the time being, I'm going to look again for another way into the basement. Maybe there was a janitor's access or something. Liz if you could stick with Bec that'd be great. She's getting a bit antsy over there. Jot down whatever you see, please."

Outside, Mark could see that the coffee shop had become very busy. Looking up at the building he noticed the flashing lights of the LRV device could be seen from the street. Surely, this accounted for people phoning their friends to come watch as things went down into the night—a gathering of ghost groupies.

Unfortunately, however, the good doctor forgot to give Mark the key to his van, leaving the extra gas cans locked up within.

When Mark returned inside, the man-in-charge could not be found. He wasn't by the stairwell, not by the elevator, and not over by the girls. Mark stood by the open door to the outside and looked across the street to a completely different world. He looked over at Liz and Bec as he propped the entrance door open, "have you guys seen Dr. Bill? He has the keys to the van."

"No, I haven't heard from anyone upstairs and Bill went off without saying anything," Bec answered as she stretched her back and rubbed her eyes "I'm about to get frustrated and say fuck this shit. Screw the credit. You know, I had a chance to take part in a study that involved just watching a movie. And I chose this 'cause I thought it'd be kinda cool."

As Bec edged at losing her patience, Liz picked up Dr. Gatreau's notes—the ones Loraine had been reading—and started to flip through them; Mark stood by the entrance of the dorms, his head down in thought.

"Alright," he said. "I'm going to go up."

"No, you're not," blurted Liz.

"Look, I'll just run up. Their radios probably ran out of battery power. They probably weren't charged or something. I'll just run up, see if they're okay, and then come right back down. That'll be it. Even if they need help with something. That'll be it."

"Well, I'll come with you," Liz offered.

"No, stay here with Becca—"

"Don't call me Becca. I hate that. And, yeah, Liz can stay here. Sounds great. But Mrs. Loraine took the last of the radios. So just head back down when you know what's up."

"Alright, and if I hear or see anything suspicious I'll come right back down and we'll get out of here."

And with that, Mark disappeared into the stairwell. Liz and Bec listened as his footsteps faded up the way.

◊ ◊ ◊ ◊

Across the street at the Haunted Café a commotion began to stir. Fingers were pointing upwards. Friends were trying to convince their more skeptical companions there was something to be seen up on the eighth floor.

"I'm telling you, it's right there. I'm looking right at it."

"It's a person standing by the window."

"I'm just not seeing it."

Josh stood outside the coffee shop, puffing on his cigarette, and trying to work up the nerve to go across the street. He glanced over his shoulder to catch Kyle saying something in Chloe's ear. Whatever it was, it made her smile. Josh looked down at the ground, taking a drag from his cigarette as the volume around him grew.

But the excitement and chatter died when the bells over at the Blessed Sacrament Church began to toll.

When Chloe looked over at him all he could do was shrug his shoulders. He hadn't heard the bells in years.

◊ ◊ ◊ ◊

From inside the stairwell, Mark could hear the thick ringing through the walls and window holes. As they chimed and chimed he took his time and watched each step he took, trying not to identify his presence, listening for any signs of the team as he went.

As he reached the eighth floor the bells came to a close and Mark rounded the corner with care. And as the echo of the ringing subsided, Mark could hear rustling from down the dim hallway: a passage lacking doors, strewn with debris, and rife with exposed wiring and rebar.

"Mark, are you there? Anyone?"

It was Bec coming through a radio—either Derrick's or Loraine's radio.

"Anybody? Come in," she called again, allowing Mark to zero in on its location. It was just halfway down the hall and on the floor. Mark approached it quietly and scooped it up. He instinctively hunched down behind something, turned the volume down, and responded to Bec.

"Hey, I found a radio," he whispered into the mic. "No sign of anyone else though."

"Come back down, Mark." It was Liz this time.

"Alright, just don't radio again. I don't want to call attention to myself."

But up ahead the lights were flashing in the room and the rustling sound continued. They had to be up here somewhere. The sound he heard was like a desk being moved over a dusty concrete floor—metal grinding on coarse grit—it was coupled with a heavy breathing and a wet knocking. It couldn't be but just a few rooms ahead.

Mark decided to simply peek around the corner, and if there was any indication there was anyone else he hadn't seen before he would bolt for the stairwell, grab the girls on his way out, and call it a night. The professors and assistants seemed nice enough but they were all adults and, well, best wishes to them.

Finally, he came to the room where the LRV machine was flashing away in the empty space. There, on the floor, was the unplugged system of cables which were supposed to be attached to the data relay that went downstairs to the first floor computer system. He looked over his shoulder—didn't see anyone—reached down, and plugged them back in.

"Hang on, I got something," said Bec through the radio. Mark quickly grabbed at the volume knob and turned it completely off this time.

As he crouched down again, he rounded the corner to leave the room and head back to the stairway. That was when he saw the strange configuration randomly appearing in front of the lights. It was a large shoulder-width blip that came and went in the flashing. The LRV device was located to one side of the room and aimed at the opposite wall. As it flashed its lights it illuminated the bare walls, counter ledge, and window frames—not an incredible amount to take in. But, sure enough, every few seconds a mass of haze would appear in its sights.

"Alright, fuck this," he whispered to himself as he slowly left the room, checking the hallway to the left and right. Still alone.

He worked his way back to the stairs and, once inside, turned the radio back on to call down to Liz and Bec. Still whispering, "Hey, I found the machine and plugged the cables back in. I'm heading down."

"Mark, the data is processing but, so far, what I'm seeing is pretty crazy."

"Any sign of anybody else down there?"

"No, I thought they were in the test room with you. I mean, according to this…"

Mark turned the radio down a tad while Bec trailed off and he looked back down the hall. He concentrated on his surroundings: the rhythmic flashing of the LRV, the sound of metal scraping against the floor, and the wet thuds. And then came the distinct murmur from the back of someone's throat.

It came out of the last room.

◊ ◊ ◊ ◊

Downstairs, Bec quickly jotted down the findings coming from the newly connected data stream as well as the time (including the questionable whereabouts of the rest of the team in relation to the experiment). Liz had Dr. Gatreau's notes in her hand and had taken to reading the pages where Loraine had left off. As she poured over these notes her eyes dotted from page to screen, trying to keep up with two things at once. But then she came upon an interesting bit of information at the back of the binder, causing her to leave Bec to her note taking.

Up on the 8th floor, Mark crept back down the hall with the idea in mind that maybe this was all part of the experiment: a covert conspiracy to see how people react when they think they're in a supernatural situation. This was only at the back of his mind, however. Someone was obviously down at the end of the hall from what he could hear. But it was dark—the city and street lights that drizzled in through the open window holes only provided so much light. Just a simple peek would be enough, and then he'd head back downstairs and be done with this.

He passed the room with the LRV device and edged the corner to the last room at the end of the hall. Here, the sounds became clearer, more pronounced and defined. A moist thump followed by a scrape-thump, scrape-thump, scrape. Mark, with his back to the gray concrete wall, drew his attention to this rhythm, to the padding wet sound from around the corner. It sounded like a wet fish falling down stairs, a beggar gimp being spanked with a sirloin, or a bat wing slapping a baby's face.

Mark slowly peaked around the doorway to catch a glimpse of this pattern.

Downstairs, as Bec had her eyes glued to the data stream—her note taking, forgotten—Liz busied herself with rifling through Dr. Bill Gatreau's notes. She skimmed over words and skipped around, getting the gist of what he had been doing, to the culmination of what they were researching tonight, when she came upon an interesting detail.

"Hey Bec, did you know that he's done this experiment before?"

"Huh?" she responded absently.

"Yeah, he's done this before on a much smaller scale.

Actually got some results."

"Oh, yeah, he told us about that. He just ramped up the lighting module. Are you seeing this?" she asked, pointing at the screen. "The more this goes on, the more these forms are becoming increasingly pronounced. They pop up and go away—masses of disturbances by the opposite wall."

But from what Liz was reading she could see it might be more than that. With a combination of what she was reading and what she had heard in his lectures, it had all started to make a bit of sense. It was more than just finding a reading: collecting and capturing a glimpse of something.

"Bec, I think he figured out a way to actually coax things out—to bring something over for a moment. He has a theory about a frequency disturbance protocol or something." Liz put the notes down, touched Bec on the shoulder, and added, "I don't think he's trying to stumble upon a supernatural event. I think he's trying to force it out into the open."

The round-faced girl turned her attention away from the computer monitor, stood up, tossed her clipboard down on to the counter and said, "That's it. I'm out."

◊ ◊ ◊ ◊

By the window and looking out into the distance from the eighth floor perch, was Derrick. He stood motionless, swaying only slightly as his body involuntarily fended off the effects of gravity—like a hollow pine tree in the wind. But the dull thudding continued, and over by the side, as Mark's periphery cleared the door jamb, he saw its origin: the side of Loraine's head as it violently thrust upon the crotch of Shawn—his docile cumbrous frame limbered back-and-forth to the work being played—the fingers of his right hand were wedged into his mouth, clenching his bottom jaw; the left gripped the right wrist and yanked down in spurts of effort.

"Mark, according to these readings if you're—"

He quickly reached for the radio to turn off the sound of Bec's voice coming through, but it was too late. He had their attention.

Loraine's head stopped bobbing and moved away from the belly which obscured the entirety of her head. As she looked over in Mark's direction she exposed her face to the open, revealing an almost cartoonish cave to her mouth. Her lower jaw had been dislocated and hung down loosely to her collar bone. Her tongue lolled out like a single sock sticking out of a drawer. The eyes in her face were wet, bulged in black-rimmed bruising, while the lower lids drooped as if they had been microwaved; the open wound of her maw leaked drops of blood on her already toxic liver spotted old arms.

She stood up slowly as Shawn turned to the sound of the radio as well. His hands worked at his jaw to rip it free of the joints and mumbled something between the fingers which were stuffed inside—tears leaked from the edge of his globular eyes.

Derrick stood unaware by the window, motionless, still swaying only slightly as his body involuntarily fended off the effects of gravity—a tree about to topple.

Mark turned and ran down the hall. He heard a commotion coming from the direction of the stairwell ahead—a noise of something being shifted or moved. So he turned into the nearest room and hid behind a large tub. It was one of the tubs still not yet placed in its bathroom home, leaving the hole in the floor exposed.

From behind the tub he heard the sound of a joint popping, a wet hollow snap followed by an exhausted exhale resembling that of climactic relief. They were moving down the hall, approaching the room of Mark's hiding place.

As they passed, Mark caught a glimpse of the blood stained crotch of Shawn: the area Loraine had been smacking her gaping face against. The red-smeared khakis, still zipped up from having never actually been rent open, was the lascivious canvas worked by some broken automaton possibly attempting to reenact something remembered from long ago. Their gait was almost newborn-ish, like something wasn't used to the operational controls. And their eyes were vacant, as if disconnected or vestigial.

Once they had passed—and Mark was reasonably satisfied he wasn't in ear shot—he found the hole in the floor, got on his belly and climbed through the tub sized opening. His body dangled between floors and with a swinging motion he was able to drop to the floor beneath, avoiding a continuous fall. He decided in lieu of the stairs he would have to sneak back down this way.

Drop by drop, floor by floor, he worked his way to the bottom landing; crawling through each tub hole, dangling over the bathroom, swinging and then dropping to the ground beneath, it must've taken him three times as long to accomplish the task than by way of the stairs—but it felt like an hour.

As soon as he had worked his way to the first floor he went directly to the make-shift office space where Liz and Bec had been. But it was empty. He stood there panting in the lonely room, covered in dust, his hands torn up from his efforts. He called out their names only to be met with silence ringing back. So he left the office space and moved toward the front entrance, still propped open, and looking out to the bustle of activity across the street. From up the uneven road he saw Josh, the barista, jogging up the drive path. He was just in time to join Mark at the dark entrance as the generator decided to sputter and die.

"What the fuck happened to you?" he asked from the look of Mark's dusty covered clothing and hair.

"Did you see anyone leave here?" Mark asked while out of breath.

"Actually, just the big girl, why? What's up?"

"No one else? Just the one?"

"Yeah." Josh motioned over to the dead generator with his hand as if to ask if Mark needed a hand.

"The gas is locked in the van. I don't have the key."

They stood without saying a word. Mark, breathing heavy, the generator cooling off in the tall grass. And then they heard a familiar sound from within the confines of the dormitory building.

—*ding*—

Mark and Josh's eyes narrowed as they heard the all too recognizable tone of an elevator arriving. They turned their heads to look at the elevator sitting in the darkness. Josh took a step forward, closer to Mark and closer to being inside.

—*ding*—

It sounded again. This time they were sure: it was from the elevator. And as the doors began to slide open there came a grinding sound of metal rubbing against a sandy grain; a shower of dust broke free as the two panels separated and a dim light filled the foyer opening, exposing an object in its interior cell.

"What is that?" asked Josh, standing closer to Mark now.

"That," Mark began to answer, "is my girlfriend's backpack."

◊ ◊ ◊ ◊

The cables holding the lift in place creaked and moaned as the lights flickered inside, illuminating the green canvas book bag in the corner. After a few seconds the doors began to close again, until slamming shut with a thump, returning the first floor to darkness.

As Mark began to go toward the elevator, Josh grabbed his arm... "What are you doing, man?" But Mark wrenched his arm free and moved toward the elevator as the doors began to open again, spilling its dim light to the floor.

Mark poked his head into the lift's entrance, holding his hand to the side to keep the doors from closing again. He gave the inside a cursory glance, inspecting its state. After retrieving the book sack he looked over to the buttons on the panel. It seemed that the "B" had been pressed owing to the fact that the dust on the button had been smeared away.

"I think she went to the basement. Maybe with Dr. Gatreau or something."

Josh looked off through the dorm's entrance doors and to the gathering of people at his coffee house—scanning the crowd for Chloe's face. He seemed to mull it over for a few seconds before coming to his final decision. "Well, let's make history," he suggested with a seemingly excited kick to his voice, adding a wry smile.

"Here, hold the door. There's something I gotta get."

Mark ran to the office space and picked up Shawn's cellphone, searched for his custom app, and ran back to the elevator.

Once inside, he hiked the backpack over his shoulder, pressed the "B" and glanced over to Josh. The elevator doors closed and the machine began to move.

◊ ◊ ◊ ◊

The short elevator ride came to a creaking halt. Once the doors began to open, and Shawn's cellphone app finished initializing, they were met by the darkness of the basement hall. It was an all-encompassing blackness once they stepped off, entered its constricted space, and stood in front of the closed elevator doors. The only light was from the cellphone screen. *Why would Liz come down here*, Mark thought to himself.

He called her name out as Josh stuck close to his back. But there was no answer. So he tried her name a second and third time—nothing.

As they got closer to the end of the hall, Mark noticed that Shawn's cellphone app started to act up. The screen displayed what looked like an odometer: a red circle with a pointer that jostled slightly in the middle. It was when they got to the end of the hall that the top of the circle turned green, the pointer positioned itself in its center, and an "EVP" icon lit up to the upper right, quite possibly pointing them to where they wanted to go.

Every so often, Mark pointed the cellphone's screen in front of him, shining the light out, illuminating what was ahead. There wasn't much to the basement facility, but there was a door just up ahead, slightly cracked open with a sliver of light bleeding through. And the closer they got the more they began to hear a set of voices coming from within. Once at this door, the cellphone app's circle turned completely green, pointing at their very location, signifying they were in the thick of it.

"It'd be great if it was a surprise party, huh?" asked Josh in a whisper over Mark's shoulder.

But Mark didn't answer. He turned the cell screen off, put it in his pocket, and edged the door open.

The door whined open to a street-light lit room: its lamp source, the windowless bays at the top of the wall—not the second LRV machine, unplugged & in the corner, its lamps still cooling. This cataract pall cast a glow into the room and the flock contained within it: dozens of people resting upon pews: half on one side of the room, half on the other. They sat facing forward with their backs to the opening door. Every one of them held a black umbrella up to conceal their faces, creating a line of dusty black fabric.

They faced a podium where a male figure stood. This shape also held a black umbrella up, hiding his face. His right hand rested on the podium edge and as the door slid open, Mark could see his chin move to his direction.

But there, just below the podium, was Liz. She was wearing a dirty white veil in her hair which flowed back behind her. And on her face, just above her nose, was a mask of stained silk fabric—attached from ear to ear—draping down past her chin, covering her mouth. Her white tank top shirt had been wrenched free from her pants and still held the clenched-fist wrinkle marks at the stomach. She looked off in the distance, unaware of the door opening—unaware of herself.

Mark quickly opened the door the rest of the way and rushed over to Liz, leaving Josh behind. "Liz, come on. We're leaving. We have to go." He reached out and grabbed her by the wrist. But as he shook it to rouse her out of whatever spell she was in, he caught a glimpse of the audience from the front. He could tell they must be drifters, squatters, and lost teenagers; a testament from their clothing being dirty, unwashed, and having not been changed in a long time.

But at the back of the congregation he could see one set of clothing was practically new. It could only be that of Dr. Gatreau. He sat still, holding an umbrella up to cover his face.

"Dearly beloved," the man at the altar began. Mark's head snapped in his direction. "We are gathered here today…"

Josh had seen enough and bolted off down the hall. As soon as he broke into a sprint a ragged looking parishioner stood and gave chase. This person held on to their umbrella and ran after Josh at an alarmingly quick speed, their hard-soled shoes beating on the pavement floor. The door to the congregation slammed closed behind him, leaving the sound of pounding footsteps trailing off into the distance.

But the footsteps ceased, followed by a dull thud. And then there was nothing.

"…in the presence of these witnesses…" the man at the altar continued. His voice was airy, deep and distant as if from some far-off radio broadcast.

"Liz, come on. We have to get out of here," Mark urged. But she stood there, staring off vacantly. Her eyes were dead eyes—wet but clouded over. "You're not yourself. Liz, wake up."

Mark yelled his last batch of words into his girlfriend's face. But she remained oblivious. He had enough of the nonsense and was done with all of this. Mark tightened his grip on his girlfriend's wrist and pulled on her as he went to dash down the aisle.

He stopped in his tracks when his attempt to flee was met by the entire congregation quickly standing to their feet in unison.

And again the bells began to toll.

◊ ◊ ◊ ◊

The patrons at the coffee shop stood—rising on their

feet when the bells at the church began to toll again. The flashing lights from inside the dormitories had stopped, the sound of the generator rolling had died off, and for a while there was only silence. But now, the bells began to toll and there was an electricity in the air.

The tolling rang and rang and rang. With each beat, the patience of the public tightened. Their coffees were set down. Their phones were put away. Their conversations had ended.

And when the bells finally fell silent it passed an infectious tone across their faces. All were at attention and a hush fell upon the pass as the street lights were snuffed out.

There was a movement at the Zilo dormitories entrance. Something was moving about inside. It looked like dark waves—indecipherable in its ripples.

There was a sound: a collected inhale taken from all the coffee shop patrons as they watched a congregation of black umbrellas proceed out of the dormitory entrance. All the regulars at the Haunted Café moved to the edge of the street for a better look, emptying out the establishment and watching in rapt attention.

Two files of people, two-by-two, came out of the dormitory doors in an organized procession. Male figure coupled with female figure—each in file, each in step, and each held up a black umbrella to cover their face. It was like the old derelict building had finally coughed up its dead flowers.

And as the procession came to a close, a woman in a dirty white veil emerged at the tail. She had crimson hair which fell in flows to the back as her chin was pushed up high in pride. Her hands circled round and round on her full belly: a false bride great with a fake child.

With no movement and no traffic on the street, the

sound of their feet crunching in the gravel and grass was all that could be heard. That and, having finally figured out the muscle control to lean his body over the edge, the heavy plop of Derrick's body hitting the ground from its high perched drop. The procession left the confines of the Terry Zilo property line and spilled off into the street where they cut a path to the north, Liz taking up the rear.

It was quite the parade.

And it was when she, the blushing bride, finally came to cross paths with the adoring attendance that she graced them with a better look at her wonderful gift. For there, stuffed under her cotton white shirt, was the severed head of Mark.

From underneath her shirt his nose pushed out from the stretching fabric like a distended belly button. Each circle her hands made around his mantled brow pulled the fabric back across his sunken eyes. His hay blonde hair was matted to his face and shifted about as the surrogate corrected its position with every few steps. Her lap was a stigmatic stain designed by the dribble of blood from Mark's cleaved neck.

And as Liz passed by the crowd at the street's edge, just an arm's length away, all eyes moved down to her stomach. The boys were all smiles, some tearing up at the sight of her. There were few girls in attendance, but one moved to the front of the file to get a better look. Liz, passing from face to face, finally came to pass Chloe. The girl reached her hand out to caress the side of Liz's bloated stomach, across Mark's shirt-covered face.

It was when the parade passed that the crowd began to stir. Without looking at one another they stepped into the street and joined in line, each stuffing a hand into their mouth, pulling downwards to let the visitors in.

And on they marched to slip away down the beat of

Rue la Barriere.

DOG KILLER
by Nathan Pettigrew

His father reeked of body odor and bourbon—the sweaty armpit and acidic stink bringing Roland back to those nights when his father would throw his mother against the refrigerator. The impact lasting for years, Roland felt it again now for the first time in over a decade.

He unwrapped himself from his father's arms. "Where's Mom? She okay?"

"She's fine," the man said, looking into his son's eyes with a bloodshot stare behind dirty glasses. "She's back at the house getting things ready for you. She's doing just fine."

Or maybe doing her damnedest to appear fine in long sleeves on a scorching southern day for the sake of hiding bruises.

"Are you hungry?" his father asked. "We can head into that bar before we go down to get your luggage."

Roland nodded toward his rolling duffle. "This is it."

"That's it?"

"All the traveling I've done for school," he said. "Got used to packing light."

"I see," said the man with bloodshot eyes. "Then let's get you home. We can pick up some fried frog legs on the way."

The two overpasses crossed at thirty feet above the swamp, matching the exact mental image which Roland's mind had held onto. The world hadn't taken that from him, though it had given him the cold, hard truth. The world is not a friend. The world is a fight—you win or you lose—but we all get a corner to come back to between each round, and that is home.

If change and death were the only guarantees in life, then they weren't worth a dried up drop of pelican shit in Cajun Country, the stench of hot marsh still dominating the swamp air—that rotten egg smell of mud and decay.

Like Roland's father—the man looked the same as he had a year ago. Shit, he looked the same as he had five years ago. Not a single brown strand around the back of his bald head had gone gray, and beneath his chin, the red flab still buried his neck while sagging, but no more or less than it did in Roland's memories of trying to yank it off as a boy.

"You're a vampire. Aren't you, Dad?"

"A vampire?"

"You don't age."

"It's probably the exercise," his father said. "Your mother and I get to party naked a lot more now that your grandma's out of the house."

"Jesus, Dad. That's—Never mind."

The bald man chuckled, his shoulders bouncing above that no-neck of his, that flabby chin—Mr. Head and Shoulders.

Growing up, his mother would always say Roland was his daddy's spitting image, seeing how they had the same eyes, lips and noses, the same hands, but sitting side by side today as men, Roland couldn't see himself.

"What about you, son? You're looking good. You staying out of trouble?"

"Yeah, Dad. I'm not sixteen anymore."

"I guess not," his father said, taking the exit for Highway 90.

Roland smiled.

Ol' 90 brought folks everywhere south of New Orleans. For hours. Places most out-of-towners don't know exist. Small towns and city parishes with populations of 30,000—all accessible through a barren flatland of highway with only a ditch of uncut grass dividing the two sides of double-lanes. The gateway to the bayous. The memories…

And unfortunately, the pollution.

Seemed as though they couldn't drive fifty yards without seeing shreds and pieces of torn up tires along the side of the highway—the one sight down here that Roland didn't miss.

His father's hand started shaking, and for being hungover, the man was fast; he caught Roland noticing and took his hand away from the wheel, closing and opening a fist, and then again, stretching out the shakes.

"Dad. I'm just gonna come out and say it, okay? 'Cause I hate this awkward shit, but I know you're drinking again. You reek."

Roland's father lit a Winston while his glasses reflected its flame. "No one's buying our shrimp," he said, putting a crack in his window and exhaling his first drag. "If it comes from the Gulf, they won't touch it. Oysters, too. Nothing's selling and the moratoriums aren't helping. People who had nothing to do with the spill are suffering. Men with families." His father took another drag, this time exhaling the smoke through his nose. "I mean at this rate? Watch. A year from now, you won't even recognize the seafood industry down here. And companies like BP will go on thriving."

"I'm—I'm sorry, Dad. Mom didn't say anything about

y'all being in trouble."

"We didn't want you to worry."

"Oh, so I'm supposed to worry less with you drinking again?"

"I'm fine," his father said. "I stopped off for a Bloody Mary at Spahr's on the way out, but that was well over an hour ago."

"Hold up. You drank today, Dad? Are you freakin' serious? I just thought you were hungover."

"The Bloody Mary helps with the hangover," his father said, and then he kissed the Winston for a long drag.

"Dad."

"Relax, boy. I said I'm fine."

"Don't tell me to relax. Pull over. I'm driving."

The Infinity went off the road and into the gravel on his father's side leaving a cloud trail of rocks and shell fragments.

"Jesus." Roland grabbed the armrest on his door.

His father steered them back onto the road. "I got it, son."

"No. You don't got shit," Roland said. "You're going off the road. Now freakin' pull over. I'm driving."

Rather than pull over, Roland's father pulled a fifth of Jim Beam from the carpet space between his seat and the door. He unscrewed the cap and took a sip, his eyes off the road, head tilted back.

"God. What are you trying to prove here?" Roland asked.

The Infinity went off the road for a second time blowing through the rocks and shells, the machinery dragging more than driving.

"Damn it, Dad."

"Come on. I'm just having fun with you," his father said, steering them back. "Like I used to, remember? Just trying to give you a good scare is all."

"Is that all? 'Cause it's working," said Roland. "Okay? Now please. Pull over."

His father closed and opened another fist, stretching out those shakes, again and again.

"Dad."

"All right, boy. All right. Just wait until we cross the canal."

Keeping a steady ascension on the narrow bridge, his father flashed yellow stained teeth through a grin.

"You've been up north too long. You know that, boy?"

"Is that right?"

"You're just like them now," his father said. "You don't know how to let things roll off your shoulders."

"You're the asshole who sent me away and I don't recall you giving me a choice in the matter. So enough with the shit, already."

The grin on his father's face fell away. "Take it easy, son. I'm just teasing you."

"Whatever. Just watch the damn road."

A gunmetal Malibu parked off to the side of the highway came into view on the other side of the bridge, the driver knelt down next to the rear tire, changing a flat.

"Holee—Look at that guy," said Roland. "A Tiger Woods doppelganger. Looks just like him. That's uncanny."

His father came off the bridge and veered toward the median beyond the Malibu.

"You're stopping here? Guy's gonna think you're pulling over to help him."

First flicking his cigarette butt through the crack in his window, Roland's father used a finger to push his glasses up on the bridge of his nose and continued onto the median, slowing fast.

Roland pointed ahead. "The exit for 182's just right there. Why don't you wait until we're off 90?"

"You wanted me to pull over. I'm pulling over," his father said.

"You know what, Dad? You're right. Just—Watch out for that mess."

The man stopped inches away from another abandoned rubble of ripped up tires—and so many of them—like a tire graveyard next to the marsh.

"Damn," Roland said. "The parish can't come out and clean this up? I mean, look at this. No wonder the rest of the country thinks we're ass-backwards."

"That's Jindal for you," his father said. "The man's gutted our entire state—everything from public schools to roads."

"It's always been this way, though," said Roland. "'Least as far as the roads are concerned. I don't know. I thought you liked him. You campaigned for him. What changed?"

"The state did, son. For the worst."

So the currents of change had crossed the homeland of Cajun Country after all. Roland's upgrade in status from exile to a welcome son returning home wouldn't be much help in a head-on collision with a people and a place he no longer related to as much as he'd thought.

"Well that's it, then," he said. "I think I've seen enough for one trip. Go ahead and take me back to the airport."

His father chuckled. "Come on, boy."

They got out to switch sides, and it wasn't three seconds before Roland brought his arm up to wipe his forehead. Hair that once curled out from his arm lay flat and pressed wet against his skin. Humidity had hijacked the air leaving no room to breathe, and no room to think, really, save for thoughts of suffocating and drowning both at once.

His father's Jim Beam bottle remained shoved down into the carpet space between the driver's seat and door that Roland closed with a muted thud. And damn. The Infinity. Roland hadn't driven her before. Her midnight blue interior gleamed that Armor-All shine.

He put her in reverse, backing away from the tire graveyard and giving himself some room to pull out.

"Hold on a minute, son. I think that man does need help. He's coming to the car."

Roland heard the words, but not his father—it didn't click. He continued to reverse.

"Son. Watch out!"

"What?"

The rock bashing sound of the impact and the Malibu man getting crushed beneath the Infinity's rear tire sent Roland into a dizzy state of hyperawareness, his heart racing into an abyss of butterflies.

No.

The road behind was a short distance of concrete before a bridge with no one coming down.

Out in front were miles of grass dividing a highway with no one coming from the other side.

Roland shoved his boot into the gas, the tires screaming through another bump when searching for traction.

"Son. Son, what are you doing?"

"It's all clear, Dad." His eyes flipped to the rearview, and there in broad daylight lay a man as still as the pavement beneath his body.

Roland wiped his eyes. Salt drops trickling down from his forehead refused to slow down, and then sped up— even with the A/C cranked. Tears blurred his vision at the thought of children looking through a window, waiting, and then seeing their world come to an end when a police cruiser pulled into the driveway instead of their father's Malibu.

"Stop the car, Roland."

"I know," Roland said at first. "I mean—Hold on." He took the exit for 182. "We're okay, Dad. I can make it."

"You can't," his father said. He grabbed the wheel.

"No." Roland jammed an elbow into his father's upper lip and watched the man fall back against his headrest while holding his mouth, his glasses unbalanced and his eyes bunched up.

Roland flinched with every breath thereafter, unsure if his father intended to strike him or make another grab for the wheel.

"You're panicking," the man said, and he was calm. He took off his glasses.

"No. I'm not panicking. I'm going home. Okay? I'm making a conscious choice."

"Son. I want you to listen to me. Okay?"

Roland's hands were shaking. He took one from the wheel, closing and opening a fist.

"I know you're scared, but you can still come out of this. Okay? You have to turn the car around. You hear me?"

"No one saw us, Dad."

"Just trust me, son. We're not even a mile yet from the exit back to 90. Turn around and go back before it's too late."

"Yeah? And what if it is too late? What if someone's there right now? Then what?"

"We'll have to cross that bridge when it comes," his father said. "But you're not helping yourself by staying the course you're on."

By staying the course he was on?

The course he was on, as far as Roland could see, meant freedom.

"I'm going home."

"No. Face the music," his father said.

Roland let off the gas, easing down to 30, 20. He pulled over, slowing to 10 before breaking.

Then he parked, and faced his father. "What? Afraid I'm gonna go home and find Mom all roughed up? Only this time she won't be able to stop me from doing something about it? Is that it? Afraid she can't protect you anymore?"

"Those days are long behind me," his father said. "Beside, none of that has anything to do with this."

"I can make it, Dad. Okay? Please? Will you trust me for once? I know I can make it."

"Son, you're not thinking. You're running."

"Yeah? Well we wouldn't be in this mess if you had just pulled over when I asked you to," said Roland. "I mean, you say I'm running, but you're drinking again. That's not running?"

"No, you're right," his father said. "You're absolutely right. We both stop running. Starting now. What do you say?"

"I say it's easier for you because you're not the one going to jail."

"I'm trying to tell you it doesn't have to be that way. But you won't have a chance unless you face this like a man."

"I am a man, Goddamn it. When are you gonna recognize that?"

Flecks of spit from Roland's mouth made his father flinch. Seeing how close he was, Roland sat back and brought his attention to the windshield, to the flatland, the marsh life, where everything sinks eventually.

"We're running out of time," his father said. "Now come on. You can do this. I know you can do this. It was an accident. It's going to be okay."

Bullshit it was. That's the same thing the man had said about the dog Roland hit in high school. The baby schnauzer. Foolish for even going to his father that day, Roland could've gotten away with it if he hadn't let his guilt determine his decision to confess. But his father, always wanting his son to face the music, had Roland return to the scene and stand before a crying little girl who gave him every last tear of anger she could shed, and all for every neighbor on the block to see. Roland was just a junior that year, but he'd faced it like a man, just like his father had wanted him to, and where did it get him?

No one wanted to believe it had been an accident. The rumors just wouldn't have been as juicy that way, and the people in their small town with their no-lives wouldn't have settled for anything less than the best cut of meat to sink their teeth into.

He wasn't noble for owning up to it. He was Roland Thomas, the dog killer—a label he wouldn't be able to live down—not after a few months, not after a year. It even went into his senior yearbook. Dog Killer.

But hey, at least his father was proud, the man having succeeded in forcing Roland to face the music.

Who on hell's worst day was he to question, judge, or interfere?

Like today—he refused to give Roland a choice. That's who he was, the hypocrite, and he wasn't going to let his son get away with this.

Roland let out a dented sigh, prolonged and exhausted. "You have to do it," he said, looking at his father, shaking his head. "'Cause I just can't, Dad. It has to be you. You have to drive us back."

"It's okay," his father said. "I'll drive us back, and then we'll call for help, okay? Come on."

Roland reached for the bottle of Jim Beam. His father wasn't getting another drop. If the man insisted on standing in his son's way, he wouldn't get to numb himself while doing it. He would suffer every hard breath and beat of a heavy heart Roland did.

He stepped out of the car, and when he started to go around from the front side, Roland went the opposite way, circling the Infinity from the rear end while nearly drowning in his own sweat.

His father just had to go and make a federal case for doing the right thing, all while the man himself had regressed into living however he wanted instead of living by example. His promises about Roland's chances to stay free, about his mother's safety—all bullshit. The man couldn't make promises—not when he was breaking promises already and drinking again.

Roland dumped the bottle dry before getting back into the car.

Situated behind the wheel, his father reached down into the space between his seat and the door, and when feeling nothing, he looked down to see nothing.

Drunk or sober, the man's self-righteousness remained an agonizing itch only violent scratching could stop. Roland's thoughts were fire ants feeding on his own composure and his determination to keep his mind in a careful state of reason.

"Looking for this?"

The man's heavy, hungover eyes became aware, concentrating on the bottle in Roland's hand.

"They can't find this. Can they, Dad? Or else you're in trouble, too."

"What are you driving at, Roland?"

"I'm not driving at anything. You're the one driving. You're the one behind the wheel. Drunk. And I'm begging you. Please. Pull over."

"We are pulled over, son. What are you talking—" His eyes widened. "Roland?"

"No, Dad. Please. Please pull over." Roland's chest caved in before blowing back out, almost breathing without him, convulsing. "I—I love you, Dad. You hear me? I love you."

He slammed his father's bottle into the radio, and then again, and nothing—just bouncing.

"Roland, what are you doing?"

He slammed the bottle into the radio again, and again, harder and faster, bursting into tears while the bottle shattered into multiple instruments of jagged glass.

"What in the hell are you doing?"

Roland drove the spike end of a longer glass shard into the red flab beneath his father's jaw, the stream of blood shooting out in spurts, again and again—it wouldn't stop.

His father's mouth wide open but making no sound, and then it came, the gurgle.

"Jesus, Dad. Are you okay?" Roland held his father's face against the window and looked down to keep from having to watch him suffer. He closed his eyes while humming his father's favorite song, *When The Saints Go Marching In*, to drown out the gurgles, the struggle. It went on for too long, much longer than Roland had imagined it would. Minutes. And it was fuckin' way too messy, his father's shirt and khakis too red and too bright, same as Roland's hands. But Roland couldn't look at him. He couldn't break.

These were the final moments of his father's life, and he would've wanted his son to be a man about this. Roland was no longer on deck; he had to strike out on his own now, and when his father stopped making sounds, Roland let go.

His father didn't renege; he was gone. Dead and gone.

From somewhere above now, his father could look down on Roland and see the truth. He could see his son the dog killer. Roland as a junior in high school, his father could see him accelerating in his Acura that day at the sight of the schnauzer. He could feel the rush Roland felt when seeing no one around, no owners, no witnesses.

No one wanted to believe it had been an accident—no one except for Roland's father. The man believed in his son, but the things his son had told him that day about not having enough time and slamming on the brakes were missing from the reality he could now see from above while the blanks were filled in with Roland not hesitating or so much as tapping the brakes.

Roland ran the dog down on purpose sending a bump to his tire and a jolt of quenched thirst to his throat. He'd swallowed the ultimate power allowing him to shed his skin, his innocence—a boy becoming a decider of fates.

His victims today were no longer doggies or animals, and if the Malibu man had in fact produced offspring, then Roland owed those children the courtesy of the truth. He owed them a reason for their father's demise. He owed them a debt of so much more.

True, Roland carried remorse for taking life from other men, but if the kids who lost their dog back in the day had refused to accept his apology, how could he expect sons or daughters of a man he killed to act differently?

They would look at him just the same and grow up associating his face with evil.

Could Roland blame them?

How many killers go above and beyond expressing remorse to the families of their victims, if they even do so at all? How many prove it? How many break the cycle of serving time in the place of justice?

At least Roland had drawn enough blood to pay his debt. In this moment he existed on a plane truly equal to the one belonging to any and all children who the Malibu man may've left behind. No, they weren't going to see their father again, but by his own hands, neither would Roland.

Eye for an eye. Father for a father.

But the question remained: was the dead man looking down and judging Roland as harshly as he had judged his father?

Not that it mattered all that much anymore come the end of the day. His father was no longer the one who Roland needed to fool.

Dialing 911, his focus shifted from the rearview mirror to the road ahead.

"Hello? Yes. There's—There's been an accident. My— My father. He's dead. And so is another man. I don't know him. Please hurry."

Static and gibberish in Roland's ear were all that came back in response, the syllables of the words being spoken in a woman's voice.

"Sorry. My phone's cutting out," he said. "What's that now?"

His location. She wanted his location.

"Right. No, I'm in a car pulled over on 182. About a mile from the exit to 90. Please hurry."

After disconnecting, Roland pulled the shard from his father's neck and placed the blood-soaked glass against the dead man's palm before closing the fingers to make a fist with the point sticking out from the bottom. He lifted his father's fist in the air, and then he drove the shard end down into his thigh and screamed, the slice burning his flesh, tearing muscle and mowing tissue.

Roland lifted the fist from his leg, and brought it down again. He screamed. He lifted. Though he needed more injuries, Roland wasn't sure where to stick his stomach. One pierce to the wrong place, and he was as good as his father.

He gashed his forearm, wide, the red falling out instead of seeping to the surface at a crawl; it came fast and Roland thought for sure that he wasn't far from passing out. He had to stay alert. Couldn't go under. Couldn't let the cops think his father ran that poor man down on purpose. No way. His father was the best man Roland knew.

But the man behind the wheel today, that man was a stranger. That man was... So drunk. And so angry. Yelling into thin air about his company. The spill.

Roland had no idea what to do—he shouldn't have gone for the wheel. But when his father started swinging that glass at him... Roland couldn't believe it. His own father... He couldn't believe they didn't crash.

But the man didn't give Roland a choice. He'd insisted on scaring Roland, on pushing Roland, and ultimately on cornering Roland.

His own father.

He didn't give Roland a choice.

DYING DAYS: RALLY CRY
by Armand Rosamilia

Amber was shocked and amazed, in this day and age, people could still think like this. The crowd around her was screaming insults and threats, but she wanted them to shut up so she could hear what crazy thoughts were issuing from the mouths of the Ku Klux Klan members standing on the Baton Rouge Capitol Building steps. She'd read on Yahoo this was the first Klan rally in the Louisiana state capital since 1969. Only hours ago they'd won a court hearing about freedom of speech and were now allowed to talk for two hours, before a crowd of mostly hostile people.

A couple of assholes she'd gone to school with were off to the side, Nazi saluting the sixteen KKK members on the makeshift stage. Amber knew the guys, all in their mid-twenties and unemployed losers. They were doing it for the shock and to have some fun. She wasn't surprised when she saw a mason jar with clear liquid being passed among them. Someone had gotten into their daddy's moonshine stash again. With the amount of police presence today, it would be sooner rather than later for them to get thrown out or arrested.

The KKK members were shouting about interracial couples and how it was an abomination. Amber bristled at their words, because she was dating a black man and she had never been happier. The trailer-park trash white boys in her neighborhood had never been attractive and never inspired her. Brett understood her and pushed her to get out of Baton Rouge and Louisiana and pursue her dreams, even if it meant never seeing him again.

Amber didn't want to look too closely at the crowd, because even though the vocal majority of them were screaming and trying to drown out the Klan, there were too many in the audience quietly listening and agreeing. She was afraid how many of them were going to be her neighbors, who always gave her dirty looks when she walked hand in hand with Brett down to the park, or sat with him and ate chicken fingers and nuzzled together in the booth.

"Nothing attracts a crowd like a crowd."

"What?" Amber turned to see who was talking to her. Ugh. It was some Podunk white boy trying to hit on her because she had curves. He probably saw her as some trailer-park whore who would be an easy lay behind a dumpster. She went back to watching the rally, doing her best to ignore him.

"I said... aww, forget it. My name is Ellis. What's your name?"

Amber wasn't interested and hoped he got the hint before Brett showed up, because he could be stubborn and quick to throw a punch to defend her.

As if on cue, Brett approached and put a hand on her shoulder while staring at the white boy.

"Babe, you ready to go?" Brett asked. He hadn't wanted to come down here, but Amber had been insistent. While he'd walked off when he saw some of his college buddies, she'd stayed riveted to the spot.

"Give me a minute. I want to hear this bullshit." Amber was also curious to see if anyone would do something against them other than the yelling. It was like watching a NASCAR race. You came for the crashes.

"Exactly what it is. Why sit here and listen to their shit? Babe, they're telling you not to date a black man. As if it's any of their damn business." Brett squeezed her shoulder before walking away.

Amber had been taught to never ignore bad things in the world. Find out why they are the way they are when it came to ignorant people. Her mother and father were poor when it came to money but not with their morals. When she'd told her parents she was dating a black man, her father's only questions: Is he good to you? Does he have a destination in life and a job right now?

Brett had an academic scholarship to LSU. He'd given up playing sports in high school when it was obvious his grades would suffer if he kept playing. He was focused on getting a good education and becoming a businessman utilizing his many skills.

Amber knew as he matured he'd lose his hostility toward people he thought slighted him and those who looked down on him. Amber thought it funny all of her friends (the real ones who didn't mock her for dating him) said she was a Cougar, since she was twenty-six and he was only twenty-one. But age didn't matter, because it was the rest that counted.

"You got a fucking problem, redneck?" Brett said somewhere loudly behind Amber in the crowd. She glanced back and saw he was confronting the white boy who'd tried to hit on her. Great. He'd make a big scene and embarrass her. And here? At a Klan rally? Wouldn't they just love that?

"No. Do you?" The white boy was saying, but Amber pushed ahead a few rows so she could distance herself from the impending fight. She wanted no part of Brett's macho bullshit today.

The crowd parted in front of her and she stepped right to the front, just to the left of the stage. One of the hooded men turned to her and his eyes watched her, probably some hillbilly more interested in her boobs right now than what his cloaked brothers were saying.

When it was obvious he wasn't going to stop staring she covered her chest with her arms and gave him the finger. She could see his belly bounce as he laughed and turned away.

The Klan members were still telling the crowd about their twisted doctrine when Amber heard a gunshot in the distance. Was this going to get out of hand? And why was she so close to the front and danger?

Amber turned to push to the back and noticed most of the crowd was already turned, looking around. There was a disturbance of some kind.

She needed to get as far away from the KKK and the stage if there were gunmen shooting at them. She knew what the news headlines would be: an innocent white girl standing at the rally was gunned down, caught in the crossfire, while the Klansmen escaped unscathed.

But there were more gunshots, and they were at the back of the crowd. Was there a crazed gunman, taking shots at bystanders? The Klansmen finally stopped yelling into the microphone and the crowd stopped yelling at them.

Amber walked up four steps, curious to see what was going on, despite the danger she was putting herself in.

Like dating Brett, she thought. There were always going to be haters, even in her own family. Half of her friends had stopped talking to her. She wondered how many of their fathers stood on the steps near her right now, too.

Another crowd was moving toward the Capitol

Building slowly. What had the redneck said about crowds?

But something wasn't quite right. The way they walked... the way they stared ahead, bloody and...

Amber smiled. Of course. They weren't here to protest the KKK being in town, they were going to bust into a flash mob at any minute. They'd do the Thriller dance and everyone would join in and make the KKK look like idiots, as black and white did the steps side by side. Brilliant.

But why were the police officers drawing weapons and pushing the crowd back? Or at least trying to.

"Holy shit, did that lady just bite that guy?" A Klansman closest to Amber said. "What's going on?"

"I think we need to pack up and go," another one said.

Amber couldn't tell exactly who was talking because of their ridiculous costumes, but she knew they were scared. Now she really hoped this was an amazing choreographed act. *Please let this be a joke.*

Another Klansman stepped down from the wooden stage and onto the step right in front of Amber. "Seriously, people are biting other people." He covered his mouth, even though he was still wearing the white hood and it looked like a cartoon. "Is that guy... taking his pants off?"

Amber looked away when she saw what he was looking at, disgusted. This was anarchy. People were getting attacked and dragged to the ground, where they were being bitten and violated. Gross.

She looked around for an exit but on the three sides in front of the steps was chaos. Police were now openly shooting into the crowd, and people were falling over one another in their haste to run away.

"Sonofabitch," Amber said when she noticed Brett and the white boy in the parking lot escaping. Some loyal boyfriend he was. He'd left her here to die.

That was a sobering thought. What if these maniacs

caught her, pulling off her clothes and brutalizing her body?

Amber turned and saw the Klansmen running up the steps toward the front doors of the Capitol Building. She didn't agree with their words or their politics but she definitely agreed with their game plan right now.

◊ ◊ ◊ ◊

She ran inside just in time to see an elevator packed with white robes and hoods and the door closing. Amber decided she'd take the next one or the stairs. But to where? She knew being on the ground floor during an attack would make her a target, but she didn't want to go too many flights just in case something really bad happened to the building. What if this was an organized terrorist attack and not just a riot at a Klan rally? Thoughts of 9/11 flooded her head.

Amber ran to the stairwell and went up three flights of steps before getting winded. She decided if she lived through this nightmare she'd lay off the Twinkies and eat healthier, because her legs and thighs were hurting after only three flights.

The door opened into a hallway with cubicles before her and office doors to either side. Amber went directly to the window, which faced the opposite direction from where the rally was. There was nothing unusual going on behind the building. Maybe she could escape through a back door?

She heard the elevator ding behind her and turned just as two men in white robes and hoods stepped out, looking around.

One of them fixed on her as she stood by the window. "Are you alone?"

"My boyfriend went to get help. He'll be back in a minute," Amber said quickly. Grown men in hoods were unsettling. "He's got a gun," she added and felt stupid for saying it.

"Good. We could use some protection," the other man said. "What's going on out back?"

"Nothing," Amber said, trying to keep her distance as the two men approached, but they were more interested in looking out the window than her.

When she turned she frowned. "There was nothing a second ago."

A group of people were running through the cluster of trees below and a stream of slower ones stumbling in their general direction. Amber watched as a young woman fell and two men pounced on her. Even at this height and with the glass between, she could still imagine the screams and looked away.

"This is awful," one of the men said. "But maybe they've cleared out of the front and we can slip out?"

The three went to the other side of the floor, but there were only closed office doors on this side. They tried them and every one was locked.

"I guess we break a law or two today to survive," one of the men said and used his dress shoe to break down the door in three kicks.

As the two men went inside, Amber held back. As much as she thought safety in numbers was a good thing, she didn't want to stay with them. They frightened her.

The two men went to the window and looked down.

"Are you going to keep those hoods on? Isn't it hot?" Amber asked.

They both looked at one another and Amber thought it looked funny, like a comedy routine.

Both hoods came off slowly and then the robes folded

neatly and put on the desk in the office. They were wearing suits.

And Amber recognized both men. They were neighbors on her street, two older men with families who'd she'd waved to when she walked down the street with Brett hand in hand. Neither men had ever let on how much they opposed the interracial couple. Amber thought it was a good thing, but now she questioned the rest of her neighbors. Did this racism still exist today? Widespread? Or was it just a coincidence two people on her block were hiding behind masks? Now she wished the rest of the KKK members had come with them. No doubt it would be a block party.

The men either didn't recognize her or were making pretend they didn't know who she was. They went right back to the window.

"It doesn't look good down there," Mr. Waterman, the first man who had spoken to her, said. "In fact, I don't even see a clear path to the cars. This is terrible."

"Where are the police?" the other man who Amber didn't know by name asked.

Amber went to the window and looked down. "The police are either gone or dead."

Neither man said a word, everyone watching the action below. Amber sucked in her breath when she spotted her boyfriend's car, a Ford Focus, smashed between two police cars. But the car was empty. She hoped Brett had escaped.

"Where's the military? The National Guard? State troopers?" Mr. Waterman asked. "I thought they'd have backup a few miles away because we're in town. This is completely disorganized."

Amber was annoyed. She knew she should be quiet but she couldn't help herself. "If you hadn't gotten all this attention and put this together, none of the innocent people below would be dead right now. There would've been no one at the Capitol Building to attack. Most people would've been home or at work today."

Mr. Waterman grimaced. "Don't you dare blame this on us. If the world was a better place, we wouldn't need to protest all the atrocities in this country. If citizens did what God wanted them to do, we'd be a much happier country."

"So, because blacks and whites date, we deserved this?"

Mr. Waterman put his hands up. "All I'm saying is mixing the races is wrong. You know it, I know it... God knows it."

The other man, still looking out the window, nodded. "This is God's work. He is punishing Baton Rouge as a modern day Sodom. I knew this would happen. We're too late to change the course of history now. It has begun."

"Doc, don't start spewing about Armageddon again," Mr. Waterman said. "This isn't the apocalypse."

"It is." Doc turned to him. "Look outside. It's a zombie apocalypse. And we're going to join them soon enough. Like God intends."

Amber decided to stop watching the grisly scenes below and find something else to do right now.

◊ ◊ ◊ ◊

She was back to the window two minutes later, once the two men had wandered off to check out the rest of the offices. Amber stared down at the craziness below.

An older man with a white cowboy hat was shooting two pistols as he calmly walked down the road before getting into the driver's seat of a yellow cab and driving off like nothing else was going on. Amber had to laugh at the balls on the guy.

When she looked at Brett's car, smashed between two

police cruisers, she sighed. He was gone and he wasn't coming back. So much for true love.

Amber wanted to settle down, get a good job, and let him finish college and make plans to spend the rest of their lives together. Brett had talked a good game but now she wondered if he'd only done it to get in her tight pants or get up close and personal with her cleavage. He'd said all the right things and told her how special she was. Maybe he was talking to her girls when he said it, though.

Bastard. She felt used. Was he really in love with her, or just in love with the thought of dating a white girl? Amber hoped she saw the dick again so she could slap him.

Amber turned away when she heard the elevator ding.

◊ ◊ ◊ ◊

There was shouting and chaos as several people piled out of the elevator and spread out, and none of them looked well.

Amber slipped back into the office and got under the desk. It was a tight squeeze and right now she wished her ass wasn't so big. It had attracted Brett, and now she knew her ass was all he really wanted.

Someone screamed and she felt bad but her first reaction was hoping it was the two KKK members. Who else was up here? It had to be one of them. Was she wrong for thinking evil thoughts about them? She looked up to the sky, but right now it was the underside of the desk. *God, give me strength*, she thought. *And stop these bad thoughts about who should and shouldn't die.*

The back of the desk, facing the door, wasn't all the way to the ground. Anyone looking from the hallway would see her. Amber poked her head up and looked around.

A bloody woman, dragging a nearly severed leg behind

her, shambled past but didn't look into the office.

Amber grabbed the stack of papers and everything off of the desk and placed it to block the gap, knowing anyone smart would see it out of place. Were these monsters smart? What were they? The neighbor had called it a zombie apocalypse. There was no way this was happening. Right?

She held her breath when someone shuffled in the hallway and then stopped right outside the office door. Amber had pulled the chair close to her but she was taking up all the room under the desk, so it wasn't much protection. If someone came even around to the side of the desk they'd see her.

Whoever it was moved into the room, not masking their movements on the carpet. Amber began to panic, covering her mouth so she didn't scream and she closed her eyes as tightly as she could. She didn't want to see what was coming for her.

Whoever it was banged into the desk and Amber banged her head. She shoved her fist into her mouth to keep from screaming, biting down on her knuckles. Now she could hear the person (she knew it wasn't someone alive but she couldn't bring herself to imagine a zombie wandering around the office looking for her) shuffle around the desk and at least one more in the room.

Amber was going to die. And the worst part was she was trapped under the desk. She couldn't spring out quickly because she was wedged in, so when they found her it would be quite the feast as she tried to escape.

She heard the elevator ding again and the zombies (*people, dammit, people*) shambled away and out the door. Amber could hear them in the hallway now.

Someone screamed but it was far away.

I need to get out of here or else, Amber thought. She took her sweet time getting out from under the desk, and when her wide hips slapped against the desk she'd stop and listen. What felt like forever took only a couple of minutes and Amber let out her breath when it was finally done.

She knew she needed a weapon, but other than a few ball-point pens on the desk, there was nothing heavy to use.

And now someone was coming slowly down the hallway.

The chair legs were plastic and all one piece. Even the desk was wood-covered but really light. There was nothing to help her escape.

"Help me," the KKK member said as he fell into the door to the office, white hood still on and his white robe stained with blood. His arm, poking out from the robe, was ripped apart, chunks of meat dangling as he moved.

Amber stifled a scream and saw something she could use. She unplugged the phone from the desk and went up to the man, who was bitten and would probably turn into a monster soon. Plus, he was making too much noise and would attract others to him.

As he fell forward and slammed into the desk, Amber brought the phone down on his head. She knew she was doing something very, very wrong but it was kill or be killed right now. God would understand, right?

Four smacks to the back of the head and the Klansman stopped moving. But now the phone was in pieces and useless.

Amber stuck her head out of the office. She could hear movement everywhere but couldn't see anyone right now. She glanced in the direction of the elevators. Could she make it? Would she dare?

The decision was made for her when a bloody nightmare stepped out of the office next to her and stared blankly with one good eye.

She ran in the opposite direction without thinking, away from the elevator bank. As Amber rounded a turn she ran right into a woman, who was obviously already dead. Now Amber was glad for her extra weight because the blow knocked the zombie to the ground.

At the next intersection she spied a Klansman hiding under a desk in a cubicle. She ignored him when he stared at her and mouthed *help*. She had no time for saving anyone except herself.

A small ornate wooden desk was in the hallway with a vase filled with fake flowers. Amber picked up both as weapons and kept moving.

She was a hallway off from the elevator when two zombies appeared and locked bloodshot eyes on her. "Here we go," she mumbled, trying to think of something funny to say before she screamed and fell to the floor in the fetal position and let them rip her to pieces.

Both stumbled at her, bumping into each other. The one on the right was a step ahead so Amber put the table down and hefted the vase with both hands. The flowers were in her way so she pulled them out and threw them at the zombies. Not surprisingly, the plastic flowers did nothing to stop their advance.

The vase did, however. Amber smacked the lead zombie in the face with the vase, and it knocked it off its feet. Amber was expecting the vase to shatter but it didn't, so she slammed the second zombie's face with it. The vase exploded in her hands, shards cutting her hands and arms lightly.

It cleared a path but now the table, which she was going to use, was behind her. If Amber went back for it she might have to start the fight over with a new weapon.

Amber ran.

The scene in front of the elevators was chaos. At least half a dozen KKK members were fighting other KKK members who were no longer allies. It was hard to tell who was who, and most still had their hoods on. Amber shrank against the wall, worried the two zombies she'd just fought would catch up soon.

When the fight slowly moved away from the elevator bank, Amber decided it was now or never. She ran, again using her weight to bump into a KKK guy. She didn't know if he was a zombie or breathing and she didn't really care.

One of the living no longer wearing his hood saw her and began fighting a zombie between Amber and where he stood. "Wait, we can escape together," he yelled.

Amber wasn't interested in helping him. She was going to escape on her own.

She ran to the elevators and hit the down button, expecting to wait forever and have to fight off zombies. But it immediately dinged, which was a relief and a curse.

Most of the zombies stopped fighting and turned at the noise.

The three or four living KKK men used it to their advantage, punching and kicking to get the zombies to the floor.

One of the doors opened and Amber sighed when she saw it wasn't filled with monsters. She rushed inside and stabbed at the first floor button.

The doors weren't closing and the fight was coming right at her.

Mr. Waterman, who she'd first seen when she'd been on this floor, was still alive. He was also squaring off against two zombies in front of the elevator. He turned his head to her and realization dawned on him. "Help me push them away so we can go."

Amber shook her head and used her palm to slap the first floor button. How long did this really take for the doors to close?

Mr. Waterman was pulled down in front of the elevator and Amber looked away.

He was a racist pig, she thought. *I am justified in what I did. God will save me.*

One of the zombies who had pulled Mr. Waterman down was a KKK member still wearing his hood. Most of it was bloody and ripped off to expose his gore-encrusted mouth.

He stepped into the elevator just as the doors closed.

BLUE BELLY BAYOU
By Ambrose Stolliker

I never believed in ghosts until I met Alisha Strangeway. I knew her for less than twenty-three days, but in that short time, she opened my eyes to a world I had always dismissed as nothing more than silly superstition. The shrinks here say we have to face down our demons if we want inner peace, but inner peace isn't why I'm writing in this journal. I'm writing because I want people to know who Alisha was, and what she did for me and the world she believed in—that *other* world—is very real. But I'm getting ahead of myself. I should start at the beginning. In New Orleans.

The spring semester was out at Tulane, and I had no intention of returning home to New England for the summer. The problem was I wouldn't have the money I needed to pay the rent if I didn't get a job in New Orleans. Two days before the semester let out, I saw the following ad in the Tulane *Hullabaloo*: "Wanted—summer intern with an adventurous spirit to help produce weekly Web show covering the most haunted city in America. Pay: $450/wk."

I was sitting in the Café du Monde when I first read the ad, my fingers coated with the powdered sugar the place drowns their beignets in, and I remember laughing out loud because it sounded so stupid. Like I said, I didn't believe in ghosts, and it always amused me when I saw some idiot tourist coming out of one of the French Quarter's innumerable voodoo shops with a shopping bag full of useless crap they'd been told would help them reach their Uncle Murray in the spirit world. The fact was though, I was a mass media major just two years away from graduation with no experience to speak of, and I didn't intend to end up unemployed when I got out of school. So, I answered the ad. That's how I met Alisha. Strangeway wasn't her real last name, by the way. It was Perkins. Strangeway was her stage name, something she used to bolster her image as a modern-day mistress of the night, for lack of a better word. Think Elvira, but without the dumb wig.

Here's what I remember most about our first meeting, other than the fact she was incredibly hot. She spent less than two minutes asking about how much experience I had working with digital cameras and sound equipment and the rest of the time grilling me about whether I believed in clairvoyance, ghosts, demonic possession, ESP, voodoo, gypsy curses and reincarnation.

"I don't believe in any of that crap," I told her. "I just need a job to pay the rent over the summer and so I can put something related to my field on my resume before I graduate."

I'd expected her to throw me out right then, but she didn't.

"Perfect. You're hired. Come back tomorrow."

And that's how it began. We spent the next three weeks scouting a laundry list of supposedly haunted locations in New Orleans—everything from the LaLaurie House to the Beauregard-Keyes House to the Provincial Hotel. And in that time we saw exactly zero ghosts. I didn't really care, though. I was learning a lot from Alisha and, as it happened, falling for her pretty hard. I know she never loved me back, but I don't hold it against her. She was at least five years older than me and dating some douche lawyer who never called unless he wanted to spend the night, and even then, he rarely "spent the night." She bitched about him a lot, but, strangely enough, never even mentioned him by name. After a while, I just called him "The Douche," as in, "Hey, 'Leesh, how's it going with The Douche?" She always laughed when I called him that, but looking back now, I think there was always a little bit of hurt in her eyes when the subject of The Douche came up.

After three weeks of striking out in New Orleans, Alisha was about at the end of her patience (and pretty much out of time and funding.) We needed something we could put on the next episode of her show. It was called *An American Haunting* and had actually enjoyed enough success to attract a few heavy hitters from the local corporate community looking to reach a younger demographic via online advertising. Five days before we ran out of money, one of Alisha's contacts on the Louisiana Tourism Commission told her a story about a place in Ascension Parish called Blue Belly Bayou. Supposedly, the area was haunted by the ghosts of some Union soldiers who had been executed at a Confederate prison camp. We didn't put much stock in the story, but we were desperate to find something—anything—worth putting on film, and this looked like it might be our last shot at a winner. That and one hour-long airboat ride through the swamps and bayous is how we ended up on the outskirts of the tiny river town of Jubilee. In my opinion, it wasn't much to look at, but Alisha felt differently.

"It's very charming in a way," she commented as she surveyed the town. "It's only missing one thing."

"Yeah? What's that?" I asked impatiently. My arms were killing me from having lugged our camera equipment from the dock where the airboat had dropped us a few minutes before.

"People."

She was right. Something had seemed off to me as soon as the town came into sight, but I hadn't figured out what it was until she'd mentioned it—there wasn't a soul in sight.

"They're probably all inside, trying to avoid melting in this heat," I said.

"Probably." Alisha started toward the town again. "I just hope we aren't wasting our time coming here. That airboat trip wasn't cheap." She shook her head. "C'mon. Let's get something cold to drink before *we* melt."

We walked into a tiny diner called Clara's where a scrawny, bone-white man stood behind a counter that ran the length of the restaurant. He wore a stained apron and button down shirt with a black bow tie. Two people—an elderly man and woman, both droopy-eyed and sickly looking—were seated at the counter. They looked up at the tinny sound of the bell over the door ringing as we entered. The old man sluggishly turned his head to face us, a spoonful of cream-colored grits in his hand and identically colored mush falling from the side of his mouth. He continued to chew, revealing he had no teeth whatsoever, while more and more of the grits spilled onto the counter and his shirt's filthy sleeve. I shuddered and looked away. Above, three large ceiling fans rotated lazily, providing a whisper of circulation but no real relief from the heat. The man behind the counter turned, wiped his hands on a dirty towel and nodded at us.

"Help y'all?" he asked. Like the old man and woman, he had rheumy eyes, the eyes of someone who was constantly fighting off the flu or some other type of infection. His name tag read "VIRGIL".

"Just a few sodas for me and my one-man crew here," Alisha replied.

He stuffed the towel into a large pocket on the front of

his apron. "Crew? Y'all airboat pilots?"

"No," she said, sitting down at the counter. "We're film makers."

"You mean for the cinema and such?"

"No. We have a show on the Internet."

The man behind the counter regarded her like she'd just spoken complete gibberish to him.

"You know," she went on, trying to explain. "The...uh...World Wide Web?"

"Worldwide what?" he shook his head. Then, having apparently decided to move on to more important matters, he informed us, "Soda fountain's broken. All's we got is lemonade."

"If it's cold, I'll drink it," I said, sitting down at the counter.

"It's cold." He eyed Alisha and waited for her to sit down at the counter. "Y'all want the same?"

"Actually, do you have any iced tea?"

"Soda fountain's broken," he repeated. "All's we got is lemonade."

"Just ice water then, please," she told him.

"Mmm hmm." He went through two swinging doors, then emerged a few minutes later with a tray and two glasses.

"Y'all hungry?" he asked as he placed the glasses down in front of us.

"No, thank you," we answered, almost simultaneously.

"That'll be three twenty-five," he said.

"Pay him, Josh," Alisha said.

I dropped a five—my last—on the counter, and told Virgil to keep the change.

"'Preciate it," he said, though his voice made it clear he couldn't have cared less. "Let me know if I can get you anything else."

"Actually, there is one thing," Alisha said, her voice going into full charm mode. "What can you tell us about Blue Belly Bayou?"

The man frowned and started to fiddle with the towel in the front pocket of his apron. "Good cat fishing. That what y'all here to film? One o' them fishing shows?"

"No. Our show's called *An American Haunting.*"

The man stopped playing with the towel. The corners of his mouth formed the thinnest trace of a smile, revealing yellowish-brown teeth. His eyes narrowed even more. "Y'all wanna know about the legend, don'tcha?"

"Would you mind?" Alisha asked. "All's we know is that your little town here is supposed to be haunted by some Union soldiers who were executed on the bayou."

"That's right," Virgil said, almost proudly. "Y'see, the Rebs, they called the Federal soldiers 'blue bellies' on account their uniforms had a lot of blue in them. Navy blue overcoat, light blue pants, dark blue kepi. Anyway, this all happened a few days after the war ended. Back then, most towns in Loozeeanna didn't have telegraph wires, so it took time for word of Lee's surrender to get to the Confederate prison camp all the ways out here in Jubilee. They killed those poor bastards after hostilities had officially ended. Just shot them and dumped their bodies in the bayou. The 13th U.S. Cavalry Regiment. About a hundred of them, if I remember right. Anyway, that's why it's called Blue Belly Bayou, because it's full of blue-bellies."

"That's quite a story," I observed. "But I didn't hear anything about ghosts."

Virgil scowled at me. "Y'all didn't let me finish."

"Uh, sorry."

"Go on, Virgil," Alisha said. "We're rapt."

Still glaring at me, he continued. "Well, they say those Yankee soldiers were right pissed that they were shot down with the war so close to ending. Can't say I hardly blame them. This was 1865, y'see, and by then even the most ignorant country boy in the Confederate Army knew the South was whipped." His eyes grew dark. "Those blue-bellies, they begged Johnny Reb for their lives down to the last one, but the man in charge of the camp—a Lieutenant Jordan—he wasn't having it. Most historians say he killed about twenty of those Yankee boys with his own pistol."

"Jesus," I said.

He glared at me again. The man did not like to be interrupted, that much I can tell you.

"Please continue," Alisha said, shooting me a dirty look.

"Thank you," Virgil went on. "Where was I? Oh, right. Lieutenant Jordan. He ordered those Union boys killed on a night with a full moon. Y'all can check the historical records if you don't believe me, and that's a fact. Next full moon comes around and those Yankee soldiers come up out of the bayou and fall on that prison camp like a pack of wolves on a herd of sheep. As the story goes, they tore Lieutenant Jordan to pieces and threw what was left to the gators. Then, they reclaimed their weapons and returned to the water. Ever since then, some say, the blue-bellies come on up outta that bayou every full moon."

"Have you ever seen anything out there on the bayou?" Alisha asked.

"Never seen any ghosts if that's what y'all're after," he answered.

"No?"

He let out what could have passed for a laugh, then leaned over the counter and said, "Ma'am, that's why they call it a *legend*."

"Right," she said.

Virgil turned his attention to his other two customers

while we finished our drinks. When we got up to leave, he turned back to us and said, "I'd advise stayin' at the Magnolia. That's where all the visitors to Jubilee end up."

"Thanks, Virgil," Alisha said. "We'll do that."

Outside, I suggested, "We should find the spot where this Lieutenant Jordan killed all those soldiers. Full moon isn't till tomorrow but it wouldn't hurt to get set up there and see what we can see."

"Good thinking," Alisha said.

"Maybe there's some information on the prison camp's exact location in the town hall."

She regarded me with a smile. "He's on a roll! Let's head for the town hall!"

We walked across the street, gear in tow like a collection of sweaty vagabonds, and entered the town hall. We found the tiny lobby deserted. An empty receptionist's desk stood to the side of a staircase. On the desk were an assortment of flyers and maps regarding the Confederate prison camp and the legend of Blue Belly Bayou. I took one and examined it.

"The camp's just a little more than a quarter-mile from here," I said, reading from the brochure. "There's a trailhead or something nearby."

"Okay, let's check into the Magnolia and then go find this place," Alisha said.

We walked across the street to the inn. The sign on the door read OPEN – VACANCY. Inside, the concierge desk was empty, but there was a shiny silver bell with a small handwritten note next to it reading 'RING FOR SERVICE'. Behind the desk was a doorway covered with a velour curtain. The inn's interior was furnished with what appeared to be mostly Victorian pieces, all of it made with walnut, mahogany and ebony veneer finishes. I gave the bell a few taps and we waited. A few moments passed before the same old man we'd seen seated at Clara's came through the curtain.

"Let's make this quick," he said. "I wanna finish my grits back at Clara's and they's probably gettin' cold by now. Y'all will be wantin' a room, yes?"

"Yes, sir. For two nights, maybe three," Alisha answered.

"Rooms're fifty dollars a night, plus tax."

She started to hand him a credit card and he held up a hand. "Cash only, missy. We's a little behind the times here in Jubilee as you may've noticed."

She smiled at him. "I hadn't. And cash is fine." She reached into her backpack and pulled out the money.

He took the bills and stuffed them into an ancient till. "Two rooms, right? Y'all don't look like a couple to me."

I scowled at him, not caring whether Alisha noticed.

"That's right. Two rooms, please," she said.

He handed each of us a room key. "Name's Caleb. Y'all need anything, don't bother ringin' the bell. Just drop by over Clara's. That's most likely where I'll be."

"That's fine. Thanks, Caleb."

He gave us both a dirty look, obviously annoyed at being separated from his grits, and then disappeared through the velour curtain.

"Remind me to give this place zero stars on Yelp," I said.

"We're not here on holiday, Josh," she said, picking up her stuff. "C'mon."

I sighed and started after her, lugging the camera and sound equipment up a long flight of stairs and down a dimly lit hallway. Our rooms turned out to be directly across the hall from one another.

"Be ready to go in five," she said, closing the door to her room behind her without waiting for a response.

Maybe someone else might have taken her brusqueness personally, but I didn't. It's just the way she was when she was hot to get something done. I didn't give it a second thought and, five minutes later, we were on our way.

◊ ◊ ◊ ◊

We could easily have missed the remains of the Confederate prison camp were it not for a sign which denoted a clearing at the end of the trailhead as such. The sign looked ancient, its metal corroded and rusty, rendering the words on it extremely difficult to read. I squinted, leaned in close and read aloud, "On this site on the night of April 12, 1865, three days after the end of the War of Northern Aggression, Confederate Lieutenant Josiah Jordan ordered the executions of 111 Union soldiers from the 13th U.S. Cavalry Regiment held prisoner at this encampment." I turned to her. "The War of Northern Aggression? Seriously? These friggin' rednecks are still fighting the war."

Alisha didn't say anything. She turned to face the bayou. The clearing sat at the edge of the water. It was about fifty feet in diameter in all directions, and bordered by huge cypress and ash trees. We were close enough to hear the water lapping gently against the muddy shore. The bayou's opposite bank lay about five hundred feet to the west and was dominated by the same gigantic trees.

"There's no way they could have kept a hundred men imprisoned here," she finally said. "The original camp must have been much bigger than this one little area." After a moment, she added, "okay, this is where we set up shop. Let's do it."

It took nearly two hours for us to set up the sound equipment and position the camera. Darkness fell on the bayou a little after nine o'clock. As the intern, I drew first watch while Alisha rested. The flap to her tent was closed, but I don't think she was sleeping. She rarely slept when we were in the middle of an investigation. I was tired, but I didn't mind drawing first watch. It gave me a chance to work the camera and sound equipment without her hovering over me and telling me what I was doing wrong. I turned my attention to the bayou. Though the moon wasn't yet quite full, it was a bright night, and I could see almost clear across to the opposite bank. The water appeared black in the moonlight, the surface as still and calm as obsidian, while all around me I heard the sounds of the bayou's inhabitants. The baritone songs of frogs pulsed in the air from a nearby, low-lying flat of lily pads. Every so often, there came the sound of some creature slipping into the water for a late-night swim. Insects pushed this way and that into the night, becoming momentarily visible when they passed through the glow of the moon. It was all almost enough to lull me to sleep.

I spotted the first one at just after midnight. Its head broke the surface so gently I might not have even seen it had it not been for the glowing yellow eyes. At first, I could only see the upper part of the face, but as it approached, the nose and mouth, then the shoulders, gradually emerged from under the water. I blinked a few times to make sure I hadn't fallen asleep myself and considered calling to Alisha before thinking better of it. I didn't want to scare away whoever it was out there by raising a ruckus. I slowly moved to the camera, my eyes on the bayou the entire time, and positioned myself behind the lens. The camera was perfectly aligned and in focus. I took in a deep breath and pressed the RECORD button, exhaling as the camera started to whir.

The figure continued to approach. Then, another

almost identical one broke the surface, then another and another.

"Holy shit, what the hell are those things?" I whispered to myself, my voice shaking. I took in another deep breath, trying to get my heart to stop pounding. "Relax, Josh. Relax. This is not what you think it is."

They were within fifty feet of the bayou's edge when the one in the lead stopped, looked upward and pointed to the moon. The others followed suit. After a moment, all of them slowly fixed their bright, yellow gazes on me, or at least it seemed like they were looking directly at me, and I felt the sudden urge to break and run or to yell out to Alisha. I didn't though. Something in the back of my mind—a cold, hard voice, said: *Don't you move. Don't you dare move. Keep recording. That's your job. Keep recording.*

They stood where they were, unmoving, for another moment or two, then slowly disappeared into the bayou. It took me several minutes before I realized I was still recording, and several more before it hit me how much I was shaking. I depressed the RECORD button and stepped back from the camera, trying to clear my head. The same voice that had told me to keep recording a few minutes before piped up once again. *Watch the video. See what you recorded.* I played it back. It had recorded everything. The faces, the glowing yellow eyes, the sounds of the bayou—everything was crystal clear.

"Alisha," I croaked.

She didn't answer and I realized I'd barely spoken above a whisper.

"Alisha!" I called out.

I was right. She wasn't sleeping. Her tent flap zipped open, and she came out wide awake.

"What is it? Did you see something?"

Instead of answering, I simply gestured at the camera.

"Did you record something?" she asked, her voice full of hope and excitement.

"Look... Look at the video," I said hoarsely.

She frowned at me as she moved to the camera. "You okay?"

"Just look at the video," I said, still struggling to find any strength in my voice.

She removed the camera from its tripod and played back the video, gasping when she saw the footage. "Look at all of them!"

"We should run a diagnostics check on the camera, make sure it's working right," I insisted. "The software on the damn thing could be screwy, you never know."

I'd expected her to argue, but, as usual, she surprised me. "You're right. Check the camera. Make sure it's running properly. I don't want anyone to be able to use hinky software or faulty lens alignment as an excuse to dismiss what you just filmed." She handed the camera back to me and then ruffled my hair like an older sister would do to her younger brother. "Good work. Way to keep your head about you. Now, let's get back to the Magnolia. I can't wait to call The Douche and tell him about this."

Here's the thing: When she said that, I wanted more than anything to tell her not to because I knew The Douche would ruin it for her. It was what he did. Anytime she got excited about something that didn't have anything to do with him, he belittled her and made her feel like crap. In the short time I knew her, I had more than a few late-night discussions where she ended up teary-eyed on my doorstep, her lower lip quivering. But I didn't say anything. I knew she was totally in love with the asshole, and nothing I did would change that.

◊ ◊ ◊ ◊

I didn't really need to check the camera to make sure it was working right because I'd given it a complete diagnostic before I'd started shooting that night, but I went ahead and did it anyway. It checked out fine, just like I knew it would. And for the first time in my life, I was really scared. I didn't know what it was we'd stumbled onto in Jubilee and, for the most part, I really didn't want to stick around to find out. I was on my way to tell Alisha I thought we should leave when there was a knock on my door. It was her. Teary-eyed, lower lip quivering. She didn't even wait for me to invite her in to throw her arms around my neck and bury her head in my chest.

"God, I hate him sometimes," she sniffled.

"Uh, come on in." I pushed the door closed. "Listen, Alisha…"

"He just doesn't get me, y'know? Everything has to be a fight with him!" She looked up at me then, meeting my gaze. "Why can't he just be happy for me? Is that too much to ask?"

I shook my head. "No. Look, 'Leesh, I've been thinking…"

She cut me off again and wiped her eyes. "I mean, this thing could send my show over the top, really bring in a bigger audience, and he shits all over it! What's with that?"

"I don't know. I—"

"I mean, *you* get it, right?" She sat down on the edge of the bed and kicked off one shoe, then the other. "That's what kills me! You don't even *believe* in the supernatural, and you understand what a big deal this is!"

"Yeah, about that –"

"Why can't he be more like you? You *get* me, y'know?"

"I guess. Maybe he had a bad day or something –"

"Josh."

The no-nonsense abruptness of her voice cut me off again.

I looked at her. "Uh, yeah?"

"Are you gonna make a move or what?"

I practically ran to the bed, and we were naked in about two seconds flat. For the next twenty minutes, I actually forgot how scared I was about what I'd seen that night on the bayou. When we finished the first time, I tried to bring it up again, but she fell asleep, and, eventually, so did I. The only time we were awake the rest of the night was when she rolled over and pulled me close for another round. I'm not going to lie. As scared as I was, I got manhandled, and I loved every friggin' second of it.

I woke the next morning to her tugging gently on my toe. She was already dressed.

"Wake up, ghost hunter," she said. "Did you check the camera last night?"

I pushed my hair out of my eyes and said through a yawn, "Yeah. It's fine. In fact, it was working perfectly the whole time."

"I knew it!" She clapped her hands. "Hot damn! The real show starts tonight."

"Huh?"

"Full moon," she said. "That's when they come out of the bayou, remember?"

"Oh. Right." I pushed the sheets aside and pulled on my boxers. "Listen, Alisha, about last night..."

"Oh, for Christ's sake, we don't have to *talk* about it, do we?"

"No, I just —"

"Look, it was what it was. Leave it at that. We have a job to do here, remember?"

"Yeah, about that..."

"*What*, Josh? I want to get back to that camp and get

set up."

I pulled her close and looked into her eyes. "Aren't you the least bit scared?"

She frowned. "Whoa! What happened to the skeptic I hired? The guy who didn't believe in the supernatural?"

"I just…"

"What?"

"I have a bad feeling…"

"About what?"

"Everything. This place. All of it. I don't like it here."

She pulled way. "I don't get it. You shot some awesome footage last night. We're this close to finding out the secrets to this place," she said, holding up two fingers. "Now, all of the sudden, you want to pack up and leave? C'mon. I need you, Josh."

I think if she'd chosen any other words than those last four, I might have insisted upon leaving, but when she told me she needed me, something took over, and, once again, I forgot I really was scared. Looking back now, I think Alisha probably knew that was all she'd have to say to get me to stay. I don't hold it against her. Not after what happened to her. It was just the way she was. When she wanted something, she went after it, and if she had to manipulate me to get what she wanted, well, that's what she did. I don't think she was even aware of it, and I don't think she could have helped herself, even if she was.

"Okay," I said, forcing a laugh. "You're right. Forget it. I'm bein' stupid. What's the plan for today?"

"Easy. We sit tight 'til nightfall and then see what we can see," she said.

I nodded, then got out of bed, brushed my teeth and ate breakfast—a few stale bread rolls and half a bottle of orange juice we'd picked up from a place called the Jubilee Mercantile & Sundries the day before. It wasn't much, but the truth was, I wasn't really that hungry. I spent most of the day resetting the camera and sound equipment back at the camp and took a little time to capture some of the wildlife on the bayou with the camera on my mobile phone before it ran out of juice. I shot a thirty-second video of a water moccasin threading its dark, silky body through a layer of dull green lily pads and about a dozen other short shots of the bayou's local denizens. By ten o'clock, the full moon hung high in the night sky like a pale white orb, casting its glare down on the bayou below. Once again, the waters were calm and inky black. Unlike the previous night, however, Alisha hadn't dared go to sleep. We were both in our designated positions, keeping a watchful eye for any strange activity or movement.

The first ones appeared at a few minutes after ten. Just like the night before, I saw their eyes first. I pressed the camera's RECORD button and, though my heart was already pounding, said in an even voice to Alisha, "It's started."

Her eyes widened and she pulled out a small hand-held camera we kept for redundancy's sake. The zoom lens on it was for shit though. "Damn," I heard her whisper, "they're still too far away."

They moved slowly, as if every step was a struggle to dislodge their feet from the muddy bayou floor, if they even had feet. At that point, I wasn't sure. Several minutes passed, and then I hissed, "I'm picking up sound! I can hear them moving out there in the water!"

"They're getting closer!" she replied.

Soon, their heads were visible, then their shoulders. There were only a dozen or so at first, but then more appeared. Strangely, they seemed to slow down when they reached the shallows, almost as if the effort of wading through the deep waters in the middle of the bayou had tired them out. The first ones reached the edge of the bayou and suddenly fell down, crawling on hands and knees, as if they couldn't go on. I continued to film, though it took all the concentration and self-control I possessed to not be distracted by the lump of fear forming in my throat and the nausea welling in the pit of my stomach. The interlopers had skin as white as alabaster and wore the ragged remnants of dark military uniforms—torn tunics and pants, rotting belts, shredded leather boots—all carrying the rusted, faded insignia of the 13th U.S. Cavalry Regiment. Some were armed with corroded swords and rifles, the wooden stocks of their guns cracked and decaying. They grunted as they fell to their knees, the decomposing flesh sloughing away from their hands and fingers when they tried to pull themselves up out of the mud.

Alisha and I retreated deeper into the camp, and soon, the bayou's edge was lined with the prone forms of pale-faced men seemingly drained of whatever dark instincts had propelled them from the water. It was too dark to get an accurate count of how many there were in all, but I counted more than fifty myself just in the immediate area where we'd set up operations, and I could see and hear more coming out of the bayou. The sight of them had jarred us into utter shock and silence. We were too scared to move, too scared to speak, and it felt as though we were holding our collective breath, waiting for the beings before us to make their next move.

At last, one of the soldiers managed to get to his feet. He had on a long, dark coat which might have been navy blue at one point 150 years before, but now appeared quite black in the moonlight. He took one step out of the water, then two, and his wet boots, or what was left of them, touched dry ground. The toe on his right boot and both heels had disintegrated long ago, revealing half glimpses of bone where the skin, sinew, and muscle had broken down. He pulled a long, curved sword from a filthy scabbard, holding it out before him as though he were about to charge an enemy position. Then, he opened his mouth, his yellow eyes skyward, and let out a cry which sounded like a horse with sandpaper lodged in its throat whinnying in hellish agony, yet agony tinged with unmistakable triumph.

A chorus of howls went up then as the others joined the man with the sword, whom I was convinced was their captain. That was enough for Alisha. She broke and ran, the mini-camera clutched tightly in her hand. A few seconds later, I pushed away the sound equipment and made a break for it. One of the soldiers swung his rifle at me, and I felt a rush of air close to where it almost nailed me broadside in the back of the head. Another crescendo of cries echoed through the night. The cries made my ears ring and momentarily drowned out the sounds of the bayou. I wanted to cover my ears, but I couldn't because that calm, cool voice which had echoed through my thoughts from time to time the day before kept repeating: *Don't drop the camera. Don't drop the camera. Don't drop the camera.*

The creatures were slow, however, and as soon as we were some distance away, I was able to hear again. I emerged from the woods and found myself alone at the trailhead. Alisha was nowhere to be seen.

"Alisha!" I yelled out. "Where are you?"

When no answer came, I trudged toward the only source of man-made light in sight—Jubilee. Through the thick branches of the cypress trees, I could see the glow of a few scattered lights in the town's small collection of buildings. *She must have gone into town.* Suddenly, the shrieks of the soldiers grew stronger. *They're coming,* the voice observed again. Then, with more urgency, *Run, Josh, run!* I ran, rounding the corner of the intersection at Hill Road and Honeysuckle Lane. When I came to Beauregard, I was only a few hundred feet from the center of town, but something made me stop short, a sense I might be heading into worse danger than that which I'd just escaped. I caught my breath and proceeded at a cautious pace. At the corner of Beauregard and Cypress Street, I hid in the shadow of the tiny alley between the Jubilee Mercantile & Sundries and Clara's and waited.

Where the hell is Alisha? The soldiers didn't get her. That much I knew. From where I was hidden, I had an unobstructed view of the town hall and, next to it, the Magnolia Inn. The inn was well-lit and looked inviting. What's more, it looked safe. I searched the dark corners of Beauregard Street for any sign of the soldiers. It was deserted. *Head for the inn, Baker.* I took off as fast as I could and reached the wooden steps of the Magnolia less than thirty seconds later. Inside, I gave the service bell at the concierge desk a series of desperate taps and waited. At the far end of the room, a fire blazed in a massive hearth. When no one appeared, I slapped the bell again repeatedly, then yelled out, "Hello! Is anyone here! Hello? Alisha! You in here?"

Caleb appeared from behind the velour curtain. "Y'all need something?"

"Oh, Jesus, I'm glad you're here," I told him. "They came out of the bayou and tried to kill us!"

"Calm down," he said.

"Calm down? They're coming! I have to find my friend!"

"She's upstairs."

That stopped me. "She is?"

"Got here a few minutes before you did."

"But why didn't she answer when I called?"

Caleb shrugged as if he didn't have the foggiest notion, but something in those bloodshot, droopy eyes of his told me different. I turned away for a second and listened for any sound that might indicate Alisha was there. That's when I noticed I was covered in sweat, and not from the run away from the bayou. The inn was scorching hot. I turned back to Caleb.

"It's got to be eighty-five degrees outside. Why do you have a fire going?"

"They're always cold when they first come out of the bayou," he answered matter-of-factly.

I started to back away from the concierge desk. "Where's my friend?"

Caleb didn't answer.

I bumped into something and whirled around, coming face to face with Virgil. He had his arm raised, and in his hand, a club of some kind. Before I could even think, he brought it down across the side of my head and everything went black.

◊ ◊ ◊ ◊

I woke up on the floor of a dimly lit room. It only had one window. Through it, I could see the full moon glowing high above. The camera was gone and it hurt to move. A noticeable lump had formed where Virgil had hit me and my head throbbed in pain. I used a shelf to my right to steady myself, and slowly got to my feet and looked out the window. It overlooked a swift moving creek which had somehow escaped our attention when we'd first come into Jubilee. After a few minutes of trying to get the window up, it dawned on me it was nailed shut, and I gave up.

Muffled voices could be heard coming from the other side of the door—which, of course, was locked—there was no way of telling how close or far they were or where exactly they came from. I leaned against the shelf again, trying to make peace with the pulsing in my head, and noticed for the first time the shelf was overflowing with wallets, purses, jewelry, cosmetics, hair brushes, photos and a dozen other items. Frowning, I opened one of the wallets and fished through it. It contained a driver's license from Oxnut, Mississippi which belonged to one Linus Ordway. It had expired in 1962. There was no money or any credit cards in it. I picked up another one—a lady's purse this time—and found an identification card for a University of Georgia sophomore named Natalie Stevens. The card had expired in 1983. Yet another purse yielded a driver's license from Bull's Head, Oklahoma belonging to Martin Kobieski. That one was more recent—its expiration date was 2012.

I turned and gave the room a full examination. There were suitcases and overnight bags everywhere, stuffed in the corner, stacked on top of a table, and also on a huge bed with a canopy. I went across the room, ignoring the pain in my head, and started to go through the suitcases. Most contained what one would expect to find—clothes, shaving kits, shoes, magazines, newspapers, books, cameras. The magazines and newspapers were all out of date, including several old editions of *The Saturday Evening Post* and *Southern Living* from the 1940s and 50s. I tossed them aside and sat on the bed, hanging onto one of the posters when my head started to swim again. *They've been doing this for decades. Maybe longer. Maybe since the end of the war. But why?*

I didn't have time to try and figure out an answer. Someone started screaming down the hall. I listened for a moment and was pretty sure it was Alisha.

"No! Please don't do that! No!"

Her cries were followed by laughter, the kind of

laughter you might hear after the schoolyard bully steals your lunch money and pushes you to the ground. Then I heard something else. Grunts. Hard, guttural grunts. I staggered to the door and would have started pounding on it were it not for that same calm voice in the back of my head, which warned, *Don't do it. Don't let them know you're awake. Find a way out.* It hurt to do so, but I got down on one knee and peered through the keyhole. *Think, Josh. Think.* I closed my eyes for a moment, trying to block the sound of Alisha shrieking.

The lock. It looks like one of the old lever types. You might be able to jimmy it open. Christ, my head hurts. I searched the room for anything that might let me have a go at the lock. Then, I remembered the ladies' purses on the shelf. They had all contained cosmetics. I started going through all the handbags and purses, but the people of Jubilee had been thorough. Finally, after searching more than a dozen, I found what I was looking for—a lone bobby pin. As quietly as possible, I worked at the lock, trying to trick the lever and open the door. The screaming and laughing and groaning continued, making it even more difficult to concentrate. Several times, the pin caught on the lever, but no tell-tale click sounded to signal the door had been unlocked. Finally, I heard it catch, and the doorknob twisted freely. The voice rang out in my head again just before I opened the door. *Don't go out there unarmed.*

On a bedside table was a long, brass candlestick covered in dust from years of disuse. I took it in hand and went to the door, taking in a deep breath before turning the knob to peek outside. There was a short hallway with old oil portraits and antique light fixtures hanging on the wall. A bright light emanated from a room at the end of the hall, throwing shadows across the wall, shadows of men standing over something, or someone. I opened the door a little wider. The hall was empty. The screams had degenerated into sobs, but the animalistic grunting, if anything, seemed to be building to a fever pitch. *Christ, what in God's name are they DOING to her in there?* I opened the door slowly to avoid any creaks that would give away the fact I was now free and slipped through, closing it behind me just as carefully. Then, I pushed myself against the wall, trying to keep to the shadows, and made my way toward the room where all the noise was coming from.

The door to the room was wide open. When I was within a few feet, I heard the sound of creaking furniture and rhythmic grunting just below the hooting and hollering. Knowing now what I would find, I positioned myself right outside and craned my neck just past the edge of the doorframe. They had Alisha bent over the table, her eyes gaping in agony. The captain was thrusting himself in and out of her, pumping away like a mad dog in heat while Virgil and the other soldier held her down. Their shadows danced in the low light from two vintage kerosene lamps resting on a table against the wall.

Alisha squirmed, trying as hard as she could to get free. "It's cold! Stop it! It's so cold!"

Then, our eyes met. Immediately, I pulled back into the shadows, not wanting our captors to know she'd spotted me. *Do something, Josh. Do something. Anything.* I exhaled and then walked into the room, arm raised high, and smashed Virgil in the back of the head. He fell to the floor. Astonishingly, the soldiers didn't bother to stop their assault on Alisha when Virgil went down. The captain let out a final, beast-like growl from the bottom of his throat, and then fell back, exhausted from his efforts. Alisha crumpled to the floor, crying, her pants down around her ankles and her hands held over her privates as if that could protect her from further violation. Virgil continued to yowl in pain. I reared back and kicked him as hard as I could, gaining a certain sick feeling of satisfaction when I felt the steel toe of my work boot crunch what was left of the bones in his face. He did not move again.

I turned to face the one who had raped Alisha—the captain. He was leaning against the wall, and for the first time, I noticed his eyes were no longer glowing yellow, but instead were droopy and bloodshot with huge, black pupils, like great dark pits. *Oh, God. That's why they brought us here. They need women. To procreate.* A corollary chain of thoughts formed in my mind within seconds. *Which means they don't need men. Which is why they're going to kill you, Josh. Right here. Right now.* Panic swept through me. I raised my hand again to strike, and, immediately sensing danger, the captain wrapped his long, bony fingers around the hilt of his sword. Before I could move, he had the blade at my throat. He stood up straight, pressing me back against the table.

What was left of his lips formed a sort of half smile, revealing a set of black teeth, most of which had fallen away. The ice cold tip of the saber pressed harder against my throat and he snarled. *This is the end for you if you don't do something, Josh.* But I couldn't move. I was too scared and I knew what the slightest motion on my part would mean. I closed my eyes and waited for it. The captain emitted a sound resembling a snicker and raised his saber to strike. Then, there was the sound of motion elsewhere in the room. It came from the floor. Alisha had grabbed the captain by the decaying threads of his trousers, momentarily distracting him. I swung the candleholder at him. He moved to parry with his saber, but not fast enough to block a glancing blow to his head. The blow knocked off the hat bearing the 13th U.S. Cavalry insignia, revealing a head almost entirely denuded of any flesh. The captain fell back a few steps.

"Run, Josh! Run!" Alisha cried.

I shook my head in refusal and launched myself at the captain, hitting him with a football-style tackle which sent us both reeling into the wall on the opposite side of the room. Two oil portraits fell to the floor and a shelf full of books toppled over, showering the both of us with musty old volumes. The captain slammed the pommel of his saber into my back, driving me to my knees, but, somehow, I kept my grip on what was left of his stinking uniform. Then, someone grabbed my arm and yanked me back to my feet with terrible force. It was the other soldier. He threw me against the table and pinned me.

The captain moved fast. I raised the candleholder to ward off the oncoming blow only to realize I had lost it in the scuffle. The long, curved blade of his cavalry saber came down on me then, cutting through skin, then muscle, then bone, and I watched in disbelief as my right hand landed on the floor next to Alisha's face. Her screams of revulsion pierced the air in the old inn. I fell back several steps and hit the wall. The searing pain cut through me. The captain moved in to finish what he'd started, raising the sword above his head and bringing it down in a precise, murderous arc.

The only thing that saved my life was Alisha stepping in front of me. With astonishing control, the captain halted what surely would have been the death blow and moved to get around her, but she wouldn't let him. She gave me a backward glance, and I could see on her face that she had come to the same realization. *He won't hurt her. Not while there's a chance she can breed.* The captain bellowed something unintelligible to the other soldier, who made a move toward Alisha.

"You've got to go, Josh!" she yelled. "Go now!"

"Alisha…" I started.

"Go! Run!"

Pressing my right arm to my chest, I broke and ran from the room, staggering and slamming into the walls. I was halfway down to the first floor when I spotted old Caleb waiting for me at the bottom of the stairs. Knowing I wouldn't get another chance at escape, I rushed him. Downward momentum doubled the impact of my shoulder into the old man's chest and sent him crashing to the ground. Not wanting to take any chances of him pursuing me, I raised my foot and stomped him in the face just as I had Virgil. He went down for the count. Outside, I struggled out of my T-shirt and wrapped it around my right wrist, praying it would help staunch the flow of blood. The inn's porch was deserted, but the edge of town was dotted with the silhouettes of slow-moving figures on the approach. Once again, the voice in the back of my head surfaced through the pain pulsing from my right arm where the hand had been lopped off at the wrist. *The creek. Go to the creek.* I moved as best I could down the Magnolia Inn's steps and disappeared into the darkness of the alley between the inn and the town hall.

I hadn't gone more than fifty feet down the alley before I heard the sound of rushing water. Out of the corner of my eye I saw a soldier appear and point at me. He let out a cry barren of any and all humanity, alerting his comrades he had found me. I bolted and came out the other side of the alley to the edge of the creek. A broken-down dock no more than ten feet in length jutted out into the middle of the creek's formidable current, but any hopes of finding a boat of some kind—any kind—were dashed. I glanced over my shoulder. A group of soldiers was now no more than twenty feet from me.

For some reason, I looked back at the inn, and saw Alisha's dark outline at the window. She looked down on me for a moment, and if I could have seen her face, I know her eyes would have been filled with desperate, dejected fear. Suddenly, she turned and raised her arms, and I could see she had something in her hands. One of the kerosene lamps. A pair of huge, black hands fell on her shoulders and she brought her arms down. Within seconds, the room was ablaze, and one of the soldiers—not the captain— burst through the window and fell to the ground below like a fiery meteorite crashing to earth. He writhed and screeched for several seconds, then lay still, a smoking hulk of orange-glowing ember in the black night. Within seconds, the entire upper floor of the Magnolia was ablaze.

The sound of heavy boots got closer, jerking me back to my own precarious situation. I turned and faced the creek. *Jump, Josh. Jump. It's the only way.* Another alien scream penetrated the night, this time much closer—no more than a few feet from where I stood, and I jumped into the creek. The water was cool and deep, but not cold, and actually provided a momentary respite from the intense summer heat and the throbbing where my right hand used to be. Even without the hand, I was able to kick and paddle my way back to the surface. The current was swift, and carried me downstream at a pace. I turned and faced the way I had come. The fire had spread quickly, moving from the Magnolia to the town hall and the post office. I watched as the Magnolia's upper floor collapsed in a fiery billow of black smoke and flame. *Burn, you fuckers. Burn to the ground.* The sound of the explosion died away and was replaced by the howls of the remnants of the men of the 13th U.S. Cavalry. Finally, the firelight of Jubilee fell away into the darkness.

The current had taken me no more than five hundred yards or so when I spotted a fork, one feeding into the wider Jubilee River and the other toward Blue Belly Bayou.

I kicked and paddled as best I could toward the Jubilee, knowing that to end up back in the stagnant waters of the bayou would mean almost certain capture and death. For several moments, it looked like I wouldn't make it, but somewhere right before the fork, the current took on new life and pushed me downriver. Soon, I lay flat on my back, arms spread for buoyancy, and allowed the Jubilee to take me where it would. At different times over the next several minutes, it occurred to me the river was probably full of alligators, water moccasins, and God only knows what other predators, but I didn't care—I knew my wound was severe and that I would most likely bleed to death long before the night was out. I simply stared up at the luminous, full moon overhead and watched it pass through thin, gray tufts of cloud.

At some point in the night, I don't know when exactly, I lost consciousness. The next thing I knew, I was on my side, spitting up river water. Someone pounded me on my back. When my vision cleared, I looked up into the face of an immensely obese man wearing a T-shirt with the words I GAVE UP FISHING ONCE & IT WAS THE MOST TERRIFYING HOUR OF MY LIFE stitched across the chest. He had beady little eyes, a dark mustache, the bushiest sideburns I'd ever seen, and arms the size of oak trees.

"Hey, y'all're gonna make it! Just hold on now!" He looked over his beefy shoulder and yelled, "C'mon, Pete, goddamit! I said full throttle now! Let's go!"

Somewhere in the distance, I heard the hum of an outboard motor. My eyes started to feel heavy again, and I wanted more than anything to close them and rest, but the fat man slapped me hard in the face.

"Ya gotta stay awake, partner! C'mon now, stay awake! We're almost there!"

I mumbled a feeble protest and started to close my eyes again.

The man swore, told his companion to hand him something and then I felt an intense burn on my right shoulder. I was instantly alert.

"What the fuck is that?" I screamed.

The fat man held a lit cigarette in front of my face. "Y'all keep your eyes open, or you'll get it again, I swear!"

I nodded at him. My hand had gone all but numb and I felt too weak to move, but I forced myself to keep my eyes open. I noticed then the boat was full of fishing rods and assorted pails of bait, none of which smelled particularly appetizing. Soon, the outboard's engine droned lower and lower as we approached shallow water, and then it stopped altogether. The fat man and his friend picked me up then—not gently—and got me out of the boat and on to shore. An ambulance with flashing red lights waited not ten feet from the dock.

"Ya sure are lucky my buddy thought to bring his cell phone, mister," the fat man told me.

His friend finally spoke. "No, he's lucky I could get a signal out there on the river is what he's lucky for!"

I was loaded into the ambulance and hooked up to oxygen and about ten different other machines all designed to keep me alive long enough to get me to the hospital. One of the EMTs examined me, shouting information about my condition and injuries to a dispatcher while the ambulance careened down an empty country road, sirens blaring.

"Sir? Can you hear me?"

I nodded.

"What happened? How did you sustain this injury? Were you caught in the fire upriver in Jubilee?"

I started to say something and then laughed instead. He

looked at me like I was crazy.

"What's that? What're you trying to say?"

I pushed the oxygen away. "You wouldn't…" I started. "You wouldn't believe me if I told you."

He gave me a sympathetic smile. "Try me."

"You ever heard the legend of Blue Belly Bayou?"

He shook his head. "Of course. I grew up here. Who hasn't? That's just a story."

I smiled. "Yeah. It's just a story."

◊ ◊ ◊ ◊

Alisha's been dead more than a year now. I still think of her often, and I am haunted by the memory of what she endured and how she died. Sometimes I wonder if there was anything more I could've done to save her. Maybe if I'd listened to my gut that something was very definitely wrong in Jubilee, she wouldn't have had to sacrifice herself so I could live. Maybe if I'd not let my feelings for her take common sense hostage, we'd both have made it out of there alive. The shrinks here call that survivor's guilt. Maybe they're right. I don't know. What I do know is there is an entire world out there most of us never get the chance to see, that most of us *can't* see, because the thought that such a world truly exists is far too frightening to countenance. But that world is there, I can assure you. It's there, hidden beneath the veil we like to call reality, and it's there, lurking under the still, dark waters of Blue Belly Bayou.

REBORN ON THE BAYOU
by B.A. Sans

Dastardly deeds of the impoverished once took place on the edge of these waters. Poor, uneducated minds mixed with superstitious mumblings to create a sanctuary for the wicked and weak. Strange stories of witches and voodoo encircled the area like a plume of smoke never to rise, thick with cautionary advice to the visitor. These tales clung to the land of my father's father—the bayous of Louisiana. And although I was very much a visitor to the area, I doubled as a landowner by inheritance.

I had been intrigued by the stories of my father as a small boy. He would weave together tales of alligators and witchcraft into a Creole tapestry of sensational visions. His stories of dead men awaking from their eternal slumbers, old women who were cast away by society, and the ever pulling lure of the swamp itself both frightened me and pulled me in a like a moth is pulled into the soft glow of a lantern ready to zap the life from it. He had spoken of the place as though it was a magical land spliced together with the wrongs of man and the nature of evil, yet I always got the feeling that he loved it. His stories rolled off of his tongue to both glorify the bayou and condemn it. I used to hang on his words; they kept me awake until the wee hours of the night. Nothing more diminished my faith in my father's lore than the first time I actually traveled to these parts. My grandfather had passed, and the obligation of setting everything in order was my father's task to take as he was the only heir to the old man's estate. Estate—what a funny word to call this place! My grandfather had owned a large amount of acreage, but the majority of it lay within the stagnant waters of the damned. His dwelling cried shack more than southern plantation and the stories which enticed my imagination as a youth fell dumbfounded with the actuality of the swamp.

Now I just used the place more as a vacation home than anything. It had become a place to get away from the roar of my life as a financial assistant out in the real world, the world beyond the Louisiana shores. All of this had become mine with the passing of my father, and like him, I did not choose to live here. Furthermore, I could not sell it for a reasonable price. No one wanted to pay for my heritage, and so the responsibility of tending to it fell to my hands. Of course, tending to it meant that I would come down to the bayou a couple of times per year, dip my fishing rod into the water, and piss away the days with each passing can of cheap beer. I would clean up the place a little each time I came down, but it wasn't really worth the effort to spend any real time fixing it up. It was a crap-hole when I inherited it, and it will be a crap-hole long after I'm gone.

That day started off like any other day in the bayou. Early to rise with a slight ache in my head from the previous day's excursion, I launched my boat out into the swamp with nothing but my fishing gear and some lager to keep me company. The warm wet air of an early August morning lured me out of my bed with the rising of the sun, and I knew the best fishing always took place at this time of the day. I found that I enjoyed the peacefulness of the random animal sounds of the early morning and the stillness of the glassy water, which was the reason I continued to keep this place in my thoughts and possession. The fishing ranked among the best I had ever encountered, and so every summer I took a week off to come down to the bayou, clearing my head of the hustle and bustle of life at home.

Drenched from the summer sun, I began my ritual of cheap canned beer and relaxation. The bitterness of my drink, something I would not let touch my lips in my city life to the far north, made me feel more like I truly was a local. Hour after hour, I felt tugs on my fishing rod with each one becoming less and less of a priority to me. The midday sun beat down upon my skin. Plunging my soul into the ice cold refreshment in my hand and letting my attention fade away from the fishing, I noticed that I had become exceedingly tired. My head began nodding and I realized the beer was slipping from my hand. I decided to set down the can and let the Sandman take his hold of me. Closing my eyes and dreaming of the clouds overhead, I felt my body relax. My arms and legs felt heavy, and gravity seemed to multiply tenfold. This is what I came here to experience. This was the reason I kept this place. It wasn't the fantastic tales of Creole superstition. It was the slight hum of the swamp singing its lullaby that pulled me into inebriated slumber.

Awakening to pitch blackness with only the sound of the frogs croaking and the ringing in my head to welcome me, I took a second to look around and gain a grasp of my present location. Everything came back to me quickly as I felt the parched knives of dehydration stab at my lips and tongue. At night the bayou looked so unfamiliar and bizarre. The trees with their draping moss and malevolent shapes along with the thousands of shining eyes, seemed so unknown and mysterious, like they were plotting my demise. The low growl of the swamp creatures began to grow in an ominous chorus of agreement, almost as an eerie prophecy of impending condemnation. It was easy to see why such stories of ghosts and goblins were born here. The combination of land, water, and brush silhouetted against the foggy backdrop of the untamed bayou was enough to create fear in the mind of even the strongest willed people. The air laid thick on my being.

I looked around for some sort of familiarity. This area of the swamp was not something I had ever seen before, but I couldn't understand how my boat drifted so far away from my estate. The water was practically without current. Desperately I yanked the cord to the small outboard motor on the rear of the craft. After a few spastic jerks, the engine sputtered and coughed. For a few seconds, I felt as though my salvation lay within the purr of the engine, only to have that moment of deliverance die with the sound. I pulled again and again, almost to the point of complete exhaustion. I slinked into the boat as my hopes sank into a void, almost as pitch black as the bayou around me. As I felt enough energy to tackle my situation again, I looked around for any signs of rectifying my situation. Within the trees, I saw a faint light burning lightly in between the branches. It glowed there like an ominous beacon, but at that moment it appeared to be my only salvation.

The stories of those who lived in the swamp shuffled through my mind as I looked at the light shining in the distance. I had heard of witches who had sheltered themselves in the backwoods, free to practice a magic that was as black as their cold hearts. Those unlucky souls who had wandered into the swamp to never return were often the victims of these dark enchantresses, at least as the stories went. Whenever tragedies befell those in the bayou, the locals would tell tales of almost unspeakable acts at the hands of these fearsome recluses. Fear was overcome by the basic need for water though, and I began paddling my boat to the water's edge. I was sure the people of the area, although uneducated and poor, would not be the monsters that they were portrayed to be in the stories of my youth. People were just people. I was confident that anyone who lived at the source of the light would be at least courteous enough to give me a glass of water. My boat reached the bank, and I clumsily fell onto the muddy soil as my feet skidded on the moist earth.

Regaining my composure and my feet, I anchored my boat to land and began making my way toward the light trying to be very cautious of the wildlife that may have been waiting around for an evening snack. It had not been unheard of to pick up a local newspaper and read about some drunken idiot who got bit as he stepped on an alligator. I did not want to be that drunken idiot tonight. As I emerged through a thick line of trees, I came upon a little shack buried within the heart of the swamp.

Every stereotype any person had about dilapidated shacks in the bayou was confirmed to me simply by the existence of this little building. Every vision from every movie with a swamp shack was confirmed by the appearance of this place. It looked as though it had been made by one of the three little pigs, and not the one who was smart. Bent wood formed the structure as it rotted and collided with earth at unnatural angles. Artifacts of long lost lives which had existed here were found about the yard in bits and pieces. As my eyes scanned the ground, I saw dirty and broken items of home life that had not seen use in at least a decade. Old buckets, metal pipes that bent to make structures of no rhyme or reason, ancient clothing stiffened to almost a petrified state with mud, and various other odds and ends were abundantly thrown about. The urge for water once again became too great for me as I noticed light in the shack through the slightly gaping boards that made up the exterior wall.

Venturing around the perimeter of the would-be house, I came upon what could only be thought of as the door. The splintered edges of the frame lashed out in jagged curves waiting to snag any passerby. Splattering tints of brown intertwined in a picture of decay.

I calmly knocked on the door not truly expecting any response.

"Hello," I called out. "Is there anybody home?"

As I expected the only response came from the wild of the woods behind me in the form of insects buzzing and other various animal sounds which I could not place. I knocked again for good measure but then pushed on the door. It easily swung open to reveal the same disarray within that carpeted the landscape outside. I peered within.

Beside a residual flame lingering in a makeshift wood burning stove, the place looked utterly deserted.

"Hello?" I called out again. There was no reply, so I entered.

I found myself in the midst of a backwoods living room. A small antiquated table accompanying a feeble looking rocking chair were the only inhabitants of the room. A dark hallway lingered in the back, and I felt like I should announce myself again. The sign of fire in the stove signaled that someone must live here which made me even more wary of who could possibly inhabit the residence. I didn't want some guy named Jeffro to bury the contents of his shotgun in my back. I went to call out again when I realized that a glass on the little table contained water. Without thinking, I grabbed the glass and poured every last drop through my parched lips. I suddenly heard a noise.

Quickly turning around, my eyes only saw something moving toward me. Out of reflex, I brought my hands up but pain in my skull signaled the lack of my speed. Dizzily, I felt my legs weaken and then nothing.

The room spun as my eyes opened. Blurred images of the room began to come back into focus as the smell of smoke filled my nostrils. I felt myself propped up in a chair. The heightened flame of the stove was the first object that my eyes fully saw. Then to the left of the fire, I saw her.

"Aw, we're awake, my Chester," an old woman said noticing my arousal. A spark glittered in her eyes. She appeared older than the house itself. Deep lines of hard life etched themselves on the canvas of her face. Her smiling lips, chapped and broken, only accentuated the wrinkles.

"I'm sorry," I spoke. My voice barely cracked at an audible level. "I'm not Chester." My head ached more than it had before I had found the shack. Splitting pain tingled about my skull. "Why did you hit me?"

"My poor, poor Chester," she answered in a rough, cackling voice. "I had to hit you. I wasn't sure if it was you at first, but I prayed to Him asking to bring you back to me, and He has."

"What are you talking about?" I roared. "I'm not Chester! My name is Steven. I don't know who Chester is, but I'm not him. Please just let me go."

"My Chester, so confused," she replied as she got up and fussed about with something. I was expecting her to pull out a gun or an axe; something to finish me off. I braced myself. Fear pulsed through my veins. She turned around and showed me an old black and white picture.

Within the old picture were a middle aged woman and a middle aged man. Both were definitely offspring of the area as clues such as missing teeth and backwoods clothing stood out. I assumed that the woman in the picture was the freak in front of me when she was younger.

"See, it's you Chester," she croaked. "You've come back to me. I asked Him to bring you back, and you've been reborn."

"Who did you ask? I'm not Chester!" I screamed. Still groggy but slowly regaining some of my bearings, I realized that I was not secured to the chair in any way. I could overtake this lunatic. I just needed to wait for the right chance in case she had a gun or a knife on her that I couldn't see. I decided to play along to buy some time and possibly gain some trust.

"Wait, it's all coming back to me," I lied. "I must have been confused, but the truth had been in front of me the whole time. I was lost in the world beyond home, beyond the bayou. Something kept calling me back, like a whisper in my ear that gradually transformed into a constant screaming in my mind. Something here was luring me back, slowly just like fragmented memories of a far off place when awaking from a dream. I have now opened my eyes and can see the world beyond the dream, the world that had been waiting for me all along. Yes, I was Chester, and I was reborn. His words have always spoken to me, but it was not until now that I have realized that his words were my words, buried deep within my soul. I thought it was Chester who had told me to come to you, but it was me who was speaking the whole time. Since I am Chester, I was telling myself to come here, so we could be together as one for eternity."

The old woman's eyes sparkled beneath the age of her face.

"Oh my darling Chester, I knew it!" she screeched. "I knew you would finally come back. It will be like old times, forever. Let me get it. I'll be right back."

She sprung down the darkened hallway behind her. I

didn't want to wait around to find out what she was bringing back. This was my chance. I put my hands on the arms of the rocking chair. My body felt numb, and I couldn't really feel my grip. Pushing up with my hands, my body crumbled beneath my weight. I toppled to the ground as searing pain echoed through my legs. I didn't hear the old woman come back.

"Oh my Chester, you should let me help you," I heard her say. I felt her hands under my armpits and with incredible strength for an old lady, she lifted me into a seat, but it wasn't the rocking chair. I was staring back at that dilapidated piece of furniture from a new seat. My head spun as I tried to make sense of the situation.

"You know you can't get around without your wheelchair," she spoke. Confused I looked down. Horror filled my very being. My feet were gone; amputated below the ankle. I screamed.

"Just like old times, my beloved Chester, you never did get used to losing your feet," the old woman cackled over my pain. "But I will always take care of you just like before. I promise. Forever and always."

SELENE
by Edward Moore

My dad owns a real scum pit named the Afterlife. The only thing marking it as a bar is the old Jack Daniels ad in the front window and the stuttering neon sign which says "tavern". The toilets are always backed up and the place perpetually smells like piss. During the day it's your typical local dive serving barflies and truckers heading south to New Orleans, but Friday through Saturday it changes as local field hands and rig workers pass through, pissing away their paychecks on watered-down beer and jukebox blues.

Not much usually happens there, but the other night was different. After all was said and done, I had to clean up the spoils from one mean ass, knockdown, drag out fight. I was in complete awe as I watched my dad beat the crap out of Butch Dumbronsky.

Dumbronsky's one of those big oilrig workers who thinks they should be anywhere but here. Typical former jock, all-state football, basketball, and more. Stories went that back in high school he put this postage stamp town on the map. State football championship, slipping tongue with the head cheerleader, all the while getting money and scholarship offers up the yin-yang from everybody and anybody. His future looked good except for one teeny weeny thing – the fact that book-wise, he was dumb as a post.

Eventually, LSU won his "services", and Lord knows how he stayed eligible. In the end it didn't matter, because after an all night drinking binge, he drove a booster's car right into Beaver Bayou. Drunk and driving into the bayou they could handle, having a booster's naked fifteen-year old daughter in the car with him – that, they couldn't handle. LSU dropped him like a snapped jock strap, sending him home, dumb, bitter and in disgrace.

My dad never liked him. Said he was a whiner, always angry, blaming any of life's misfortune on everyone but himself. With a nasty temper to go along with an impressive physique, people were scared of him. The slightest thing could cause him to go upside your head in a minute, especially after he had a few drinks in him. Still, my dad tolerated him because he was good for business, running up a huge tab and promptly paying at the end of the night.

◊ ◊ ◊ ◊

Booze makes people stupid; especially fools like Butch. He said something about my mother to Daddy and all hell broke loose. Dad punched him square in the face, and I flinched as Butch's nose exploded, splattering blood and teeth all over the bar. The punch dropped Butch to the floor with a gangster movie sounding thud. When he tried to get up, Daddy kicked his feet out from under him and began stomping all over his legs. People were yelling and screaming as he continued to slam his bootheel into the back of Butch's legs until the man's knees were mush. Finally, Daddy hit him across the head with a bottle, putting Butch out until the ambulance arrived.

"Guess we won't be seeing much of Butch around here

anymore," my Uncle Danny said as he hoisted another beer to his tobacco-stained lips.

"She may be dead but nobody talks about her like that. Not to me. Next fool says something like that, I'll put my foot so far up his ass that when I wiggle my toes, I'll tickle his nose," Daddy said with a satisfied chuckle.

With that said, the bar maid, Gap-Tooth Sue put a song on the jukebox, and people started drinking and playing pool again as things returned to normal. After getting the eye from him, I promptly started cleaning up the mess. Later that evening I helped him close up for the night before I went home – alone. Daddy left with Gap-Tooth, shoving a couple of bucks in my hand and telling me to go get a haircut in the morning.

I'm a Brooklyn immigrant with Hungarian roots as my father is fond of telling me, and I've got to admit that Thibodaux is a bit much to get used to. It really isn't a city unless you want to use the term jokingly. It's mostly a scared speck of land, littered with ramshackle moss-marred clapboard buildings; snaked with gravel roads crisscrossing patches of pockmarked Louisiana swampland. Beside my father's place, it has a few small shops, your typical hardware and feed store as well as a couple of restaurants and upscale bars. The lone gas station is next to the local whorehouse and has a sign warning people to fill their tanks before leaving because the swamp's full of alligators.

Beside being boring, it has this creepy fog which never seems to go away. It just hangs over the place like a dingy shower curtain. Walking through it is not like walking through misty droplets of water—it's something different. It feels like I'm walking through walls of wet muffled sounds. The grownups say it's a spirit sent by God to watch over the children of the Delta. I don't know what it's supposed to protect us from, I just know that from the first moment it touched me, something about it bothered me.

The morning air was humid; thick with bugs, and every breath I took felt like I was sucking jelly into my lungs. As I left the house, I noticed strips of orange and lemon colored leaves clinging to the blackening limbs and twigs of boscages dotting the road in front of the house.

The morning fog hadn't lifted as I passed the post office heading for the barbershop, my mind on the streets and sounds of Brooklyn. I had just gotten back a couple days before and couldn't help thinking about playing blacktop basketball, smoothing with the ladies, and dancing to the sounds of Buddy Holly, Little Richard, and other great Yankee music. Best of all, that's where I first heard my new favorite song, Fats Domino's "Blueberry Hill," which I was happily humming to myself, when Jimmy Ranes ran up to me, panting with his tongue hanging out like some parched barfly who'd had too many salted peanuts.

"Rick," he gasped, as he leaned against me, catching his breath. "We thought you'd never get back from vacation."

"Who's we?" I asked.

"Me and Pascal."

Pascal's my cousin, and along with Jimmy, we are the biggest horror nuts in town. Unbeknown to our parents, we snuck into theaters to watch the latest monster movies, read magazines like "Terror Tales", "Dime Mystery", and our favorite, EC Comic's "Horror Stories". On Friday night we told our parents we were going over to Pascal's house for Bible study. Instead of studying the Good Book we'd be up in Pascal's room watching "Haunted Movies at Midnight."

Jimmy sweated buckets and his hands twitched like a crapshooter pinched while using loaded dice. Behind his thin speckled glasses his eyes darted around as they checked to make sure no one stood too close to us. He used his tee shirt to wipe sweat from his face, and then he jerked his head and indicated he wanted me to go behind the post office with him.

After we got there, he nervously looked around and whispered, "There's a vampire at Pascal's house."

I was stunned and gave him my "Do I look stupid" face.

"Don't look at me like that. I'm telling the truth."

"Whatever," I said as I turned to walk away, "Got to go get my haircut."

"Wait, what about the vampire?"

"Stop it. You think I'm an idiot or something?" I sighed.
"C'mon – Count Dracula in swamp country?"

"No, it's true. Come see for yourself," he said, his voice dropping as his face scrunched into a baby-like "please you gotta believe me" expression.

I briefly felt a little sorry for him, before I started thinking about how him and Pascal were most likely pulling a prank to make me look stupid. "I ain't got time for this. Just got back from vacation and my dad told me to go get a haircut."

"Bring anything back?"

Now it was my turn to look around, making sure nobody could see us. After I was satisfied no one could, I said, "Yeah. Just this knife my cousin gave me."

Then I pulled it out, and flicked it open so fast, Jimmy's glasses almost fell off, when he must have jumped three feet away from me. He stared at it all bug-eyed and everything as he asked, "Is it silver?"

"Quit it," I snapped. "Your gag is old, and I need to get a haircut."

"No … no this is good. You getting that knife, like

you're psychic or something."

"Like I'm what? What're you talking about?"

"C'mon. I'll show you."

Against my better judgment I started walking with him toward Uncle Fergus's sugarcane field. It was a short distance away on the east bank of Lafourche Bayou.

As we trudged through the wispy patches of fog, I felt like something or someone beside Jimmy was with us. As we got closer to the field, I started hearing faint, echoing whispers. They sounded like nothing I'd ever heard. Not words, just sounds. Violent sounds. I knew it was the fog whispering to me with that frustrating voice I couldn't understand. I didn't say anything to Jimmy about it, but those sounds, their echoes, gave me goose bumps.

When we got to my uncle's field, we hopped the fence. Brushing one or two bugs away from my face, I watched Jimmy as he searched for the path he wanted me to follow. By the time he located it, one or two bugs had become thirty or forty and I felt the first sting of bug bites on the back of my neck. I slapped the spot and noticed my fingers were dotted with blood.

He finally located the path and motioned for me to follow. Being careful to keep low to the ground, we blazed a trail through rows and rows of sticky sweet smelling sugarcane.

Jimmy surprised me, because he was running faster than I'd ever seen him run. I was having a hard time keeping up with him, but as we got closer to the center of the field, his pace started to slow. Finally he stopped and began moving his head like an out-of-control-jack-in-the-box, looking around as if he was afraid someone might have followed us. "We're almost there, just a little further," he whispered to me.

"Almost where?" I asked as I held up my hands

signaling for him to relax. "Slow down or you'll pass out from this heat." In reality I was the winded one who needed a break. Pausing to catch my breath and wipe some sweat from my eyes, I noticed there were no longer any bugs around.

What kind of field doesn't have bugs in it?

"I'm okay. Just got to show you the grave."

The what?

Without saying another word Jimmy pushed through a clump of stalks that crackled like dried bamboo sticks. After following him for a couple of more rows, we stopped and I stood before a mound of fog moistened dirt. It was an ugly, black, pile of dirt clods drying to a grayish brown texture beneath the hot sun.

The absence of greenery around the mound made me think of the bald spot on Uncle Fergus's head. Snotty yellow in color and sprinkled with speckles of black dots, it always made me think of a bull's eye because of the silver circle of thinning hair surrounding it.

As I stood there staring at the mound, I realized something was very wrong with this field. It had been ready for harvesting for at least a week, and yet my uncle hadn't done it. With the cane stalks being so green and leafy he needed to burn this field to get it ready for harvesting.

My uncle was a skinflint and one of the most devoutly religious men in town. Like Dumbronsky, he enjoyed lording over anyone he thinks he can dominate. As an assistant pastor of our church, he's always preaching about discipline and how people shouldn't tolerate foolishness, from child or adult – business or personal. My dad once said Uncle Fergus holds onto his money so tight he must squeeze the buffalos off the nickels. He would never waste an opportunity to make a buck; so putting off harvesting wasn't like him.

Uncle Fergus was my father's former brother-in-law and to me was almost as scary as any vampire could ever be. He had the palest skin I'd ever seen – so pale I could see the blue veins of his arms and nose. Daddy told me he was an albino like his mother, whatever an albino was. On Sundays he taught Bible school, where he'd often get the Holy Spirit. Then his thick black Buddy Holly glasses would start inching up and down his long hawkish nose, and his eyes – one gray, one blue – would swim in opposite directions in his head. With spittle flying from the corners of his mouth he would start talking so fast nobody could understand what he was saying. When that happened, us kids got scared to death, but the grownups just told us that was only the Lord talking to us through him.

The nerves in my neck were twitching as I circled the mound of dewy dirt. I couldn't help but notice that beside Jimmy and me, there were no other living things in sight. My eyes scanned the area looking for snakes or lizards skirting about, field mice or cats flitting through the stalks, but saw nothing. It was as if anything living was afraid to be near it. Hell, I wasn't too keen on being near it.

As the sun disappeared behind some clouds, my mouth went dry, and the only sounds I could hear were the thumping of my heart racing in my chest along with Jimmy's, my heavy breathing and the chirping of far away crickets filtering through stalks of sugarcane.

As I crept closer to the 'grave', I started thinking about how it looked like a huge, dirty sponge with spiky hair sticking out of it. Survey stakes, forks, kitchen knives along with some fancy stuff that must have been pure silver, were poking out of it. Someone had also laid a cross on top of it.

Then the realization of what I was looking at hit me. I knew this was no ordinary mound. This was a grave, a vampire grave.

I don't know how long it was before I noticed a thick milky looking mist crawling over the mound. The mist rose, swirled then began convulsing like something dancing to the tune of a snake charmer. In its middle I could see a vague, shimmering shape of a man – tall, thin and smoking a cigarette. He turned toward me as the mist changed colors from vanilla white to amber yellow.

Backing away I couldn't take my eyes off him. Strangely I wasn't afraid, more curious than anything. Everything was fading in and out of view like some bad UHF reception, as the mist began swallowing snippets of light away from the mound, finally blanketing it in a shroud of chocolate darkness.

Suddenly the rest of the light was sucked into the mist and changed the green leafy field into a strangely milk white ghost-like world. A world devoid of all color or pretense of life. I saw shapes taking form, floating inches from my face, first a moon, then a cross and finally a cloth bag. I looked around for Jimmy but couldn't see him. I shouted his name, but the sound of my voice was drowned out by a great roar, and in the blink of an eye, the mist twisted into a tornado-like funnel and knifed into the mound.

"Jimmy what was that?"

"What was what? I didn't see anything. You see something? Hear something?"

"No. Must be my eyes playing tricks on me. Let's get outta here. Go to the house, see Pascal."

Before leaving the field I took one last look at the mound. Its pin-like stakes were brown, hard and smooth, and with the hilt of knives glistening in the morning sunlight the clumps of earth looked like little dead fists.

From the road my uncle's house looked like something from your hack artist cliché painting—large white antebellum surrounded by hundred-year old trees. I'll admit it looked good, having stood the test of time through three or four generations. I knew a few coats of white paint every couple of years along with skilled carpentry work contributed to its longevity. As a child I always thought there was something about the way it rested beneath those trees that helped protect it. Not that day. It looked small and trapped, like an animal ensnared by wooden gnarly arms, all twisting inward toward it, holding it down like a parent force feeding a child medicine he didn't like.

When Pascal answered our knock, he didn't look good. There was a purplish welt on his cheek, and his eyes were red. Jimmy began whispering too loudly and Pascal held a finger to his lips.

"My parents are gone," he said. "Pop's in town and Mom's gone to see Grandma in Houma. Doctors don't think Grandma's gonna make it, and she won't go to the hospital." He opened the screen door, "Come on in but be quiet."

We followed Pascal through the living room. It was depressingly barren, no TV, hi-fi, magazines or flowers, just like a room you'd expect no one to live in. All it had was my uncle's worn rocker, a few stiff high back chairs, an oak table with his bible opened to the Book of Exodus resting on it, and a huge wrought iron cross hanging over the fireplace.

I tried to make some small talk, and asked Pascal where my cousin Lori was. "She's upstairs asleep. Lately that's all she ever does," he solemnly said.

That didn't sound right to me. She was always up and about doing something. She had more energy than a hundred rabbits in a garden patch. To the boys at school she was the biggest tease, and Jimmy, he was the one with the biggest crush of all of them. It was embarrassing how he got mooney-eyed around her, and it was also a pathetic waste of time. She was three years older than us, and girls like her wanted the big dogs, not the pups.

I went to the foot of the staircase, looked up the landing, and saw the door to her room slightly open. Before Pascal could say anything, I climbed the stairs and headed toward the door hollering, "Lori."

As I got closer to the room I could see an arm dangling over the side of a bed. She rolled over just as I entered the doorway, and I could see her long black hair, blacker than a tax man's heart was how my daddy described it, and a blue nightgown dipping low over a freckled shoulder.

Lori, Pascal's sister, looked at me with eyes like her brother's, red and swollen from too many spilled tears. They caught mine, but it was like they weren't focused, as if they were seeing something or someone else.

"Frency?" she whispered. "Is that you?" she sobbed. "I'm sorry, I'm sooo sorry."

I backed down the stairs, embarrassed and not saying a word. Pascal whispered a couple of words to Jimmy before grabbing my shirttail. Turning I saw his swollen red eyes, and couldn't help but wonder what the hell was going on.

Meanwhile upstairs I could hear Lori crying.

Just as I was getting ready to tell them to step outside for a talk, I heard Uncle Fergus's car pulling up. Pascal wiped his eyes with the back of his hand and nodded for us to go out back.

Once outside he said, "We got to talk, but not with Pop around. Come meet us down by the fish dock about six. Jimmy and I got a story to tell you. Lord knows I'm going to need help getting through this. Think you bring us something from the Afterlife" he said with a "please-oh-please" look on his face.

"Bring some cups, I'll get us something," was my reply as I was thinking it must be serious if Pascal is asking me to pinch some booze from the Afterlife. We shook our heads, hugged each other, and I left to go get my haircut. All the way to the shop and throughout the day I couldn't help but wonder what Jimmy and Pascal were going to tell me.

The sun had dipped below the horizon, but a scattering of clouds siphoned its rays back into the sky spreading a hazy orange glow across town. The streets were steamy from that afternoon's shower, leaving rivulets of water to trickle down the sidewalk and into the cracked asphalt fronting the Afterlife, feeding tiny pools of oil-slicked surfaces shimmering in the falling light.

A calm had settled over the town as the evening rush of folks heading home for supper had passed, and those who would be coming to the Afterlife for an evening's entertainment hadn't yet appeared on the street. I helped my dad set up for the night and told him I was going to see Pascal and Lori, tell them about my vacation and how great Brooklyn was. He didn't need to know I'd hidden a fifth of Crown Royal in a bag by the dumpster out back. I hugged him goodbye, circled around back, picked up the scotch, and made my way to Uncle Fergus's fishing dock on Lafourche Bayou.

The fog was rolling in just as I got there. Jimmy and Pascal waved at me while using a lantern to sweep an arc of light off to the side of the dock. Their pants were wet up to their knees and they were bent over panting like they had just hauled something heavy from the bayou.

"What's going on? How'd you get your pants wet?"

"Take a look at this," Pascal said as he waved for me to come closer and see what they were hunched over.

The fog hadn't reached shore yet and from the light of the quarter moon and the lantern I could barely see the reflection of chrome handlebars and the partially mud crusted sight of a motorcycle immersed in the muddy bottom of the bayou.

I let out a low whistle before asking Pascal to tell me what was going on.

Immediately Jimmy started babbling, and I cut him off with a hard glare. He put his head down and looked sheepishly at his feet, slapping at bugs buzzing around him. Pascal didn't look like he was ready to start talking until I handed him the bag with the fifth of Crown Royal. He pulled out three plastic cups from the cloth bag he carried, and offered them to us. Jimmy took his while I shook my head no.

"I drink from the bottle," I said, "It's got more punch that way." I don't know if that was true or not, but that's the way I saw my heroes Steve McQueen and James Dean do it.

After a few sips we sat down on the dock and leaned against its rails as Pascal started talking. "I guess I was the first one to figure out what was going on," he sighed. "It was hard enough telling Jimmy the first time, and I don't really want to talk about it."

"You gotta tell," Jimmy blurted, and then shut up before I could punch him.

Pascal called for the bottle, took a big swig, and his face scrunched up like it was going to tear apart right between his eyes. He started coughing and gagging before continuing, "Yeah, I gotta tell." He stared at the bottle he'd place between his legs while he rubbed the welt on his jaw.

His eyes glazed over as he started talking about the family going to see his grandmother. How Lori was seeing some boy who wore a black leather jacket and rode a motorcycle. "In the middle of the night, I'd hear it out on the road in front of the house, full open, racing fast. I knew Lori wasn't in her room. I'd imagine her riding with him, her fingers digging into his jacket, her cheek pressed to his with her black hair blowing in the wind. I guess they headed up to wherever he was from, and come back a few hours before Mom and Pop would be getting up."

The pained look on Jimmy's face was wrenching as he listened to what Pascal had said.

"I heard it, too, loud and full open, flying past my house on the way to who knows where," Jimmy said. "Your mom didn't like him at all. I told you how she came by the house and talked to my mom about it. Overheard it all. She was just a fussing. Talking about how evil that boy was, and if she didn't get Lori away from him, he was gonna suck all the blood and grace of Jesus out of her. Mom told her he weren't no good and that he was dragging Lori straight to hell and the devil himself."

"Your moms can be pretty wild with all that fire and brimstone stuff," I said. "I'm sure they've said worse about me."

Pascal kept rubbing his jaw as he started talking in a real low whispery voice, distant like it wasn't a voice at all, but a machine that had clicked on inside him. "Everyone went to Houma to see Grandma, everyone except Lori. She said she wasn't feeling well. Whispered something to my mom about how she felt, mom blushed, then told her it was okay to stay home."

As he continued talking, my brain was feeling the numbing buzz from the scotch and my mind had started to wander as the fog crept up over the dock. Paying no attention to Jimmy and Pascal I saw the fog starting to dance in front of me. I strained to focus my rapidly drooping eyes on a pocket of what looked like amber colored smoke wrapped in white mist. While raising my hand to touch it, the smoke changed into two daggers and plunged straight into my eyes.

When the smoke pierced my eyes, a shearing pain

exploded in my head, and I could now imagine what Dumbronsky felt when my dad's fist broke his face. My first instinct was to panic, since everything had gone dark, and I believed the fog had blinded me. I tried to scream, but my throat wouldn't let out any sound as I desperately rubbed my eyes, all the while silently praying I wasn't going blind.

Upon opening my eyes I could see I had returned to that strange milky white ghost world I saw at the mound. This time it had a moon, and the air was cool and soothing. Outlined by moonlight was a woman, perhaps twenty, blond haired, wearing a checkered skirt, black Angora sweater, with a yellow scarf around her neck. I fancied she looked like my mother when she first met my dad. She had a small mouth that looked like it was pleading with me, as she anxiously waved to me.

"Rick, Rick something terrible has happened. We need…." Her voice trailed off as she nervously moved away from me.

"What's wrong?" I shouted.

She didn't answer as she backed away. I could still hear her voice faintly. I couldn't clearly hear what she was saying, but one word stuck repeating out over and over again.

Selene. Selene.

I'd never heard that word before. What was it? Someone? Something? Someplace?

I tried to run in the direction she had gone, when suddenly I felt weak in the knees, with painful dizziness in my head and a sudden weight on my chest. As I struggled to move forward my breath became more labored before sudden darkness surrounded me. This time I knew I hadn't gone blind as I listened and counted the chimes of a bell as it tolled twenty-three times. With each bong, the darkness faded little by little until I found myself in a field surrounded by wheat, oleanders, and ferns.

Off in the horizon, shadowed by a purple hued sun, I could make out the shape of a city with towering spires and buildings that looked like architects from all over the world must have built them. Beneath my feet was a road leading to the city, a city surrounded by mist. With nothing to stay there for and nowhere else to go, I started walking toward it.

Three quarters of a mile along the road the oleanders, ferns and wheat started to fade. The ground, at first green and soft, became dull and dark as if a rain of ashes had fallen upon it. As I traveled further along, the sky turned gray when sooty clouds blocked the sun's rays.

I blinked and scratched my head and suddenly found myself in the middle of the city, standing before a vision of what I always pictured the Tower of Babel must look like. It was built with pale, almost clear sandstone, tinged blue with a sticky honey-like film. Inside I could hear chanting, like people praying, and I figured maybe there was someone in there who could help me. I opened one of the two blue sandstone doors and entered.

I scanned around looking for anyone or anything familiar, all the while hoping to see the lady in the sweater. Somehow my eyes locked on the figure of a boy kneeling in front of an altar which was as transparent as amber and fitted together with splinters of black marble. As beautiful as that altar was, I couldn't take my eyes off the boy.

That's because the boy was me.

I watched myself as I participated in something that looked like communion. It was weird watching myself waiting for the host, before stopping to look at the 'priest' who was that shimmering figure from the mound. In one hand he held a cross while the other held the host. I still couldn't make out his face as he turned to look at me. The face was just a pool of reddish liquid that reminded me of transmission fluid. The figure paused and as the face stared at me, two dirty yellow eyes and an angelic smile appeared upon it. Before I could fully comprehend what had happened, I found "myself" before him, kneeling, mouth opened, tongue out, waiting to accept the host. My other self was gone.

My attempts to scream choked in the bowels of my throat as I realized I was paralyzed, unable to move my eyes let alone my body. Still as I looked at him, I focused more on his smile that his eyes. I noticed he wasn't dressed like a priest, wearing only a short sleeved shirt with black pants, hinged with a belt sporting a gaudy silver elk buckle.

With an angelic smile he placed the host on my tongue and gently traced his middle finger on my lips. As he traced his sandpaper-like fingers along my paralyzed lips, I looked closely at the notches between his pale almost transparent albino-colored fingers. They glistened with a web of water, looping like silver twine down his wrist until it was lost in the blue vein valley of his elbow. Seeing those blue veins on its pale skin reminded me of Uncle Fergus.

When I swallowed the host, he disappeared, and I found myself in the middle of the city, kneeling beneath a marble archway. With eyes squinting I peered between the marble columns looking at a purple sun setting over the horizon. I saw a street I thought would take me away from this weird city, and started walking down it.

With the light of the fading sun falling across the city, I heard an awful roaring sound. The sound was coming in my direction and getting louder and louder as it approached me. Turning to look in the direction of the sounds, I saw bands of reddish light illuminating six stone animals, set on the high end of the street behind me—a snake, a bat, a spider, a vulture, a falcon, and a leech. I watched in horror as they slowly moved in my direction, and I again heard the tolls from overhead bells that I could now see were made of crystal.

Panicked, I ran as fast I could, passing building upon building each resembling pictures of places my father's Hungarian relatives had lived in.

Doors flung open, and in the doorways were tall thin men with yellow eyes and pulsing ashen skin, as well as thin pale women with yellowish eyes and dark lips. They reached out of the doorways and tried to grab me, while overhead a humongous blackbird rose from the flames of a burning torch perched high above my Tower of Babel. It started singing in sync with the sounds of a far off drum whose rhythm matched those of the tolling bells. My mind listened to the voice of the woman in the Angora sweater. She was singing with the blackbird, imploring me to flee the city and get to the mist I saw at the end of the road.

Without looking back I pumped my arms and legs as fast as I could. Seeing the mist ahead I felt as if my heart were in my throat when the stink of burning flesh stung my nostrils. My neck burned as the slimy, pulsing body of the leech crawled behind my ear. To make matters worse, the bat clawed at my eyes, and I could hear both the vulture and the falcon overhead fighting with the blackbird.

I swung my arms at the bat and tried to shake the leech off of me when I saw both the spider and the snake appear on the road ahead of me, growing larger as I approached.

The spider jumped up and fired a sticky web line at me, while the snake coiled and sprang at my face. I dropped and rolled out of the spider's line of fire, and the snake, fangs dripping with purple spit, sailed past me. My fall had dislodged the leech from my neck, and the bat frantically flew straight into the air. I quickly sprang to my feet, ready to run.

Before me the spider was as big as a beaver and quickly circled around getting ready to attack. All the while, I could hear the cobra headed snake hissing behind me. From the corner of my eyes I spied those hideous creatures leaving their doorways and start making their way toward me. They appeared cautious, as if they were scared of the animals attacking the blackbird and me. I could also see that the mist was less than a hundred feet away, and I knew if I didn't get there, I'd never leave this hellish place.

With the creatures getting closer and closer, I turned to see the hissing snake coil and spring at me. Again I ducked and dropped to the earthy road, the knob of my knee squishing the leech as I landed on it. The bat was no longer bothering me as it had joined the falcon and the vulture in their battle with the blackbird.

Again the spider fired a stream of webbing, but this time part of it landed in my left eye and along my arm and shoulder. Clawing away at the webbing I saw the spider rear up its legs, readying to assault me with another stream of stinging webs. Desperately I scrambled to my feet, ran over to it and stomped the beaver sized bastard as hard as I could, twisting and grinding the heel of my shoe into the soft dirt. The sound of it crunching beneath my foot was more beautiful than any music I'd ever heard.

Despite having my eyes partially covered with spider webs and hellish creatures chasing me, I willed myself to keep blindly running straight toward the mist, all the time praying and remembering every lesson from Bible study. With the conviction of the host of Jesus in my body and God on my side I dashed away from those monsters, and as I reached the end of the road, I dove headlong into the wonderful tingling embrace of the mist.

Resting my hands and knees on the soft earth beneath

me, I hungrily sucked in the cool refreshing air of the mist, thanking God and my faith for delivering me from what I concluded was the city of Selene. As I stood wiping the remaining webs from me, someone touched my shoulders, and I believed I was about to lose my scotch in my pants.

The soft voice of the sweater woman told me to relax, that I was safe, but there was one more thing she wanted me to see.

Before I could open my mouth to question her, both she and the mist were gone.

Now the air was humid, fetid and stank of swamp water and diesel fumes. Looking around I could see I wasn't on the dock but instead in the middle of the road leading to my uncle's house. As I started to wonder how I got there I spied a pair of headlights coming toward me. It was Uncle Fergus's car. I leaped to my left to avoid getting run over, but the car passed me as if no one had seen me. It was eerie, like watching a televised episode of the Twilight Zone.

I scrambled to the end of the driveway, and saw my uncle sitting in the car with its motor running, staring at the barn, with knuckles growing white from tightly gripping the steering wheel. Aunt Florence was sitting next to him, frightfully looking at him. Pascal lay on the backseat, asleep.

Wondering what my uncle was staring at, I looked over at the barn and saw moonlight reflecting off something near its doors. Straining to get a better view I immediately understood what it was and why my uncle was gripping the steering wheel so tight. The look on his face told me he, too, had seen the motorcycle parked by the barn, moonlight reflecting off its chrome handlebars.

His eyes narrowed as his face turned red. He turned off the engine, got out of the car, pointed a finger at Aunt Florence and said, "Stay."

Afterwards he started fast walking, not running toward the house. Pascal started to wake up and ask her something, when she reached across the front seat, shushing him, then clutched his arm.

Just as I was beginning to wonder what was going on, I heard a terrible scream.

Aunt Florence was yelling at Pascal to come back as he bolted for the house. I was with him step for step as he barged through the screen door looking for Lori and his father. Once inside we dashed up the stairs to her room and were shocked by what we saw.

Lori was in a corner, naked and all hunched up as if she wanted to hide. Without her clothes on I could see what looked like bite marks on her neck and boobs. Quickly spinning around, I saw blood on the sheets and immediately began looking to see if she was bleeding. There was blood on her legs!

Uncle Fergus was also there, straddling my shimmering figure – pinning him to the floor with his knees. His face was contorted like he was possessed by the Holy Spirit, and I couldn't make out what he was shouting, as his hands swept up and down in rapid rhythmic arcs, repeatedly bashing the "vampire" about the head and chest with a wrought iron cross.

Again and again he pummeled the vampire as Lori screamed and Pascal and I stood there, mortified by what we were seeing. It was twitching and squirming as blow after thunderous blow from the cross landed again and again. After a short while it stopped moving.

Uncle Fergus got off of it and looking like he didn't know where he was, dropped the cross and left the room. As Pascal ran to comfort Lori, I crept over to the carnage to see where Uncle Fergus dropped the cross. It lay in a pit of what had once been someone's face, his shattered skull fragments ringing it and making the whole thing look like a sloppy picket fence around an open pit.

The sound of Pascal's voice shook the vision from my head as he related how later that night he followed his dad as he removed the vampire from the house. Without my uncle's knowledge, Pascal saw where he buried the body and disposed of the motorcycle.

"What are we gonna do Rick, what're we gonna do? Your uncle didn't put a stake in its heart. At least we don't think so," Jimmy said and sighed as he took another sip of scotch. "That's why we put the knives and stuff on the grave. You know what we have to do, don't you?"

I didn't answer. I just motioned for Pascal to pass me the bottle and took a huge swig from it. I settled it between my legs, thinking about what Jimmy was saying; looking at Pascal staring into space with his scotch dilated eyes. He knew what had happened. He had seen the blood on her neck. His soft whispery voice spoke volumes, "It's like they say. Them things can hypnotize folks and make 'em say or do all kinds of stuff. And the blood, all that blood on her neck...." Pascal stopped as he started crying and rocking himself back and forth against the dock rail.

Draining the rest of the scotch in his cup he continued, "You don't think it can come back?" He started shaking again as he talked, "We did the right thing, didn't we, Rick? The stakes, the cross on the grave. It ... it can't come back, can it?"

I shook my head, no, Pascal.

Jimmy put his drink down as his body started quivering as if someone put a quarter in the slot of some cheap motel's Magic Fingers mattress. "It's hard but there's nothing else we can do about it," he said as he started fingering the cloth bag Pascal had brought the cups in.

"Jimmy's right. We all know what's gonna happen next.

We can't let it happen to her, not to my sister, not Lori," he stammered between sobs.

Looking at them, I had to agree. Pascal couldn't do it. He was the son of a hard man, and he had been broken.

Jimmy couldn't do it. He was still in love, and the idea of what had to be done was too much for him.

No one said anything as I leaned over and took the cloth bag from Jimmy. My heart knew what else was in it, and as my hand touched them, I thought about Selene and what all of it must have meant. Jimmy and Pascal eyes told me to go ahead and without another word amongst us, I pulled two wooden slants from the bag, opened my knife, and started sharpening them into stakes.

INDIGO
by Anthony Watson

When Lowell Johnson took out his bottle-top slide, closed his eyes and began to play *Indigo*, a hush fell over the room. While his fingers plucked out that twelve bar blues, the glass slid up and down the strings of his dobro like it was greased, bending those notes into somethin' more than they really was, somethin' beautiful.

And then he began to sing, still he had his eyes closed, his deep, bass voice growlin' out the words. It was like everyone was transfixed, hypnotized or somethin'—the music took them away somewhere, somewhere different for everyone there, but someplace good. Wasn't like he was such a good singer all told, but it was the story he was tellin', the words themselves, which held us all in rapture. The room was full of smoke and even it seemed to move in time with the music, driftin' slowly here and there like clouds of ghosts.

He didn't open his eyes all the way through that song and not for some time after. When he finished, no one clapped—at least for a moment or two, it was like we all needed time to come back from that place he'd taken us to. We did clap though, and the sound gained its own momentum, startin' slow but buildin' to a crescendo of noise. Everyone was smilin', some was even laughin', and that was somethin' you didn't hear a lot of—not in Briersville leastways.

Lowell nodded slowly in appreciation then got up to leave the stage. It was like somehow the playin' of *Indigo* had took it out of him. At least that's how I figured it at the time. Course, now I know the *real* reason.

Anyways, just a few moments after he'd gone, the whole place erupted back into life, like the moment had never happened. Much enjoyment was had by all, long into the night and, though there was plenty more music to come, none of it came from Lowell.

That was my first ever visit to Creoles and Mr. Johnson had played *Indigo*. Seems like fate was playin' her hand even then, right at the beginning.

◊ ◊ ◊ ◊

Chester Dixon's old dog died. Just wandered out into the road, laid down and gave up the ghost. Damn thing must've been fifteen or sixteen years old so no complaints there, but the last few years it'd been stinkin' somethin' awful so—while we was all a bit sad, for the dog and for Chester who loved the thing more than any man had a right to—we're all of us just a little bit relieved that we don't have to smell it any more. Bad as it smelt when it was still livin', it isn't going to improve none layin' out there in the sun, so me and Charlie Fresneau do the business and take it away, and dig a hole for it in Chester's yard; given that he's too upset and old to do it himself. There's a cloud of flies buzzin' around the dog's body, more than there was when it was alive even, and we waved them away as we pick it up.

"I'm gonna miss old Rex" Chester says, sniffin' back tears. "We will too," I answer on behalf of me and Charlie though I don't tell him it'll be for different reasons. "Thank you boys, much appreciated" he says when we're done and dustin' the dirt from off of our pants, but we decline his offer of some hospitality figurin' the look of his place from the outside doesn't bode well for any comfort inside. We take ourselves off to the well and fill our bellies with water from there instead.

Across the street from the pump, what's left of the Lafayette residence still smolders, givin' off a heat we can still feel despite how hot it is already. Smoke still drifts up from charred and blackened timbers. Two nights since it had been put to flame and still it burns. We both stare at the ruins grimly, not speakin', not that there's anythin' worth sayin'. Eventually, we move off, back into town.

"You playin' tonight?" Charlie asks.

"Mmm hmm," I nod, "I'll be there all right." I glance back over my shoulder at the ruins. Oh yes, I'll be playin' tonight.

◊ ◊ ◊ ◊

When I woke up the mornin' after my first visit to Creoles, I was expectin' to feel a whole lot worse than I did. The joint's reputation for moonshinin' was known far and wide and those drinks I could remember takin' certainly fulfilled all *my* expectations but the hangover I'd been anticipatin' hadn't come to bear and I felt good as gold, no headache, no sickness.

My head was full of music though, all the songs I'd heard in the Juke Joint were still buzzin' inside my skull but the one that kept comin' back to me the most was *Indigo*, the words sung in that deep, bass rumble of Lowell Johnson. I couldn't shake them from my head but then, it's not such a bad thing to have a head full of song so I wasn't actually tryin' too hard.

That was the day I said goodbye to Lester Robideaux. He'd decided enough was enough and that his future lay Northwards. He was goin' to join the thousands who had already left in search of a "better life". From what I'd heard, things weren't a whole lot better above the Mason-Dixon line than they were here and, though it weren't exactly a bed of roses for most of the time, sometimes it's better the devil you know. Still, I wished him good luck and success in his travels. He smiled when he patted me on the back but I could tell he didn't feel it in his heart or soul, it was only his face movin' and even then his eyes didn't join in.

Where he'd end up I didn't know, some factory or other no doubt, workin' himself into an early grave. Sharecroppin' ain't the bees' knees but it sure fills up the days and sometimes even gives me enough money to live on.

The previous night had been experience enough for me to realize that from then on, some of that money would be goin' straight to Creoles by way of purchasin' some of their fine concoction. Oh, and to listen to the equally fine music played there too.

It had been the music that had made me high, not the moonshine, of this I was certain and that mornin' I realized just how keen I was to go back and sample some more of it.

The thoughts must have put some kind of spring in my step and some gumption in my belly because when I saw Lowell Johnson himself walkin' along the other side of the street I ran over to shake his hand and tell him how much I had enjoyed his performance.

At first he shrugged me off, seemed embarrassed by the attention I was givin' him. Up close, I could see just how old he really was, in the wrinkles which creased and folded his face, but also in his dark, brown eyes which had a look in them like he was carryin' the worries of the world on his shoulders. He thanked me politely for my words and made to proceed along the sidewalk. I wasn't so keen to see him go; I wanted to tell him everythin' about how I felt, about what his music had done to me—for me—to me—for me—the previous night. I gabbled on and could sense how tense Lowell was gettin'. Did I stop? I did not. There came a moment when I was sure he was about to strike me, so irritatin' had I become and would have had I not at that precise moment mentioned *Indigo*.

His eyebrows shot up at the mention of the song and he took a step back away from me. The tension in his face (the tension I'd only just put there) was gone, replaced by worry—shock even.

"What's that you say boy?" he asked me.

I began stammerin' in reply, a bit shocked myself at his reaction, wonderin' what it was I'd said that had upset him. "I was just sayin' how much I liked your *Indigo* song—at least that's what I think you called it…"

He nodded, "yup, that's its name." He still looked worried.

"Th-that's good then, that I remembered it right an' all…" I could feel myself blushin'.

His expression changed from worry to puzzlement. He nodded again. "And you remember me introducin' the song?"

My turn to nod.

"You'll remember the words too then?"

Still nodding.

"Shit." (Except the way he said it, all long and stretched out like, it came out as sheee-it). He raised an arm and I instinctively flinched back. I reckon the worried expression had migrated from his face onto mine at that point. He laughed, a big grin split his face showing his pearly-whites, and a huge hand clamped itself on my shoulder.

"Son, we got some talkin' to do!" he said.

◊ ◊ ◊ ◊

There ain't nothing to *Indigo* really, not in the playing of it. As far as the chords are concerned, C7, F7 and G7 is all you need. It was the chords Lowell showed me first and it took me a while to get a hang of the barre, but once I did, the rest was plain sailin'. Practice makes perfect. I'm still more of a strummer than a picker but I can handle a good few melodies now, *Indigo* bein' one of them. Thing is, it's a risky business even just practicin' that particular song so's often as not I'll content myself with other tunes even on the nights I'm gonna play it. Playing the chords is all right of course, and Lord knows there's plenty other songs use that same twelve-bar progression but it's the knowin' that you're playin' *Indigo* which somehow puts the words in your head and you can't help but sing along.

Not good.

So, even though I know I'm gonna play it tonight, I'm stickin' to the rest of my repertoire to get the fingers loosened up. No point in takin' any unnecessary risks. That said, I still don't have all the necessaries—the *accoutrements* as Lowell called them—but with this kinda thing it's best not to get too complacent, least ways that's my line of thinkin'. I smoke as I play, relishin' the hit of the tobacco. You got to die of somethin' I guess, might as well enjoy the process.

I'm on the stoop so anyone walkin' past is getting a free show. Every now and then some'll stop and have a listen but on the whole folks just get on by, too busy with their own lives to pay me any heed.

I can see the remains of the Lafayette house from here and there are a couple of kids playin' around it. I see one of them pull a blackened piece of wood from the pile and start wavin' it around like a sword. The two of them whoop and holler as they chase each other round and the sound of it's nice to hear.

I start foolin' around with some minor chords, settlin' into the melancholy air they create and end up hummin' a new melody which suggests itself from the progression. I love it when this happens, when somethin' new is created. I never knew I had it in me and I'm eternally grateful to Lowell Johnson for takin' me under his wing and nurturin' this thing that's inside me which allows it to happen. The melody writes itself and I know I'll remember it, the words take more effort and will come much later.

I strum a D minor and hear it's slightly off. The E-string is out so I adjust it, turnin' the ivory peg and tunin' by ear. That's better.

The kids run by, their fight has become a pursuit.

I strum again, the tunin' is pitch perfect now. Order and balance have been restored which is kinda fittin' cause that's what's gonna happen tonight too.

◊ ◊ ◊ ◊

"Tell me the words. You don't have to sing 'em if you don't want to, just speak 'em but go on and tell me them."

We were sat in Lowell's house (though to call it a house was probably stretchin' things, shack would be a better description. It wasn't the worst abode in Briersville but it certainly wasn't the best—though I'm guessin' bein' the owner of the best house in a shantytown ain't nothing to be *that* proud of). We'd gone straight there after our encounter on the street. He'd said nothin' more to me on our way there and I was nervous as to what would go down when we got there. Curious too though, and it was that which made me follow him like an obedient dog behind its master. It's always been a failin' in me—curiosity that is—but I was keen to find out what all this was about.

So I began, slowly at first but gainin' speed as I went on. I'd only heard *Indigo* the once but somehow I knew all the words and I could see the look of amazement on Lowell's face as I recited them perfectly.

When I was finished, he puffed out his cheeks and blew the air out through pursed lips, like a trumpet player without a trumpet.

"I didn't know I had such a good memory," I said—as much to break the uncomfortable silence that had descended than anythin' else.

Lowell shook his head and laughed. "Why boy, it ain't nothin' to do with memory – so don't go congratulatin' yourself on that score." His expression changed, became serious. He leaned into me and spoke softly. "*Nobody* remembers the words to that song, nobody. There's people been in Creoles have heard me play it ten times or more but I guarantee you this—they wouldn't be able to tell you what the tune was like or what any of the words were. They all know it, about it I mean, but not one of them could tell you one of the words or hum a piece of the tune."

I looked at him, confused like. "I don't know what you mean, I'm not sure…"

"You have a gift boy, a rare and special gift!" I swear, I could see tears glistenin' in the old man's eyes when he said it. I have to say, it was the first occasion of anyone sayin' I was gifted at anythin' so there'd have been some wetness in my own eyes too.

"You ever been to N'awlans?" he asked and I shook my head, I'd barely been beyond the county line, never mind all the way to a big city like that. He looked thoughtful at my response for a minute or two then continued. "Do you play?"

"The guitar you mean?"

"Mmm-hmm."

"No sir, I don't. It's not like I've ever had the opportunity…"

Without replyin', he got to his feet. He left the room only to return minutes later clutchin' a couple of guitars in both hands. One I recognized as the instrument he'd played in Creoles, the other wasn't as fancy, just a normal wooden guitar as opposed to a shiny Dobro, though it was colored green which made it look kinda different I guess. He handed it over to me and I half got up to take it from him. He settled back down into his chair, restin' his own instrument across his knee and strummed an open chord. The sound of it sent a shiver down my back.

"Then consider this an opportunity," he said.

◊ ◊ ◊ ◊

It's the middle of the afternoon now and the hottest part of the day. Too hot. Humid too and my clothes are clingin' to me like they never want to let go and I can feel the sweat tricklin' down my neck. I don't pass too many people on the street, I'm guessin' they all have a lot more sense than me and are stayin' inside as much as they can. It'd been my plan to get all this done this mornin' but then Chester Dixon's dog kinda got in the way of things and then when I'd gotten back home the lure of the music was too much to resist—as it always is. Result bein', here I am makin' my way up to the cemetery, hotter than a hog being turned on a spit, mutterin' all the cuss words I know— which is a lot—under my breath.

To make matters worse, the graveyard's up on a hill so by the time I reach those big metal gates, I'm feelin' fit to drop. I don't though, and after a moment or two to pull myself together, I step into the cemetery. It's surrounded by tall trees so there's a chance of some cooler air in the shade. No sign of a breeze though, that would be askin' too much I guess, the moss draped over the branches just hangin' there all limp and motionless like giant cobwebs or somethin' similarly spooky as befittin' my current whereabouts.

Winston Lafayette's grave is up at the back of the field, furthest from the gates. Plots here are taken in turn, the first ones are right alongside the gates, those that follow gradually extendin' the cemetery deeper and deeper into the field. Whoever is next to go will be buried right alongside Winston.

Me, I'm plannin' on being about a mile away from those gates when they put me in the ground.

It doesn't take too long to reach the plot, dirt still piled up on top of it. A small bunch of wild flowers lie on it, already wilted and withered away to brown by the heat of the day. The soil on top of the grave is still fresh of course, but has already turned hard and dry by the sun. I pull out a handkerchief from my pocket and stoop down over the grave. Reachin' out, I grab hold of a clump of soil, my fingers goin' down into the deep fissures either side of it, and with a small twist, detach a fragment. It feels hot.

Straightenin' up, I wrap the hard bit of ground in the handkerchief and put it back in my pocket. The journey back will break it down into a pile of soil I know, but that's okay. I pause for a moment, lookin' down on the grave, still without a headstone so recent is it and give a small nod. "I'll be seein' ya Winston," I say, as a joke, but quickly turn to go just in case he answers me.

◊ ◊ ◊

"My fingers are hurtin' somethin' bad" I said in reply to Wendell's question. He laughed, heartily, "oh, you'll get over that! Give it a few weeks and your fingertips'll get all callused, just like mine." He held up his palm, fingers spread wide to show me the patches of hard skin on the pads of his fingertips. "Soon enough you won't feel a thing!" He laughed again, "why, you've got it easy playin' that old thing there anyway, wait until you get yourself one of these," he hefted the dobro once or twice from his knee, "the strings on here are like cheese wire!"

I smiled and shrugged. The sympathetic response I'd been hopin' for hadn't quite come to fruition. I waved my hand to emphasize just how much my fingers were givin' me pain but more for effect than any real use. "I'm just saying they're hurtin', that's all."

It was a couple of weeks since that first meeting with Wendell and in that time he'd taken me under his wing and was teachin' me how to play guitar. I was flattered of course, and deeply honored but surprised too, as I'd never shown any inclination to pick up an instrument before. I was a little nervous too, knowin' as I did that his "interest" in me was all due to *Indigo,* about how I could remember the words and tune and all, and how that somehow made me *special.* Right at that moment, I wasn't feelin' overly special, my fingertips definitely weren't.

Though I'd asked on many occasions, Lowell seemed reluctant to talk about whatever this special thing was— even though it had been him who'd mentioned it in the first place. "All in good time" was his reply to any inquiries I made about it but the secrecy was makin' me nervous and not a little distrustful. The thought occurred to me I should just stop comin', give up on the whole guitar thing if he wasn't prepared to tell me anything but that woulda just been spiteful and woulda been more my loss than his—I was enjoyin' these sessions, learnin' the craft. I was bitten, well and good.

I was curious though...

"You gonna start playin' or just sit there feeling sorry for yourself?"

I sighed and swung the guitar around onto my knee. I fingered a C and started strummin'. Lowell grunted and started tuning up his dobro. I moved to A minor, an easy transition, just getting the fingers warmed up. I'd seen his guitar many times of course, but that day I peered at it even more intently. It truly was a beautiful thing, made of a deep brown walnut, the metal resonator cone shined to the brightness of a mirror. There was a name on the headstock but it was written in some foreign language, French or Spanish or some such and I wasn't even sure how to pronounce it. The tunin' pegs and the inlays between the frets were a dull, cream color and seemed to be made of the same stuff. I had to know.

"What're your inlays there made from?" A minor shift to E minor.

He paused in his tunin' and looked straight to me, deep into my eyes. "Ivory" he said, but no more.

I slipped my fingers down and across to make a G then back up to C to begin the progression again.

Lowell closed his eyes and began to nod. He let me cycle through the chords once more and once I got back to the startin' C began to pick out a melody. It was one I'd never heard before, one he was makin' up on the spot, there and then. We played on, lost in the music. Every now and then I'd slip in a seventh and I saw a smile play across his lips when I did. Somethin' swelled inside me at those moments, I reckon it was pride.

After a few minutes, he opened his eyes and I knew it was time to wind down. The melody found its way to the end and I finished on a final G, the sound of it slowly diminishin' alongside Lowell's last note. My fingertips were burnin' but I didn't care. We had created somethin' together—truth to tell *Lowell* had created something—but I'd been there too. I had contributed.

"That's good," he said and, unused to compliments as I was, I felt somethin' other than pride swellin' within me and I had to cough so as not to show it.

◊ ◊ ◊ ◊

I stopped for another drink at the well when I got back from the cemetery and find myself gulpin' down the cool water. I splash some onto my hands and face, run a wet palm around the back of my neck. The day is beginnin' to cool as evenin' approaches but around here that just means it's very hot instead of *unbearably* hot. Feelin' more cooled and refreshed, I walk over to the burnt down remains of Winston Lafayette's house. As I reach them, the solitary cloud that's been hangin' in the sky moves across the front of the sun and the light dips. "Oh Winston, don't be messin' me about none," I say quietly, feelin' my heart trippin' and stumblin', "this is plenty weird enough already without any extra strangeness going on." I lean over and pick up a small, blackened piece of wood from among the debris and put it into the pocket not containin' the dirt from the grave. "I'm goin' now," I say, this time a little louder and yes, as I turn to walk away, the sun comes out from behind that cloud.

There are long shadows in the house when I get back there and what light there is has a deep, golden color. I remove the objects from my pockets, the hanky-wrapped dirt and the burnt piece of wood onto a table. I need one more thing but I won't be gettin' that till later.

As I turn away, a bright flash catches my eye and I blink against it. Winston's ghost, come to torment me for a bit more fun? No, not this time. The rays of the settin' sun had found themselves all the way to the walnut dobro propped up against the wall, their light reflectin' off the resonator plate. That's all.

◊ ◊ ◊ ◊

He said I had a natural talent, was gifted (but in a different way to the gift I really wanted to know about) and I was only a month or so into my practicin' when Lowell asked me to play with him at Creoles. There were some mighty big nerves going on right there let me tell you but I was strictly there as rhythm, playin' in the background while Lowell provided all the magic up front. Two songs in and the nerves were gone, replaced by such a feelin' of happiness I'd not known could even exist. "Don't think about it none," Lowell had told me before we went out onto that stage, "let the music guide you, listen to it, *feel* it." Listen and feel I did—and I've never felt so happy.

And that happiness flooded up over us from everyone who was in there that night. Seemed they were feelin' the music too, lettin' it take them away from whatever version of Hell their life had turned out to be, for a few hours at least. That was the joy of Creoles, it was an escape from the harshness of life, the joker in the hand of cards most folk hereabouts had been dealt. People came together here and found that there could be happiness and it was there for the takin'. The 'shine helped of course, but it was music which took them away to that better place.

I didn't sleep that night, couldn't come down from that place so high up the music had taken me. There was no moon in the sky and as we walked back in the darkness the cicadas were so loud we could barely hear each other speak, soundin' like Jimmy Dupree slidin' his brushes over his drums, runnin' a long line of paradiddles. Not that we spoke much. "Do you ever get used to it?" was one thing I *did* say. "Nope," Wendell replied, "and I hope I never will."

I smiled. This was good news. Best I'd heard. "Me too," I said. And it was true, I didn't ever want to lose those feelin's the music gave me, didn't ever want it to become normal, somethin' I got used to. When it came time for us to go our separate ways I offered to carry the guitar I'd been usin' back to his house.

"No need for that," he said, "it's yours now" and before I had time to argue he was on his way, leavin' me with the biggest smile my face had ever known.

I played that guitar constantly. Now I could practice even when I wasn't at Wendell's and I made the most of it. Sure enough my fingertips hardened off and I wore the calluses as some kind of badge of honor. This is who I am, I would think, this is what I do.

Two days after my debut at Creoles, they found Charlie Renwick hanging from a tree. The hangin' alone obviously wasn't enough for them, they'd horsewhipped his back to a bloody mess too, and put his eyes out. The flames from the fires they set had lit up the night-time sky and the embers were still glowin' when Chester Dixon (in the days when he still had a dog) found him. If they're such God-fearin', Christian folk, how comes they think it's okay to burn a cross?

They didn't burn his house down though—probably too busy enjoyin' themselves with the killin'. We put guards on the property anyway, just in case they came back to finish off the job.

The following week, Lowell played *Indigo* at Creoles.

He did it solo, no accompaniment was required so I sat it out and watched the emotion pourin' from him just like everyone else in there that night. I watched as the audience descended into a kind of trance, slowly stoppin' movin', fallin' into silence so the only sound in the whole place was that hauntin' melody and Lowell's deep, gravelly voice. And again, that moment when the song was done and everyone came out of the trance and applauded fit to bring down the roof.

I remembered every word of it. I also remembered the dedication before he sang it.

"Are you going to tell me about *Indigo*?" I asked him when we walked home that night.

He stopped walkin', let his head droop down on his neck and seemed to wait an age before replying.

"Yes," he said, "I guess I will."

◊ ◊ ◊ ◊

It's dark out, but still some hours before I'm due at Creoles when I hear the knock on the door. I know who it's goin' to be before I open the door and I say "hello Marcie" as I do. She doesn't reply, just walks in through the door which I close behind her.

"I've brought it" are her first words to me as she stands by the table, lookin' down at the two mementoes I've collected.

I walk slowly round to the other side of the table, see the thousand-yard stare which is her expression. "Thank you," I say but nerves make the words little more than a whisper.

She reaches into the bag she's been clutchin' to her

chest and pulls out a small object. Like my grave-dirt, it's wrapped in a handkerchief. She drops—almost throws— the object on to the table where it lands with a dull thud and I suddenly realize what she's done, what she's had to go through to get it.

I begin to thank her again but my words are cut short by her own. "Play for all your worth," she says, and now she's starin' at me so I can't help but see the tears which spill out of her eyes, tears of sorrow but also of anger, "for me, for him."

"I will," I say, trying to reassure, but it's too late, she's already turnin' and goin'. I take a step after her but then stop, it won't achieve anythin'. She pauses, to compose herself and just before she steps out through the door turns to look at me and say "for all of us". Then she's gone and it's not until the door closes behind her that I realize I haven't breathed in since she uttered those partin' words and I cough and splutter as my body reminds my mind of this.

I glance down at the table, at the thing she has left me. I reach over and pick it up, unwrap the handkerchief from around it. It's a key, cold and heavy in my hand, a perfectly ordinary object under any other circumstances than these. Though I'm not sure, I can guess who it belongs to, one of many attached to a keychain hooked to his belt. I don't need to know, it's not important, won't affect anythin', but if it is who I think it is then I can only imagine the courage it took for Marcie to get close enough to relieve him of it.

Whatever, the key is perfect, exactly what I needed— the final piece in the jigsaw. Puttin' it back down on the table, I begin to make preparations.

◊ ◊ ◊ ◊

"You dedicated it to Charlie Renwick" I said, "but I'm guessin' there's more to it than just some kind of tribute."

"You would be right." Wendell was starin' at me with the most serious expression I've ever seen on his face.

"How comes no one can remember the words except me? Why can *I* remember them?" I was shoutin', I knew I was, but here I was, about to find out all about *Indigo* and what it was which apparently made me different to everyone else.

"'Cause you're special and they ain't." He paused after that and for a moment I was frightened that would be it, that the enigma would remain, that I would be fobbed off again.

"What do you mean special?" I shouted, "what's so different about me?" For a moment or two he said nothin' and it looked to me as if he was collectin' himself, gettin' ready to say some stuff he really didn't want to. Eventually he began speakin' again, his voice quiet, like he was embarrassed or somethin'. "What it is, I don't know, I just know you have it. Same as me, you have it. I been through this particular situation myself, many years ago 'ceptin that time around it was me all young and wide-eyed and Floyd Blake—a far better bluesman than I'll ever be by the way— doin' the tellin' and explainin'." His voice slowly got louder, stronger—carried within it an authority which would not be argued with. "It's a spell boy, a –hex—an old Loosyanna voodoo spell and there's only certain special people who get to use it, people like you and me boy, people like you and me."

My mouth fell open, I must have looked like a catfish on a hook. What was all this talk of voodoo and magic nonsense?

"You remembered the words boy. You heard them and you remembered them. That marks you out as special, as being one of the ones who can use the spell. Back in the day that was how I found out I had the gift, bein' as how I could remember the tune and words an' all."

"Mr. Johnson, no offence but…"

"But nothin'!" it was his turn to shout now. "It's all true boy, and the sooner you can accept that the easier this is all gonna be."

Creoles had been full of smoke, but not as much as there was inside my head at that moment. This was not what I had been expectin' to hear, certainly not from someone as, well, *respectable* I guess as Mr. Lowell Johnson. Spells and hexes? This was the kind of stuff we told each other as kids to put the willies up ourselves. And what—I was some kind of witch doctor? *I* could cast spells and do magic and shit…? I looked deep into those soulful eyes of his though, and could see that he was tellin' the truth—or a truth he believed in leastways. Eventually, my mouth started workin' again. "So this spell, what does it do an' all?"

Lowell visibly relaxed and when he spoke it was in his normal voice again, calm and measured. "Oh, I think you're clever enough to work that one out all by yourself now aren't you?"

And yes, thinkin' about it I guess I could work it out. As outlandish and just plain creepy as the whole thing sounded, I figured I knew *exactly* what that song did. The first time I'd heard Lowell play *Indigo* he'd dedicated it to the memory of Morgan Hayes, not long gone, murdered by the local maniacs dressed in their robes, hidin' their faces like cowards. Wasn't but a few days after that one of 'em was found dead. Turned out he'd shot himself, stuck a shotgun in his mouth, pulled the trigger and sprayed his brains (what little there was of them) all over his yard. As Lowell stared at me with those dark brown eyes of his, I realized it hadn't been guilt or anythin' noble like that which had made him take his life. No sir, now I was gettin' the picture loud and clear about exactly what it had been that had put that gun in his mouth.

"I'm guessin' a couple days' time we'll be findin' another body…" I mumbled, my head dropped forward on account of me not bein' able to hold that intense stare of his, on account of how I knew he didn't even have to answer me. On account of how I now knew how "special" I was.

Lowell nodded, "mmm-hmm."

The smoke was fillin' my head all over again. Havin' your suspicions confirmed ain't always a good thing, not on every occasion leastways—and this was definitely one of those occasions.

"You ready to do some more learnin'?" Lowell asked.

◊ ◊ ◊ ◊

I'm halfway through the set and it's time to play *Indigo*. There's a good crowd in and everyone's havin' a good time as far as I can tell. I clear my throat—singin' and smoke filled rooms ain't never gonna be a good combination, least not as far as good health is concerned—and begin speakin'. At first, my voice is lost amongst the hubbub.

Folks seem to know when it's time for that song though and a hush settles over everyone. My stomach does a flip, and another—this is my first time playin' *Indigo* and all the times I've been up here on the stage, all those times with Lowell before he passed away, even the months I've been up front, playin' the melodies and singin' to all of the crowds who have come here to have a good time haven't prepared me for this.

My voice falters, but only briefly and I step back,

coughin' into my hand to try and cover up my nervousness. Lowell's dobro swings around my neck as I move and somehow the feel of it, the weight and solidity of it give me confidence. He left it to me after he passed on, wrote a letter out and everything explainin' that the guitar was to come to me and nobody else. Turns out he didn't have no family anyways, none that were livin' at least, but he'd wanted me to have the instrument and had made sure it was gonna happen. I'd read the letter and it brought a tear to my eye as I did. He'd been a man of few words but what I read in that letter was to me like a poem of some kind, somethin' more than just words on a piece of paper. They told of a relationship I hadn't even been aware of when it had existed, Lowell had always been a stern taskmaster and compliments of any kind were few and far between—and even then given grudgingly.

Floyd Blake had passed the dobro onto him and now he'd passed it onto me. Maybe the guitar's haunted by Lowell, maybe he is here, in the room after all. Maybe it's him playin' and not me.

"Gonna play you folks a special request now," I say, and some fella out in the smoky darkness gives a "whoop" and some laughter ripples through the crowd. I twist one of the ivory pegs on the guitar like I'm tunin' it but the guitar doesn't need tunin', it's just nerves again and I twist so far one way then back the same amount to where it was in the first place. Behind me, the other fellas get up and leave, this one's always a solo effort.

"This one's for Winston Lafayette…" more whoopin' and hollerin' greets this announcement and I strain into the darkness to see if Marcie's there. She's not, at least as far as I can see. "It's called *Indigo*." I finish and reach down to the strings to strum the opening C chord. I know everyone in there will listen to the song, move along in time to the rhythm and melody, but once I'm done that'll be that, they'll have no recollection of what I've just played and sung for them. They all know what *Indigo* is, what it does, but ask any one of them to hum the tune or sing the words and they'll just look blank, give you an embarrassed smile.

And so it has to be.

They ain't "special".

Not like me.

I begin singin' and pick out the melody, feel the strings diggin' into my fingertips but feeling no pain, just a reassurin' pressure. I close my eyes and try not to think of what's happenin' right now up in the old cemetery, try not to think of what's *gonna* be happenin' later on tonight.

My fingers move quickly over the strings and I close my eyes, losin' myself in the music.

THE KING OF BELMER
by Jonathan S. Pembroke

T he Mercedes hybrid barely slowed as it left the interstate and circled clockwise up the exit ramp. Kendra's fingertips dug into the cloth of her seat. "David, slow down! You're going to run us right off the road."

"Give me a break, Kendra. I've been driving this area for years." The car merged with the eastbound traffic. The anemic horn of an old Pontiac bleeped at them, but David ignored it. He gave his wife a smug glance. "See?"

"Even a blind squirrel finds a nut once in a while."

"Be nice."

"I still don't understand why we can't go to the Lacombe Crab Festival," she said. "It's only another twenty-five miles. I never heard of this ... this ..."

"Belmer," he supplied.

"Belmer." She tapped the electronic device in front of her. "It doesn't show up on the GPS."

"My family has been coming here for decades, hon. It's a family tradition and one of Dad's favorites. Do you think we'd drag you somewhere that doesn't exist?"

"Knowing you and your father, you just might."

He shook his head. "Look, just trust me. Okay?"

She folded her arms and looked away. "The last time

you said that, we ended up in a dive in Acapulco and got our room robbed."

"I don't have to dot every 'I' and cross every 'T' the way you do. That was a spur-of-the-moment thing, so we had to settle."

"We wouldn't have to settle if you had let me plan out the trip."

David shrugged. "I like my plans to be a little more organic."

"Organic." Kendra wrinkled her nose. "The word you want, dear, is 'chaotic.'"

"It adds to the fun."

"Also means things go wrong."

"Not for me," he chuckled. "Things always work out okay for me. Always have for the men in my family."

"I know you've never had a bad break in your life, David. You might one day, so it wouldn't kill you to think ahead just once."

Another heart of another tiny town blurred past. Kendra let her eyes wander over the weathered brick and mortar buildings, many boarded and abandoned. Overall-clad rubes and beer-bellied country gents in shorts and black socks ambled along the cracked sidewalks

She shook her head. Not a Prada bag in site. Probably not a full set of teeth, either.

The car thumped over a railroad track and continued through town. David said, "Kind of quaint here, isn't it?"

"Oh yeah."

He smiled. "I could see myself living in a town like this."

"That's what I love about you, David, always thinking small."

Without taking his eyes from the road, David bent his head and lit a cigarette. "You know, you can be a real bitch when you set your mind to it."

"Never mind."

"It's not L.A., there isn't a Starbucks on every corner."

"There isn't anything here," Kendra said. Crimson irritation rose in her cheeks. "It's just some god-forsaken backwater. Nothing good ever comes from these hick-filled jerk-burgs."

David's eyes narrowed. Kendra bit her lip; David had grown up in the backwoods and she wondered if she had gone too far. Instead, her husband took a deep breath. In an even voice, he said, "Look I don't want to fight. Can't we just try and enjoy something new?"

Kendra nodded reluctantly. She adjusted the air vents, letting the frigid air pour over her face. The set of her shoulders relaxed as the cold air massaged her heated skin.

The town gave way to two lonely lanes of cracked asphalt, plunging them into the dense Louisiana forests. Small country homes and rundown shacks lined the roadside. Kendra watched them go by with little emotion. Her stomach growled. "How much longer?"

David squinted. "We should be coming up to the turn to Route 445 right about .... now. There it is."

They turned right, heading ever-deeper into the woods. Kendra saw fewer turn offs and side roads. She said, "What did you say this hoedown was called?"

"The King of Belmer Festival."

"What does Belmer mean, anyway?"

"'Good Sea,' I think," David said, scratching his two-day chin stubble.

Kendra's eyebrows lifted. "The Good Sea King Festival?"

"Yeah."

Kendra bit back a smart remark. She stretched her toes; the painted nails winked at her. "I assume seafood is a staple here."

"It's been ten years but the last time I was here, it was great: steamed crab, smoked red snapper. Even crawdads."

"Craw-what?"

"Crayfish."

Kendra blanched. "People eat those?"

"Yep. Just like a little lobster, Kendra."

"No, thanks."

The Mercedes slowed. Kendra looked out and frowned. The road ended in a gravel parking area, beyond which several docks extended into a muddy slow-moving river. A small boat sat waiting; puffs of blue-gray exhaust wafted up from the running motor. An elderly African-American man wearing khaki trousers, a white short-sleeved shirt, and a worn ball cap crouched by the boat. Kendra said, "Are we here? Where's the festival?"

"Nope, this is just Lee's Landing."

"Okay?"

David pulled the car into a slot and threw the gearshift into Park. He pointed at the boat. "We have to take the boat downriver. It's the only way to get to Belmer."

"Have you lost your damn mind?" Kendra exploded. "I am not getting in that rickety tub."

"Kendra, settle down. I rode in these boats all through my childhood. They are perfectly safe. Just be glad we don't have to take a pirogue."

"A what?"

"A pirogue. It's a bayou canoe. They are very easy to tip over. At least that boat is stable."

"That explains what happened to you—too many dunkings in that filthy river."

Something unpleasant flickered in his eyes but David's voice was smooth. "You said you were willing to try something new."

Kendra eyed the small craft. The water rippled ever so slightly, setting the skiff rocking. She fought down a rising panic. "What about alligators?"

"They won't bother us. We probably won't even see any."

"What about…"

"Hey, remember when you said you'd trust me?"

"I-I guess." She fought the urge to clench her fists.

The man at the boat doffed his cap as they approached. "Good morning, David. All ready to go?"

"Sure am. This is my wife, Kendra. Hon, this is Hank. He's worked for Dad for more years than I can remember."

Kendra put on her most charming smile. She extended her hand. "Good morning, Hank."

Hank gripped her hand. His grasp was strong and his skin was dry and cracked, reminding Kendra of ancient leather. "This way, Ma'am."

The old man helped her into the boat. As she stepped down, it rocked sharply in her direction. Kendra blanched but Hank steadied it until she was able to climb in. David hopped down with the native grace of one bayou-born. Hank shucked the thin rope from the dock and seconds later, the small craft putt-putted into the main channel, trailing a gentle wake.

Kendra fumed. Mosquitoes the size of china plates buzzed about her head and despite David's reassurances, she was certain the suspicious-looking logs floating lazily in the channel were more than waterlogged lumber. "Oh, there is going to be payback for this," she muttered.

"What's that, hon?"

"Nothing, just clearing my throat."

The boat chugged past thick tangles of pines and kudzu-laden cypresses. Hank and David engaged in a bout of reminiscences, punctuated by good-natured snickers at fond memories. Hank's Creole accent held a soothing rhythm—nearly lyrical. She listened to the melody of his speech without listening to the words and it helped relax her as the boat cruised along the canal.

They passed a number of smaller canals which branched off the main artery. Kendra glanced at each one. Other than the lapping water of the channel, all she saw were insects and verdant growth. She twisted to look at David. "Are we almost there? I haven't seen any other boats."

"Not quite, Kendra."

"We're going to end up in Lake Pontchartrain if we go much further."

"No, Ma'am," Hank said with a pearly grin. "The Lake is a bit further. We turn off just ahead."

The entrance to a wide canal loomed to their right. Hank steered them toward it. The tantalizing smell of cooking seafood reached Kendra's nose; she inhaled, driving away the smell of the festering bog. Behind her, David said, "Smell that?"

"Oh, yeah."

"That's the festival," David said. Kendra rolled her eyes and resisted the urge to tell him she had already figured that out.

The crush of vegetation on the right bank gave way to a grassy meadow. Rainbow-hued tents formed several broad pavilions. Several columns of white smoke puffed skyward and Kendra saw a large number of people milling about. Pleasant chatter rolled across the water to her ears. A collection of small boats bobbed alongside a low wooden pier. As they approached the dock, a familiar figure in a white linen suit and hat waved to them.

"Hey, Dad," David called.

"Hey, kids! I was afraid you might not make it." As the boat glided up to the dock, the tall gray-haired man reached down and grabbed the bow. Hank tossed him a looped rope, which the man secured about a post. He then bent and offered his hand to Kendra. "Good to see you again, young lady."

Kendra forced a smile to her face. "The pleasure is all mine, Sam." She took his hand and let him help her up. He gave her a quick hug.

David hopped to the dock. "Afternoon."

"You guys have any trouble getting here?"

She shot David a warning glance; for once, her husband seemed to understand. He said, "No, just a little traffic around Baton Rouge. We found Hank and he took right care of us."

Kendra glanced around. "Sam, David tells me this is something of a family tradition. He says you've been coming here for years."

"Every ten years. This is the first one without my wife." Sam smiled sadly. He motioned at the pavilions. "You guys go grab something to eat. The band starts playing at the top of the hour."

David perked up. "Is it Red and his group?"

"Sure is."

David grabbed Kendra's hand. "Come on, you'll want to see this. It's a hoot."

She did not protest as he half-led, half-dragged her off the dock. Sam stayed behind; his gentile voice drifted up as they walked away. "I'm going to discuss some things with Hank; you guys go on."

They passed a row of eight-foot high poles embedded upright in the ground. Kendra touched one as they walked past—the wood was smooth to her touch. "What are those?"

"Just support poles left over from previous years' tents."

"This close to the water?"

"Yeah. C'mon, let's go get some crab." He tugged at her hand again.

"All right, don't pull my arm off. What did your Dad mean about his wife? Was that your Mom? I thought she died when you were young."

"She did. That was his second wife."

"The one who ran off on him?"

"Yeah."

David steered them toward a large tent. The open flaps were tied back; people passed in and out, chatting and laughing. Kendra ran her eyes over the assemblage and pursed her lips.

The interior of the tent was crowded with tables and benches, though few sat at them. An open barbecue pit occupied the center; steam and smoke rose through the tent's apex. The smell of cooked crab hit Kendra again. Skewers of Cajun-spiced crab and shrimp sizzled and popped over the coals. One of the tenders saw David and nodded. "Hey, Little David."

"Lucius," David nodded. He jerked his head at the man. "Hon, this is my cousin Lucius. We used to play together while growing up."

Kendra fought to hold her composure as the smell of cheap wine washed over her. She gave the man a clipped nod. "Hello."

The man did not reply. His dark eyes were flat—almost lifeless. Instead of the unease she'd expected at the man's stare, Kendra only felt the flutter of humor, and she chuckled. David frowned; he reached past Lucius, grabbed a pair of crab-laden skewers, and propelled his wife away from the pit. Kendra glanced back. Lucius still stared at them. A tiny smile lit his lips. Kendra snorted. "That troglodyte is your cousin?"

"He is."

"And how many more of these hicks are your cousins?"

Instead of replying to her taunt, David motioned to another pavilion. "Let's go; Red's band starts in a few minutes."

"What kind of band?"

David hesitated, then said, "A jug band."

Kendra burst out laughing. "You're kidding, right?"

"No. It'll be fun."

She shook her head. "Can you at least get us some plates and napkins for these crabs? I'd rather not get it all over myself while I'm laughing to death at this ridiculous nonsense."

David stopped in his tracks. He said nothing but the narrow set of his eyes screamed both hurt and anger. Kendra sighed. She reached out and touched his shoulder. He flinched away. "I'm sorry, David. I didn't mean..."

"But you do it anyway, even though you know I love you."

"I'll stop. Let's just eat and I'll be better. Okay?"

He nodded, though the injury never left his face. "I'll find some napkins."

Kendra sat at one of the picnic tables holding the skewers, her mind wandering. She knew David loved her. Despite being a bit backwards, he wasn't bad and he made her happy. So why did she never miss an opportunity to attack him? For the nth time of her life, Kendra cursed her temper and sharp tongue, both of which she had inherited from her mother. Those traits cost her mother all three of her husbands. How many would they cost Kendra? A drop of water from the steamed crab dribbled on her hand, snapping Kendra from her reverie. She sighed again and resolved to keep her opinions on the hillbilly party to herself for the rest of the day.

While she waited, her eyes probed the details of the passersby. Though a few were dressed in stylish casual or in southern suits like Sam's, many wore faded denim, dirt-encrusted boots, and stained tee-shirts. She murmured, "This is it. I am at the bottom of the food chain here."

A well-dressed man about David's age ambled past. Trailing behind was a slightly older woman in a fashionable pants suit. Her hair was coifed and she strode awkwardly on her high heels. None of that hid the scorn on her face. "Honestly, Art, what was the point of dragging us into this swamp? We could have had the same crab back in New Orleans. And another thing..."

The two passed out of earshot. Kendra laughed. "I hear you, sister."

Her eyes locked on another couple, this one dressed in trailer park chic. The man, a middle-aged bald guy wearing a sweatshirt and oily jeans, nodded absently as his cigarette-wielding wife gesticulated and complained. With each motion of her hand, ash tumbled to the ground. The man had a look of long-suffering patience on his face, the woman, one of spoiled indolence. A twinge of guilt tickled her heart; Kendra wondered if David had ever seen that look on her face.

David returned. He passed her a Styrofoam disc and stack of folded paper napkins. "Here." His face was neutral.

They exited the tent. After a moment, Kendra said, "David ... do you think I'm a bitch?"

He gave her a guarded look. "How do you mean?"

"Am I hard to be with sometimes?"

Her husband did not hesitate. "Often."

"I don't mean to be. You met my mother. I come by it

honestly, you know."

"I know."

She tucked her arm in his. "But you still love me, right?"

"Yeah. Let's go watch these guys play."

The band pavilion was also crowded with tables; unlike the first one, these were full of chattering festival-goers. A low wooden platform occupied the far end of the tent. Mounted on the stage were half a dozen of the roughest-looking men Kendra had ever seen. She said, "Please tell me those guys aren't related to you too."

David nodded. "Distantly. Look, there's a spot over there."

They wove through the press of bodies and finally reached the bench. They were forced to sit across from each other. A grossly fat man grunted as Kendra sat next to him. Her nostrils flared; the stale smell of beer and sweat washed over her like a tide. She glared across the table at David, but he had already turned his back on her to face the band. Ignoring her impatient mind, Kendra concentrated on her stomach. She plopped a crab skewer down on her plate, cracked open a shell with an expert twist of her wrist, and picked at the sweet meat within. The morsels hit her tongue and she shivered in pleasure. At least the food was good.

A thickset man with a great red beard stepped to the stage. Kendra's eyes widened; the man was at least seven feet tall and must have weighed a good three hundred pounds. At the sight of him, a round of wild applause erupted from the crowd. "Good afternoon, friends and family."

Kendra reached over and tapped David. "That's 'Red,' I assume."

"Uh, yeah. Brilliant guess."

She flushed but remembering her self-imposed resolution, Kendra kept her mouth shut. Red bellowed, "Welcome to the Belmer King Festival. Now let's git to playin'."

His entourage hefted a motley collection of instruments. One fellow strummed a washtub bass, another pressed his lips to a comb. Kendra's lip turned, though musical by some standard, it wasn't the Metropolitan Opera. She listened for a few moments before losing interest.

Bored, she let her eyes wander over the crowd again. She spotted the gentleman with the nagging wife. Kendra thought the look on her face must have matched her own. The next table over, she saw a heavyset guy in a trucker cap watching as his portly wife stuffed pasta into her mouth with a gourmand's gusto. To their right, a standing man patiently held his wife's bag while she dug through it. Contents flew as she searched. Apparently, she did not find what she sought; she yelled something obscured by the band's song before shoving the man backwards. The calm in the man's face never wavered.

Tendrils of icy uneasiness crept into Kendra's stomach.

The band finished their primitive tune with a flourish. The crowd began clapping—rather, Kendra noted, the men began clapping. The women in the crowd looked as bored or as hostile as she felt. She looked around but could not find a single one who seemed to be paying attention.

As the clapping died down, Red and the band started a new tune. Kendra reached across and tapped David again. His brow creased in irritation as he looked back. She said, "How many of these people are related to you?"

"Huh?"

"How many?"

"I don't know, Kendra. A lot of the guys. Can I listen

now?"

Something clicked. "How many of the women?"

"What?"

"How many of the women are related to you?"

The annoyance slid off his face, replaced by an unnatural calm. "None of them, Kendra."

"None?"

"Not one."

Moisture fled her mouth; Kendra swallowed uncomfortably. She wanted to look away from David's steady gaze but found herself unable to. She whispered, "Where?"

David opened his mouth to reply but was cut short by a piercing scream that filled the tent. Kendra jumped; two tables away, a woman staggered to her feet. Blood streamed from an ugly wound on the side of her face. The man next to her stood, took careful aim, and hit her with a short wooden truncheon. She toppled to the ground.

Silence descended. Kendra felt her hands began to shake. The face of every man in the tent was stone cold – calm—the same steady look still on David's face.

A white-haired man stepped forward. Kendra's eyes locked onto the movement. *Sam.* The thought rippled through her mind, suppressing her hysteria. *Sam will take care of this.*

The man looked at David's father. "I'm sorry, Sam. I couldn't take her mouth for one more moment."

"Quite all right, Ben." Sam glanced at his watch. "A little early but I think we're still on schedule, aren't we, Red?"

"Yes, indeed we are."

Kendra's gut twisted. Red's coarse voice was suddenly urbane and silky, and all the more menacing. Kendra looked back at David. "What…"

David lunged across the table. Powerful fingers closed over her wrists. Kendra recoiled up and away from his grip. Caught off-balance, David fell face-forward onto the table. His head thunked against the boards, eliciting a sound not unlike a melon hit with a broom handle and his grip relaxed instantly.

All about her, men wrestled shrieking women to the ground. One girl—a skinny redhead in her twenties—spun free and darted for the tent entrance. But Sam was there, waiting, and stabbed at her. Kendra heard a brief sizzle; the girl's body went rigid and slumped to the ground. Sam eyed her critically, stun-gun in hand.

Kendra felt a heavy hand on her shoulder. Instinct took over. She slammed her elbow backwards and connected with something solid. She heard a grunt and the hand released. Kendra lurched to the side, falling against the heavy canvas of the tent. The interior of the tent was chaos; women screaming, men cursing and laughing. All other thought fled, Kendra's only desire was escape. She dropped to her knees and tugged at the tent bottom. Tears blurred her eyes as she yanked at the seam. A crease of daylight appeared. Kendra plunged forward. She wormed her head and shoulders through. Earthy grass smells pushed aside the seafood aroma; she wondered suddenly if the grass stains would come out of her shirt and almost laughed at the thought.

Something grabbed at her ankle but she kicked free into the sun. Kendra staggered to her feet and sprinted toward the dock. Tears streamed sideways on her cheeks and she desperately prayed the boats started the same way a car did.

She was almost to the dock when someone shouted behind her. Kendra risked a glance back. Sam had emerged from the tent; he saw her and pointed in her direction. She faced forward just in time to see Hank loom before her.

His hand arced toward her face, she caught a glimpse of something metal in his grip—and then her world went dark.

◊ ◊ ◊ ◊

Low moans reached her ears. Kendra tried to roll over, make the dream go away. Her arms didn't respond and something hard rubbed against her neck. She turned her head and was rewarded with a crippling pain along her jaw line. The agony was so strong her stomach lurched and for a moment, Kendra thought she might throw up. She opened her eyes to darkness. Pinpoints of light blinked on the periphery of her sight. She strained, slowly her vision came into focus.

Night had fallen. Flickering light from a nearby torch bathed her in a small island of light amid the sea of darkness. She was upright, against one of the poles she and David passed coming up from the dock. Her arms were over her head; when she tried to lower them, the rough bite of woven rope clamped onto her flesh. Her waist and legs were bound as well. Kendra turned her head to the left but was rewarded with another spasm lancing through her skull. She wiggled her jaw; a dull burning sensation throbbed along her jaw line. The ominous sound of grinding bone filled her ears. Instead, Kendra rolled her head to the right.

Tied to each of the poles was another woman. Most were still unconscious. A few moaned. Even as she watched, one began shrieking. Kendra blinked, it was the woman who'd been waving her cigarette at her husband. The woman's hysterical cries rolled across the green, threatening to drive any last bit of sanity from Kendra's head. She clamped her eyes shut.

The woman's screams terminated in an abrupt thump. Kendra cracked her eyelids. The cigarette gal's husband stood beside her, a truncheon at the ready. His now-silent wife quivered in her bindings. Her head lolled loosely. Evidently, he decided she wasn't going to yell anymore, he lowered the club and disappeared from view.

"Sorry about this, Kendra." She faced forward, ignoring the pain in her neck brought by the sudden movement. David stood before her. He wore the same blank look she'd seen back in the tent.

She had to force the words through gritted teeth. "D-David, what…"

"This is why we're here, 'hon.'" He spoke the last word with a snarl.

"What are you doing?"

"Remember when I told you that things always work out for my family? Well, this is why."

"I … I don't understand."

"You will soon enough. The King of Belmer will make you understand."

Panic pushed its way to the front of her mind. Tears blurred her vision. "David, please, you aren't making any sense! Cut me down from here right now!"

"He can't do that, Kendra," Sam said as he emerged from the gloom. "Your fate was sealed as soon as you stepped ashore."

"I demand to be let down from here!"

"Of course you do."

"You can't do this," she cried.

Sam shrugged. "We've been doing it for centuries."

He disappeared, leaving his son. Kendra blinked the tears away, silvery trails wound down her swollen cheek. "David, I love you."

David hesitated. He glanced in the direction his father

had gone. A sudden spark of hope flared to the surface of her mind. Kendra said, "David, look at me. David!" He did. "You love me too, I know you do."

"I do."

"David…"

"This is our burden, Kendra. We have to live with what we've done. Do you know what that's like?" His face twisted into a grotesque mask of self-loathing. "Do you know what this has done to us—what it has turned us into? You might have the easier fate."

"Then let me go."

"I can't. Not now."

"David, please…. Please don't leave me here."

Indecision warred on his face for a moment. Then he shook his head. "I'm sorry, Kendra, It could have been different. You shouldn't have been so difficult." He strode past her.

"No!" she shrieked. "Don't leave me!"

Something moved in the channel. Kendra froze, a wave of algae-bearing swamp water lapped ashore. She peered into the darkness. As opaque as the night was, she could see some blot of inky blackness standing out against the far shore of the canal. A new fear took hold. Spots appeared before her eyes; she realized she had stopped breathing and forced herself to inhale.

Another wave of canal water washed ashore, bobbing the collection of boats in the tide. Then to Kendra's horror, a massive segmented leg entered the torchlight, thrusting down into the muddy water at the edge of the canal. Then another appeared, before the body of the creature entered the light.

Kendra screamed.

It was the size of a semi. For all its bulk, the beast looked as though it could move quickly. Slime glistened from a leathery skin riddled with warts and boils. Four lobster-like claws clicked open and shut in horrible anticipation. A shark's mouth riddled with dagger-like teeth adorned a stubby, reptilian head. Its eyes were cruel and possessed of a malevolent intelligence.

From behind her, Red's lilting voice drifted forward. "All hail, the King of Belmer!"

"All hail!" rose the thunderous response of the assembled men.

"Mighty King, please accept these gifts and bless our family with good fortune and prosperity for another ten years."

Like a shock wave, the unspoken response thundered through Kendra's mind.

Granted.

The beast scuttled forward on ten chitinous legs to the nearest pole. Kendra saw that she was still—mercifully—unconscious. The beast's pincers scissored forward, the woman's body unhinged, spraying blood in a fan pattern behind her. Small clawed arms reached out, bringing the bloody remains to its eager mouth. Kendra could not look away. Foam and blood dripped from its jaws and the rending sounds of crunching bone flooded her ears.

At this, the other women who were still conscious set to wailing. Kendra was scarcely aware, as she wailed along with them.

The monster worked its way down the poles, repeating its deadly feast. Too quickly, the King came to Kendra. Its demonic gaze bored into hers. "Please, don't!" she moaned.

A rasping, dry chuckle was the answer. Pincers settled about her body, sliding between her and the pole. She thrashed and yelled but could not move.

With a sudden snap, she felt herself born aloft as the ropes gave way under the beast's serrated claws. Spines pierced her skin but in her fear, she barely felt it. The King drew her to its slavering mouth. She struggled, to no avail. Kendra twisted, she saw David, Sam, and the rest, assembled like a choir some distance behind the poles. Some wore rapt, dreamy looks, with adoring smiles and shining eyes. Other looked haunted, sickened even.

Her eyes fell on David. Tears streaked his cheeks and his lips moved. He refused to meet her gaze.

She cursed his name even as she forgave him, knowing he would not forgive himself.

INSATIABLE ANGOLA
by J.M. Lawrence

I had shucked a hundred thousand oysters by my 17th birthday and my calloused, scarred hands told the full picture of all the hours I spent at the barroom, which had wood-bladed fans on the ceiling and an ancient pool table, with whiskey stains on the cloth. It was filled with Vietnam veterans and oil men, many of whom had never left Louisiana, who told me of blown oil rigs and fingers pinched off by drilling chains, of innocent sons lost to crack dens and grandfathers who had been worked to death at Angola.

They ordered oysters by the dozen, splashing the shells and shaved ice with lemon juice and shallots and vinegar, chewing them greedily and washing them down with Jim Beam until their eyes shone with red fire and they zigzagged home in pick-up trucks to wives who trembled when the front door opened.

Why didn't I leave it all behind for LA or New York? My mother was hooked on crack and dragged a watermelon and strawberry cart through the cobbled streets of New Iberia. But there was another reason I spent my days at Napoleon's, shucking oysters and calling the cops when one of the patrons took his repressed anger out on another. My father had been convicted for a murder he didn't commit and sent to rot in Angola. He disappeared one day and they told us he'd escaped through a sewage shaft.

I felt his presence on the fringes of my mind, like echoes in an abandoned mine shaft. I was sure he was circling, hovering, waiting to make contact when the powers-that-be struck his name off the shoot-to-kill list. That's why I spent 12 hours a day in a sweaty barroom, breathing in the sickly smell of spilled beer on sawdust and shucking oysters until my hands were calloused and scarred. If he wanted to find me he would not have to look far.

The day was heat hazed and close, the smell of moldy pecan husks thick through the barroom windows, when I received the letter.

And with that my father moved from the fringes of my mind to the forefront.

◊ ◊ ◊ ◊

On Saturday morning, the air was filled with brine off the Atchafalaya. I woke up at 5am and couldn't get back to sleep. Once the sun had risen I drove to New Orleans to meet a stocky PI who frequented Napoleon's.

I showed him the letter and he read it slowly, face pinched like trodden fruit, eyes roving like clock hands that float rather than tick. His chest rose and fell gently, like waves lapping a shore. Eventually he threw the letter on his table. It slid off and drifted lazily to the floor. My mouth was dry.

"It's fake."

My head twitched. "Excuse me?"

"I said it's fake."

"Thanks. But I just wanted to know where you think he'd be."

"You don't like what I'm sayin'."

"I've not see him in three years. Why would someone want to fake it?"

"Why would anyone want to con another man?"

"You tell me."

He pursed his lips and looked out to the courtyard, where a few potted plants were roasting in the sun. Then he turned back.

"You payin'?"

"No, I'm not payin'. Just like you never paid when I gave you oysters on the finger. Or when I stopped guys about to stomp you."

He sniffed. "I got a family."

I picked up the letter and held it out.

"Yeah, me too." He held my gaze and didn't blink. I turned on my heel. The man had spent his career digging unwanted children out of garbage cans and telling fathers their sons had been beaten to death in the county jail. Who could blame him for being a cynic? But I wouldn't let his cynicism and anger stop me seeing my father again.

◊ ◊ ◊ ◊

My house had three rooms with a rotten veranda I'd always wanted to fix up. It stood downstream from an antebellum mansion which had served as the home of a wealthy plantation owner. My house was built where the slaves' quarters had once stood.

I walked through the screen door and into the living room. The wooden TV was switched on, the picture blurry.

"Ma, look at this, I heard from him. He's in town."

The pipe had fallen on the floor and scorched the wood. She was strung out. Her eyes roved over mine and to the letter.

"Ma, it's Dad. He's ready." I smiled at her. Her mouth opened slowly and closed again. She shrugged her shoulders and scrambled down to the floor to get her pipe. I turned away in disgust.

I sat down and put the letter on the table. In the cold light of my crumbling house, it looked dark and threatening. I could reduce it to memory in the flick of a cigarette lighter and go back to Napoleon's.

Perhaps that was the better way. If it was real, he would contact me again.

I closed my eyes and breathed deeply. Then I heard whimpering, quiet at first, then louder. I felt it in my stomach, like broken glass in a washing machine. My hands balled to fists. I didn't want to see her weeping over her broken crack pipe for the second fucking time this week.

When I opened my eyes, she was knelt on the floor, holding the letter in her hands, tears leaking down her face. With one nicotine-stained, blistered finger, she stroked the words on the page lightly. When she let go, the letter sailed through the air and landed face down on the ground.

I went over and pulled her against me, holding her head to my stomach. She looked up at me and in her eyes I saw pinpricks of the light which used to shine before she fell into crack, before her husband was sent to rot in Angola, before her only son threw up concrete walls to protect himself against the pain.

I picked up the letter, folded it up, and put it in my pocket.

◊ ◊ ◊ ◊

There are places in the world where suffering is woven into the air and every breath fills you with the last gasp of a dead soul. From history books and ex-cons I had learned this about Angola, that great, sucking wound in the side of the state. They closed it several months ago, and it is with universal agreement the people of Louisiana want to forget it ever existed.

Napoleon's was emptying out, the wooden blades of the ceiling fan throwing shadows across the stained pool table that danced on the edges of my vision, drawing me in, promising me secrets.

An old man sat at the bar. I had never seen him before.

I felt his eyes on me.

"You fixin' to enter the rabbit hole, you."

I blinked the shadows away and smiled at him. I was fixing to right a wrong. That was all.

"I don't blame you," he said. "A man shouldn't fear what he's destined to find." He drank his whiskey and got to his feet.

I shucked a few oysters and ate them, chewing the salty flesh slowly.

It made sense, to be honest. They had stolen his soul in Angola. It was the last place they'd expect him to hide.

◊ ◊ ◊ ◊

From my vantage point I could see the twisted claws of barbed wire, the razed and crusty soil covering the concrete foundations of two iron sweatboxes that had been used to roast prisoners alive. I could see the remains of Camp A, a bright yellow strip of housing with rusted windows and a muddy-looking roof, where slaves were originally quartered. The whole place buzzed with a dead, drifting sort of energy.

I held up the letter in my hand and read my father's words. His handwriting was different and his tone more curt, but he had been on the run for years. There were no instructions about where he'd be – just a date. He'd been kept in Camp H, so I thought I'd start there.

I walked across crunchy leaves and squashed cigarette packets toward the perimeter fence. The sun was setting like an inflamed eye on the horizon. I eased the wire into the cutters, opened a hole and slipped through onto land that had seen untold amounts of human suffering. My soul felt heavier and as I passed over the sweatbox foundations I thought I heard the groans of wretched men climb like pathetic puffs of air from the ground below.

For the first time, I was aware of my heart beating.

I carried on walking, past the sweatboxes, looking toward the ugly yellow façade of Camp H, like a row of rotten human teeth pockmarked with iron-barred windows. Many of the metal slats on the roof had been blown or stripped off.

I stood facing it and breathed deeply. The building was just concrete and paint. Nothing more. The door was slightly ajar. I stepped forward and pulled it open, allowing light to spill inside. The concrete floor was cracked and stained with food and blood. On the wall was fresh graffiti, a kid's joke, designed to scare.

LEAVE.

The paper was new and recently folded. I stepped forward and picked it up. There were two words on there: *Red Hat.* I swallowed, throat working, and stepped back outside into the light.

◊ ◊ ◊ ◊

Red Hat Cell Block was the most restrictive prisoner housing unit at Angola, constructed after an escape attempt in 1933. Inmates slept on iron bunks without mattresses and relieved themselves in steel buckets which were emptied intermittently. The block was named after the red hats inmates wore when working out in the fields.

It stood about 20 meters to my right and I turned and walked forward toward the squat building, bars as thick as boa constrictors in the windows.

Crunch, crunch, crunch went the piles of leaves under my feet, like crumbling bones.

I pulled the door and it swung open to reveal a grey corridor and solid steel doors on either side, which led onto cells so small inmates had been unable to fully stand. At the end of the corridor, on the right hand side, was a wooden door.

My heart thudded in my chest and I put my hand on the letter in my pocket.

I stepped forward tentatively, one foot after the other, feeling the doors on the walls go past me as I neared the end of the corridor. When I reached the end, I turned to my right and pushed the door open.

◊ ◊ ◊ ◊

He was older and frailer, but it was unmistakably him. I couldn't feel any part of my body when we locked eyes. We embraced and I held his thin frame tight. He felt light as air, as though part of his soul had been sucked out by the oppressiveness of his time in this hellhole. When we parted, he had tears streaked through the dirt on his face.

"Weren't hardly nothin' I could put in that letter 'less they found me."

"I know."

"I wanted to see you so bad, you."

I nodded and smiled. He put an arm around me and we walked out of the room and into the corridor. The sound of our feet echoed through the building. He gestured toward the door. "Let's go sit out and talk. There's a lot we gotta say and the moon don't judge."

Outside the night was beginning to chill. We sat on a rock and looked up into the shining face of the full moon. For a few minutes we were silent. I sensed he needed time to gather his thoughts.

"I want you to know I always loved you, Dave. You was always on my mind. I went down for that murder and nothin' changed. Nothin'."

I nodded, throat tight. "I know. I missed you so much."

He rubbed his hands on his torn, ripped trousers. "How's your Ma?"

"Bad. On crack. Sometimes she doesn't know where she is. She was never the same, Dad. We don't really talk."

He looked away, toward the moon. "I miss her. Lordy I miss you both so bad." He glanced behind him nervously. I saw the heat rise in his cheeks and the tendons in his neck tighten. He swallowed slowly and pulled me into a hug. I felt his chest against mine. He put a hand on the back of my head and held me tighter and I felt the top of my t-shirt moisten with his tears. Eventually we pulled apart.

"This is a bad place, Dave."

He smiled at me, but there was something else in his eyes. He opened the palm of his left hand – there was blood leaking from one finger. I had seen that coppery red colour once before that night.

The graffiti.

Oh, my God, I thought.

"RUNNNNNNNNNNNNNNNNNNNNNNNNNNN NNN!" he screamed. I heard horses whinny and looked round. Prison guards, clothed like overseers, were racing toward me, their bodies tensed, steam and dirt rising in gusts at the horses' feet.

I couldn't believe what I was seeing. They gained on me as I ran for the perimeter fence.

◊ ◊ ◊ ◊

Angola was coming back to life.

As I ran, hands breached the dirt of the muddy path and tried to ensnare my ankles but I ran harder, faster, away from the Red Hat Cell Block and toward the fence. To the right I could see open fields where inmates were broken by the weight of sledgehammers and the whips of their masters, cooking beneath a red-hot sun. I saw Camp H alive with faces at the window and guards walking out the door with blood on their whips.

I ran past the ground where the iron sweatboxes now stood again, getting closer to the gap in the fence. I urged myself to go faster, to escape the stampede behind me, and when I was only meters away a man materialized in front of me, blocking the gap.

He looked slightly familiar, his face slightly shadowed, with a swollen jaw of chewing tobacco. His ears were long and hairy, the cap on his head set at an angle. On his right arm was a tattoo of a gallows. He was of medium-build and not innately strong, but he had the solid midriff of someone who had built his strength with the whip and the cane.

He grinned at me, showing grimy teeth, the skin of his face taut and weathered. He held a whip and his hand tightened greedily on the handle.

"You're here now, boy, and you're gonna feed me."

When he spoke the ground groaned, like there were souls down there rotting in the darkness. I heard men screaming in pain as their backs were torn to shreds. Whether this man had ever been real was a question I couldn't comprehend. He was evil, though — that much I knew in an instant.

I turned and ran into an onslaught. The guards were coming down off their horses, whipping the backs of deranged inmates. Their faces were snarling, angry, but their eyes were filled with remorse so intense that even in my situation I pitied them.

They surrounded me, grabbed my legs and arms, their grips as hard and as strong as steel. They were synchronized and moved slowly, like it was ritualistic, and carried me like a stuck pig to one of the iron sweatboxes, its outside flecked with rust, a cigar-sized hole chiselled through the centre for oxygen.

The adrenaline burst and I started to cry. They opened the sweatbox and placed me almost lovingly inside. I trembled as the door swung shut again. It dawned on me what I was up against—the sum of all the human greed and masochism and bloodlust which defined life for so many in these parts.

And then, in an instant, agonizing heat. The sun was atop the world and on fire. The air was so hot it singed my throat as it went down. My legs went numb, and when I collapsed from exhaustion the space was so narrow I couldn't fall to the ground. I wondered how many more breaths I could take before my lungs failed to work and I crumbled into the ground and became just another soul in the evil heartbeat which consumed this place.

I felt my brain give out, my vision flash, my soul being pried from my head in a red-raw grip. I was being absorbed, to dwell for eternity in this place, a pawn to capture the innocents that feed the dark.

But the door to the sweatbox swung open and in poured cooler air. My father's face appeared, covered in welts, one eye destroyed, and he grabbed my face and kissed my forehead, light as air. The guard approached a few paces behind.

"Go, Dave. I love you."

I ran without thinking.

My father turned away and leapt at the guard, who knocked him back to the ground.

"You will suffer for this," he said. "Tie him to the stone! I will make him bleed."

I staggered across the ground, past Red Hat and Camp H, toward the break in the perimeter fence I had opened. Behind me I could hear sounds of pain and torture and when I glanced behind me I saw the guard lashing my father with a giant whip.

Then I was through the fence and outside the boundaries of Angola. I turned, and all I saw were decrepit buildings, which had once held unspeakable suffering, and the foundations which once held iron sweatboxes, all sitting dormant and silent in the night air.

The moon had returned to the sky, fat and full, as if it had been there all along.

My father had disappeared, but I knew he was somewhere, and that he was suffering.

◊ ◊ ◊ ◊

I had shucked two million oysters by my 21st birthday and had drunk more liters of Jim Beam than I cared to remember. Although I had left Napoleon's for another oyster bar, I still visited, sitting at the back near the wood-bladed fan that turned overhead.

The bartender was handy with a knife. He looked about seventeen.

A lone man sat at the bar, turning a whiskey glass with his fingers and occasionally taking sips. He wore a cap and looked hefty, like he used to be strong.

The bartender was smiling. The man looked up.

"What's brightened your day?"

"My ex-girlfriend's back in town. Wants me to meet her."

"Well, that's great. Don't ever keep a girl waitin'. Not least one wants her way with you." He winked, finished his drink and left.

I smiled at the excitement in the boy's eyes. He'd be back at work the next day with a grin fixed to his face.

Then I stood up suddenly, my heart thudding, and ran out the door. Where had the man gone? There was no sign of him strolling down the sidewalk, or a car just about to leave. I went back into the bar.

"Who was that guy?"

The bartender looked up and wiped his oyster knife on a cloth. "Dunno, never seen him before."

"He used to come in when I did your job."

He shrugged. "I never seen him."

"He had a gallows tattooed on his arm."

I went back outside and looked across to the bridge, then went down a few side roads and checked for cars, but there was no sign at all of the ghostly guard of Angola who gorged on the blood of innocents.

◇ ◇ ◇ ◇

I stood at the perimeter fence, looking out over the abandoned buildings that made up one of the cruellest places in the country.

There were other gaps in the fence. But I don't believe the prison fed on everyone who rattled around its bowels in the dead of night. It knew who it wanted. Perhaps it was only those with links to the men who had been worked to death in the fields, or roasted in the sweatboxes. I had heard the bartender at Napoleon's had an uncle who had served a 10-stretch for homicide.

I took a flask of Jim Beam out of my jacket and drunk from it, enjoying the burn in my throat, feeling waves of hate rise inside me. Unspeakable things had been done to people here. I just couldn't get over that.

Was my father still out there, somewhere, more than a wisp of memory? I wanted desperately to go and find him, but fear held me captive. If they had finished him, if he no longer existed, I would end my time in the sweatbox and become an eternal part of this horrific place.

There had to be another way. But I just didn't know what it was.

I stood there for a long time, taking long glugs of Beam and when I had finished the bottle, I threw it over the fence and watched it smashed on the dirt floor. The site stayed silent, the buildings lifeless.

"Fuck you, then."

I turned and walk away, disgusted with myself.

◊ ◊ ◊ ◊

I had shucked five million oysters by my 65th birthday but my hands were now useless and twisted. I was done shucking oysters and drinking bourbon Beam.

From my vantage point I could see the buildings still standing and the fence still intact. Something other than a lack of economic viability told ruthless developers to turn away from this place and forget they had even seen it.

Did it know what I had planned? It must have known I would try and make contact with my father again. Perhaps it had laid waiting, ready to take me, or perhaps it had since moved onto others and accepted that I had been one of the few who had gotten away.

At the perimeter I opened a hole in the fence with bolt cutters and stretched it wide open. From my jacket I took out my best oyster knife and nicked at my wrist, then pushed my wrist through the hole and held it over the ground. The first droplet of blood dripped out, and I turned my wrist over, letting it fall to the ground.

Figures rose from mist and formed into inmates. Guards came into being with a whip crack and cantered around, yelling instructions. Over by Camp H, someone was being flogged.

Then, by the Red Hat Cell Block, a man clambered out of the ground and ran forward, shaking off invisible chains. My heart fired hard. His eye was still destroyed and one arm was gone. His teeth were bared and I could see his chest heaving.

Every eye in the complex turned and looked at him run.

From behind a pile of oil drums I saw the guard with the tattoo ride out. He gained on my father, his legs kicking the horse with dirt-trodden spurs.

As my father was just a few feet from the perimeter fence, I jammed the knife as hard as I could into my throat and moved it around, doing as much damage as possible. My vision blurred but I stayed conscious. He fell through the fence and I moved forward, slipping through the gap onto the grounds of Angola. The guard rode into the fence and was thrown back, landing in a heap on the sodden earth.

I couldn't really breathe but I saw my father turn and run up to the fence, hammering on it, his teeth bared, his eyes filled with panic. He was staring at the blood I was spilling. My strength was going. I heard boots hit the sod behind me and looked up. The guard was grinning, his hand tightening on his whip, the tattoo on his arm bulging.

"Now you're mine."

He whistled, and inmates materialized and started running over, their eyes shining with pent up energy that had been carved into something hateful by their incarceration.

My life force was leaving me, but I would not be dying.

As my father pummelled the fence, his hands torn by the chain links, his face morphed into something young and human again.

As for me, I turned back to embrace my future.

That great, sucking wound in Louisiana would live on, and I would form one more wretched part of it.

That much suffering can never be erased.

WITHOUT A TRACE
by Melodie Romeo

N ew Orleans is both a melting pot and a mosaic, with its French language and Spanish architecture, mingled with African cuisine and uniquely American music. Ethnicities and races mix there as easily as ingredients in a recipe. And while the Big Easy may be best known for Jazz, Mardi Gras, and fine dining, it is also hailed as the most haunted city in the U.S. Curiosity seekers are drawn to the mysterious and macabre of New Orleans like moths to a flame—even at their own peril. Everyone knows of the numerous ghost sightings, the pinnacle of paranormal activities, the accounts of how the first vampires set foot in the New World right there in the old French Quarter—these legends are well documented, if not always believed. But the following tale, while originating almost as early as the colony itself was founded, persists to this very day, perhaps with even more occurrences since the ravages of Hurricane Katrina. But before we get to today, travel back with me to a time when Louisiana had just become a state and New Orleans was our most essential port, to a time before most of the ghosts so widely celebrated had been created, to a time when science was beginning to replace superstition. What mystery lurked in the shadows along Grunch Road?

◊ ◊ ◊ ◊

Southern Louisiana, 1830's

The night was as black as death, cloaked in a shroud of steamy humidity and stillness. It was as quiet as a tomb—no chirp of crickets, croak of frogs, nor hoot of an owl; no breeze rustled the leaves and no moon or stars illuminated the opaque sky. Raoul, his wife Janette, and their young daughter Arabella lay sleeping under mosquito nets with windows open wide in their modest farm house in Little Wood. Suddenly through the silence sounded the bark of a farm dog; then another, louder, more frantic. The commotion was so loud and insistent that it woke the Hernandez family from their slumber. "Mon Cher, shouldn't you go see what the matter is? I have never heard the dogs barking in that tone before," said Janette, brushing her long strands of brunette hair back from her face.

Raoul sat up, running his fingers through sandy curls and rubbing his eyes with the back of his hand. "Could be a coyote or thief." Just then the bleating of goats and lowing of cows added to the din. Raoul pushed the net aside and climbed out of bed. "I'll check." He slipped his feet into boots while Janette lit a lamp.

"Take your musket, and I'll get you a lantern. It is as dark as pitch tonight." She moved with ease around the house in her long white night gown.

"It's probably nothing," he muttered, but continued to prepare to scare off whatever intruder was disrupting his farm.

Janette handed her husband a lit lantern then touched her hand to his. "Be careful. Don't you recall a few weeks ago when the Lavigne's livestock were killed by something?"

His steel blue eyes locked on hers of deep brown. "I will," he promised, and then strode out the door into the blackness. Even though past midnight, it was still quite warm outside in the marshy, southern Louisiana summer. With his father's old musket in one hand and the light in the other, he took steady steps toward the dog pen. "What is it, fellows?" he called to his two herding dogs. As he neared he could feel their distress, their need to chase away whatever was out there. Raoul opened the gate and the two canines bolted toward the small pasture where the livestock were kept. Primarily Raoul planted sugar cane to generate cash for his moderate farm, but he kept a small herd of goats, a few cows, a horse, and some chickens and pigs as well. Janette managed a small vegetable and herb garden. But the swampy location of Little Wood, just a few miles down Grunch Road from the city of New Orleans, made a large-scale operation impossible.

The dogs were out of sight, yipping and yelping, snarling and growling. Then one let out a high pitched cry of pain; as he made haste in that direction, Raoul was passed by his other dog, running back toward the house. That worried him. He had never known his dogs to flee; they were bred and trained to protect the herd and protect their master. There was less bleating and lowing now, but that, too, unnerved the farmer. He held the lantern higher as he proceeded with more caution. "Who's there? I have a musket and I know how to use it," he called forcefully. Raoul's father had come to New Orleans from Spain as a youthful soldier during the city's Spanish period and had taught his son to shoot.

Raoul almost tripped over the body of a goat lying on the ground in front of him. It was lifeless, but still warm, with blood trickling from three holes in its neck. For the first time, a twinge of genuine fear started in his chest and he swallowed hard. "I will shoot you!" he called louder into the foreboding night. After a few more steps with the light raised he spotted something in the distance–a pair of glowing red eyes. In a flash he aimed and fired his weapon at them. The report was followed by the sound of rustling in the brush. Raoul took a moment to reload and then followed. "A coyote, no doubt," he muttered. "Killing my animals. Well, we will see about that." As he breathed in, Raoul scrunched his nose and skewed his mouth. "What is that awful stench?" But he didn't have time to worry about that. Weapon and lantern in hands, he marched forward, leaving the clearing of his pasture into the wilderness that surrounded it.

The shot awoke Arabella, and she rushed to find her mother. "Mama, what is it?" she asked, rubbing sleep from eyes which peeped out from under long, red curls.

"Something is outside; Papa is going to chase it away," she said as she took the six year old into her arms. "It will be alright. Now, back to bed for you."

But it wasn't. She waited and waited, but her husband did not return. She paced the hardwood floors all night and at first light dashed out back. The one remaining dog refused to come out from under the porch. She ran across the dew covered grass to find several dead goats covered in blood, but no Raoul. Next she gathered the neighbors for a search of the area, but they found nothing. It was as if he had disappeared without a trace. Determined, she asked one of them to stay at the house with Arabella while she went to town for the constable. After hitching their horse to the buggy, she set off up Grunch Road toward the Crescent City.

A rap sounded on the guardhouse door early on Sunday morning. Constable Charbonneau was napping at his desk and had intended to keep doing so. No one was supposed to be bothering the constable on a Sunday morning; they should all be at mass. But he wasn't; he had been ordered to post, probably as some sort of political punishment for not voting "properly" in the mayoral election. He waited, hoping whoever it was would just go away, but instead the pounding grew louder and more insistent. "I'm coming," he grunted.

All six-foot-four of the constable lumbered over to the door and opened it. He hulked over the petite woman yet she immediately took charge, invading his post like an enemy army. "My husband has gone missing," she declared in French, "and you are going to find him—and the others." A few stray brunette strands had escaped her knot and cascaded down to land on her blue and white dress which was covered with a full-length bibbed white apron. Janette was the daughter of a French fur trader and his Native American consort. She felt lucky indeed to have found a nice man like Raoul; she did not intend to just let him disappear into the blackness without a complete search and rescue.

His graying brows shot up, brown eyes blinking. She strode in right past him and proceeded to take up residence in his office. The aging Charbonneau did not have the energy to traipse about trying to find an errant husband.

"How long has he been gone, Mrs. ... ?" he inquired, speaking his native tongue as well.

"Someone, or something, was disturbing our livestock last night," she explained. "He went out with his musket to investigate and never returned. I am Mrs. Hernandez; and you are?"

"I am Constable Charbonneau, at your service." He inclined his head even if his speech sounded a bit sarcastic to her. "My dear Mrs. Hernandez, your husband has not been gone long. Perhaps he got lost."

She stabbed him with an intent glare. "Goats and cows are being killed and people are going missing all in the vicinity of Grunch Road, Constable; he is not the first. And no, he didn't just get lost; he grew up here. Now I want a missing person's report filed and I want people out looking for him—or whoever killed or kidnapped him." It was at once evident in both her dress and manner that Mrs. Hernandez was country folk.

"Mrs. Hernandez, I am with the New Orleans Police Department and you are obviously from a rural community. Why not go pester your sheriff?"

She straightened and raised her chin even higher. "Little Woods is too small for its own sheriff and in such close relation to the city that it falls under your jurisdiction. I demand that you perform your duty."

He shot her a look of annoyance and sighed, running a hand through his salt and pepper hair. "Alright. I'll fill out this report and assign an officer to the case, but I can't guarantee he can start today."

No sooner had Charbonneau sat down and taken out pen and paper, Janette placed her hands firmly on his desk and leaned over him in a menacing fashion. "I may not be upper-crust society, Constable, but I know my rights and your duty." Her brown eyes darkened with sheer determination. "I am not leaving until someone comes to search for my husband."

He raised his eyes to meet hers. "Suit yourself." Then a big hand began to scribble down the report. Charbonneau did not consider women to be men's equal; he generally didn't consider them at all, but there was something singular about this exotic, demanding wife who spoke fluent French and would not take "no" for an answer.

Satisfied, Janette retreated a few steps and took a seat, feeding the constable the information for his report. When he was done, he pushed himself up from the desk and lumbered over to the door. He poked his head out peering up and down the street. "François," he called in an authoritative voice and motioned for the boy to come.

A lanky black youngster of thirteen, all arms and legs, snapped his eyes to Charbonneau and trotted over. He wore sandals, calf-length tan pants, a blue shirt, and a wide-brimmed straw hat over his closely cropped wool-like hair. "Yessir, Massa Constable." He popped instantly to attention in front of the law enforcement officer. "Wha' do ya need?" François was a free Negro who earned his keep running errands, making deliveries, and the like in that part of the city. He was trustworthy—as far as any white person was willing to trust a darky.

"Do you know that new officer, Mr. Thomas, from New York?"

"Ya means da one wid the round, gold eye-glasses?" he inquired making circles out of his fingers and holding them up to his big, round eyes.

"Yes, that one. I need you to go find him and bring him back here right now. The sooner you get him here, the bigger your tip will be."

His eyes lit up as a wide grin revealed snow-white teeth. "No one's faster dan me, Massa Constable. I'll have 'im here in a jiffy." With that the lad sped off toward St. Louis.

François was true to his word returning in short order with Quinton Thomas in tow. Charbonneau smiled to himself as he thought of the small triumph of dumping this case on the new man—one who nobody liked. Thomas was a young college graduate from New York with the fancy title of "detective." Everything about him made the natives nervous. He talked with a strange accent, didn't know a word of French, and had a way of making himself look smarter than the other officers.

"Good morning, sir, Constable Charbonneau," he greeted eagerly as he sucked in air after trying to keep pace with François. "What is the emergency?" Quinton stood in sharp contrast to the man shadowing over him. He was only five-foot-eight with a slight build. His black hair was cut short and his youthful face sported a fashionable mustache and goatee. Instead of a uniform, he sported civilian clothes of brown trousers and a white shirt with an intricate cravat. He had given up on wearing a suit coat as he would have in New York. He removed his spectacles and ran a handkerchief over his sweaty face as he awaited a reply. The Yank was certainly not accustomed to the direct sun and high humidity of southern Louisiana. He felt as if he was trying to breathe under water and found he could not stand it outdoors without sitting in the shade periodically. The locals had taken to making him the butt of their jokes. But at least Thomas was good-natured about the teasing, admitting he struggled with the heat.

"This young lady's husband went missing last night from their farm in Little Woods along Grunch Road. Apparently there have been several unexplained disappearances from that area recently. I am giving the case or cases—you'll have to look through the files for the others—to you. You are a detective, so I expect you to detect what has happened to these individuals. Personally I suspect they have been eaten by alligators, but it is also possible they were kidnapped by pirates and pressed into service, or murdered by some madman who lives in the swamp. This is New Orleans, Mr. Thomas; do not discount any possibility, no matter how absurd it may seem."

"Yes sir, I will do my best," he replied and replaced his glasses.

"Thomas, this is Mrs. Hernandez." He presented the young man to his determined guest, glad to no longer be dealing with this nuisance of a woman.

Quinn took a seat beside her and listened while she recounted the tale again. Then he informed her he needed to look up the files on the other disappearances before proceeding out to the scene. "I will be out to your place later today," he promised before they left.

Detective Thomas carefully sorted through the files. There was one from last week, two from the week before, and three more over the past two months. "Hmm," he said in a soft audible voice. "They seem to be getting more frequent since the first disappearance." Charbonneau ignored him. "But they aren't all men, and one was even a small child, so I don't think we are dealing with pirates seeking a crew." As he continued to investigate the files he also spotted reports of livestock killed, drained of their blood and bearing a mark of three holes in the shape of a triangle. "How odd," he mused, not initially thinking the cases could be related. "This area has all sorts of strange things occurring." It suddenly occurred to Quinn that no one was listening and he was essentially talking to himself. After that he kept his musings in his own head.

After about an hour of researching the files, Detective Thomas walked over to his boss who was eating little square pastries covered in powdered sugar and drinking coffee. "Has anyone been investigating these disappearances? Have any bodies been found?"

"Eh, and no."

Quinn scratched his head. "They just disappeared without a trace. Shouldn't these instances have received more attention?"

"I'm giving them to you; now, give them attention," he barked. "If you haven't noticed, the city is rampant with crime. Important citizens are being robbed and assaulted. We are short of manpower and have to prioritize. Residents of the city take priority over the rural bunch." Then he narrowed his eyes, speaking softly and intently to the young newcomer. "I have seen this kind of thing before, about fifteen years ago. There was a rash of disappearances on Grunch Road. The constable then looked into it and he vanished as well. Before you proceed, I would strongly advise to you learn more about some of the local lore."

"Lore, sir?" he inquired, quite puzzled.

"Go see Madame LaRoux on Descartes. She is a local authority on all things strange and bizarre. And Thomas," he said in a tone of warning. "Watch your step."

"I am a student of science, Constable. I don't see how bizarre folklore can help."

Charbonneau sighed. He didn't want the Yank dead. "Just talk to her before you go out there."

"As you suggest." Quinn inclined his head and exited the guardhouse on his way to find this Madame LaRoux.

◊ ◊ ◊ ◊

A little bell tinkled when Quinton Thomas entered the shop at 524 Descartes Street. As he gazed around the room he felt as if he had left America and traveled into some foreign world. The room was dark, lit by candles with heavy curtains drawn against the sunlight. There were shelves with jars of chicken feet and something that looked like tiny eyeballs, claws and teeth hanging on cords, masks, little dolls, dried leaves and powders of every color. There were colored crystals and pots and baskets. To one side was a round table with strange cards and a large opaque crystal ball.

"Hello?" he questioned. "Is anyone here?"

For a moment the strange shop was still, quiet like death. He could smell incense coming from somewhere and felt uneasy, very out of his element. "This was a bad idea," he muttered to himself and turned toward the door but was stopped when he perceived a presence enter the room.

"Going so soon?" The voice was low and smooth, with an exotic Caribbean accent.

Quinn turned to face a most singular looking woman. She was taller than he by an inch and twig-like. Her cheekbones and high arched nose looked Caucasian but her skin was a dusky color a shade darker than the Italian and Greek olive tan. He couldn't see her hair as it was wrapped in a bright orange scarf on top of her head, but her eyes were brilliant amber. She had a powerful presence which filled the room leaving little space for him to occupy. "Wha - - I mean who are you?"

An amused smile tugged at her lips. "I am Madame LaRoux and I presume you are here to see me. You are not one of my regular customers and you do not have the appearance of a mere visitor to our fair city."

Madame LaRoux was a quadroon, one quarter Negro and three-quarters some variant of white. The Crescent City abounded in racial and ethnic variety. It was also home to the largest free black population in the nation. There was a very complex social structure which thrived upon exceptions to every rule. Still, mulattos, often referred to as 'high yellow', occupied a rung on the social ladder higher than some white residents—particularly the poor. They were bankers, shop keepers, ship captains, even slave owners. And often the slaves didn't even act or live as an outsider might expect, having free reign of the streets and taking on extra jobs to earn cash money. Quinn Thomas was a long way from mastering the intricacies of the new society into which he had been flung.

He breathed a sigh of relief then tilted his head to one

side in curiosity. "You sound rather like a detective."

"I am a seer," she replied modestly, inclining her head. "As it says on the window." She motioned and he looked over his shoulder to spy the word *fortune-teller*.

"Ah." As a scientist, Thomas believed that all fortune-telling was false, but if she was really observant she might pick up things about her customers through a good job of deduction and fool them into thinking she knew all their secrets. "I am Detective Quinton Thomas. Constable Charbonneau sent me to see you for background on a case I'm working on."

"Yes, the good constable. It is wise you have come. Please," she motioned toward the table. "Have a seat."

"Ma'am, I'm not here to have my fortune told, nor do I believe anyone can truly tell fortunes."

"Don't worry, Mr. Thomas. I would not presume. I am just offering to make you more comfortable while you ask your questions."

"Oh," he replied with an embarrassed frown. "Thank you."

"Would you like some tea?" she offered in hospitality. "I have a pot ready in the back."

"No thank you; I won't keep you long. Now then, to the point." He pushed up his glasses and then looked into her face. He could tell she was a much older woman, but it certainly did not show in her smooth features. The hands; that's where he could see her age, but not the face. "There have been a number of unexplained disappearances of people along Grunch Road leading out of the city in recent months, the most recent being yesterday." He registered recognition in her eyes and expression. "Have you heard about them?"

"Not this time, but before, many years ago." Thoughts, memories flooded in. "And I have felt uneasy since ..."

"So," he continued without waiting for her. "What do you know about them?"

"What do I know? Nothing and everything; everything and nothing."

Quinn scrunched up his face. "Madame LaRoux, you aren't making sense."

"Well, you see, I don't know anything specific about them, but I do know a secret. Some people attribute all mysterious disappearances to vampires, but I know they like to stay close to the city." She paused, eyeing his dismissive expression. "But it could be someone, or something else. *They* may be angry again."

"They?"

She gazed at him in such a way as to measure his response. "The albino dwarves, a reclusive clan who are said to hide from normal people to avoid abuse."

He gave her an incredulous stare. "Albino dwarves? That sounds like something from a fairy tale. Has anyone actually seen one, or are they just part of someone's vivid imagination?"

She rose slowly as if her joints ached and walked to a nearby cabinet. She opened a drawer, withdrew a paper flyer, and bringing it to the table, handed it to the detective. He adjusted his glasses and took a look. It was an advertisement for Colonel Payne's Menagerie and Sideshow. "See the amazing albino dwarf," he read printed there along with a hand-drawn picture of a stubby man with abnormally disproportioned head and hands, skin as white as cotton, and pink eyes. "I don't believe most of these side-show freaks. Most are regular people made up to look weird; some may be unfortunates who cannot find any other employment."

"But," she interjected thoughtfully. "What if this fellow was captured and taken against his will to make money for the menagerie?"

"If that was the case," Quinn mused, tapping his fingers on the table, pondering the possibility. "I imagine they would be angry."

"Angry enough to take some *regular* people in retribution do you think?" Her brows raised expressively in emphasis. "Let us see if the white dwarf is real and if he was captured." Madame LaRoux focused her gaze on the crystal ball in the center of the table, moving her hands around it but not touching it. She hummed a single tone and then closed her eyes in concentration.

Quinn glanced at her and frowned. Smoky strands began to circle inside the globe and immediately he closed his eyes. "I do not wish to be hypnotized, mesmerized, or be-spelled in any way," he declared sternly. Before he dared open his eyes, his other senses told him that something most unexplainable was happening. At first just a whiff, the aromas grew stronger: roasted peanuts, taffy, and peppermint sticks ... animals and manure ... smoke from cheap cigars. He could hear the sounds of children giggling, people talking, the clip-clop of horse hooves. At the loud trumpet of an elephant Quinton's brown eyes popped open wide. He knew he was sitting at a table in Madame LaRoux's shop, but then again he wasn't—he was at the traveling Menagerie. There were tents and wagons and people bustling all about.

"Step right up folks and see the amazing Faulk Brothers easily command the largest creatures on Earth!" a man wearing a top hat and waxed mustache announced. Quinn glided through the crowd with the impression they could not see him at all.

"This way, curiosity-seekers," a short stout man called. "See the strangest aberrations known to man. The fat lady, over 600 pounds, as big as a carriage, and the strong man who can lift her up. See the beast-boy of the bayou, so hairy he appears part bear, part boy. And ladies and gentlemen, for the very first time in our show, see the freak albino dwarf—a full-grown bearded man a mere three feet tall and whiter than cotton."

That caught Quinn's attention; that is why he was in this trance, or whatever it was. He decided to pursue the questions of how this was occurring later and focus on the matter at hand—to determine if this albino dwarf was real. He slid easily past the stout man unseen and into a striped tent. Inside was a wagon constructed with bars like a cage for animals and a lock on the door. Inside was a sad little man with skin as white as a New York snowfall. Quinn immediately began to study him. A few white hairs sprouted from his oversized head and a bristle of whiskers protruded from his square chin. He sat on a wooden bench, short legs dangling above the floor, stubby fingers hanging from short arms intertwined in front of him. His downcast pink eyes displayed the sorrow of one without hope. He was dressed only in dark trousers speckled with dirt, his disproportionate feet, each bearing six toes, jutting out from their hem.

A pang of compassion swept over the detective as he examined his subject. He was alone and caged like an animal. Suddenly he found himself in the midst of a group of paying inquisitive patrons thrusting themselves up to the bars. "Wow," one uttered in amazement.

"Ooooo," squealed another. "He's so weird looking."

Utterances of, "What a freak!" and "Can he talk?" "Where did he come from?" and "He can't be real," poisoned the air within the tent. A cruel boy poked the little man with a stick to get him to move.

"Come on, Crum," prodded the stout Menagerie worker. "Stand up and let them see you better. Say hello to the nice people." With a sallow expression, he slid off his bench, took a few steps, and turned slowly in a circle. Then he said a few words in Cajun. Quinn thought he was wishing them "good day." Like a mist the crowd faded away and only the freak-keeper remained. "Here, Short Stick," he said with a sneer. "Eat your gruel." He slapped down a bowl of something, which did not look or smell edible, on the plank floor of the wagon cage. "And if you don't perform better tomorrow you won't even get this!"

Quinn closed his eyes, bile rising from his belly in contempt for how this unfortunate was being treated. He had seen enough. When he opened his eyes again he was back in the fortune teller's shop sitting at the table which he had never left.

"Well?" Madame LaRoux inquired. "Was he real?"

Quinn rested his chin in his hand propped by an elbow on the table. "I am not even going to ask how you did that. I am not convinced it actually happened, or what it was I think happened. But Constable Charbonneau said to keep an open mind because strange things happen in New Orleans. It would appear that the albino dwarf is real, was taken against his will, and is being mistreated. I suppose his clan may in truth wish to enact vengeance."

Her eyes glinted at him with a knowing sparkle. "That is indeed the case, Mr. Thomas. So keep that open mind while I tell you of another impossibility. The old Spanish who had come up from Mexico used to tell of a rare creature who appeared like a cross between a reptilian and a canine. It was about four feet in size, weighing a hundred or more pounds, and could either walk on all fours or just its hind legs. They say it would kill livestock by piercing them with its three fangs—two upper and one from its lower jaw—and then drain their blood." Between the hypnotic rhythms of her voice, the incense wafting through the shop, and all of the peculiar artifacts lining every shelf and even hanging from the walls and ceiling, Quinn began to feel a spooky unease; yet, he could not help but listen intently to her tale. "The Spanish called them 'chupacabra', which means 'goat sucker'. But when similar incidents began to be reported here, oh maybe forty or fifty years ago and periodically since, they were always in the same locale—near or along Grunch Road. So locals who are inclined to believe such a creature may exist call it the grunch. It could be conceivable the albino dwarfs, who some just call 'swamp people', imported or conjured one or more of these chupacabra to guard them from members of civilized society who think nothing of kidnapping and exploiting unfortunates. It is said they raise goats to feed their beasts and they often attack people's livestock as well."

"Conjure?" His pecan-brown eyes widened. "Surely you don't believe anyone could conjure a creature, especially some uneducated, inbred albinos?"

"Perhaps they would not have the skill or intelligence to do so, but Marie Laveau certainly does."

"Who is that?"

Madame LaRoux made a dramatic pause before continuing. "She is the Voodoo Queen. Surely you have heard of her. She is very powerful," she stated with conviction.

"I do not mean to give offense, but I am an educated man of science; I do not believe in Voodoo, Hoodoo, or fortune-telling for that matter. But as a man of science I am forced to admit that new creatures are being discovered every day. It could be possible that this chupacabra migrated north from Mexico and now inhabits the swamp near Grunch Road. It must be shy or rare or more sightings would have been reported. But surely a grown man would not be its best target for a meal. It would be logical for a creature that size to stick with goats, pigs, small animals and the like. And if it is that reclusive, why would it venture out onto a frequently traveled road or populated area?" Quinn voiced his contemplations, as was his habit.

"Good questions for you to consider, Mr. Thomas. But if the albinos trained them and reward them for keeping passers away from their camp ..." Her voice trailed off as she offered the suggestion.

Quinn still held the circus flyer. "May I keep this?" he asked.

"Yes, you may," she answered politely with a nod. "You intend to go looking around, do you not?"

"That is my job, Madame," he answered matter-of-factly.

"Then you will wear this talisman," she said as she rose and selected a leather cord with a small gray leather pouch, an alligator claw, and a few feathers strung on it.

"As I said, Madame, I do not believe in talismans, curses, or any such things. I would feel foolish to accept it."

"You would be more foolish not to," she insisted in a commanding voice, her eyes flashing.

The shop room seemed even darker to Quinn than it had when he came in despite his eyes having time to adjust. "That is very kind of you, but I don't see how it could ward off dwarves, albinos, or blood-sucking swamp creatures. I have a pistol and I believe it will do quite nicely." He smiled at her confident in his knowledge and ability.

Her shoulders slumped and she lowered her head placing the talisman on the table. "As you wish." When she raised her gaze to him he could have sworn she suddenly looked older than the woman he had been conversing with.

Quinn rose from the table and addressed his hostess politely. "I do want to thank you, Madame LaRoux, for your hospitality and for answering my questions. You have been most helpful indeed. With your historical knowledge of the area, I am sure I will have a need to call upon you again in the future."

"I do hope that will be the case," she replied, her voice uneasy. "But I must warn you, do not go alone. Surely there is another officer who can accompany you in your investigation."

"I will look into it. If anyone is available, I promise not to go alone." He smiled an almost boyish grin at her.

"Arabella!" her mother called out the back door when she returned from town.

"I swear, Mrs. Hernandez, she was right here on the porch a minute ago." Beatrice, the youthful neighbor girl who was supposed to be watching the child, wrung her hands, worry and fear drenching her features. "I have been watchin' her real close, and lands sake, I don't know where she could've runned oft to!"

Janette gave the tow-headed girl a stern glare. "Bella come on in the house now," she called again. She battled to keep dread at bay; after all, it was mid-day, and who or what would be out at high heat? She held her breath for what seemed like minutes, but in only a moment the jovial, red-haired little girl came bounding out of the bush into the short grass skirting the vegetable garden.

"Mama, you're home!" she beamed.

Janette cast serious dark eyes on her. "Where have you been and why did you leave the yard without Beatrice? She is here to watch you while I was away. That was very wrong of you." Despite her anger, relief flooded Janette and she scooped the child into her arms for a hug.

"Sorry," she offered apologetically. "I was just down at the creek playing with my friend Mona."

"You know I don't want you going down to that creek

without an adult. There are snakes and snapping turtles and alligators and who knows what all that could hurt you. I don't know why Mona's parents would let her go down there."

Arabella's bottom lip poked out and a pronounced frown covered her face. "They don't let her either; she just sneaks off every now and then so we can play together."

"Well you can play with her in the yard or in the house," her mother stated emphatically. "I don't recall meeting Mona; is she black, white, or brown?"

"Oh she's REALLY white," Arabella replied enthusiastically. "And she's littler than me and she's funny." The child giggled, her green eyes twinkling. "She has six fingers on one hand. But they all work," she added. "Sometimes they don't all work but hers do. And she has the prettiest pink eyes. Mama, can I get pink eyes, too?"

Color drained from Janette's face. A lump caught in her throat and a sick feeling began to rise from her belly. Beatrice thought Mrs. Hernandez was about to faint. She reached a hand to her arm to steady her and gave her a concerned gaze. "Are you alright?" asked the sturdy blue-eyed blonde teenager.

Janette dropped to her knees and grabbed her daughter holding her tight. "You aren't allowed to see this Mona anymore," she demanded. "Those people are dangerous!" Her eyes were wild with terror at the thought of the albino dwarf swamp people taking off with her only living child, and the thought that they may have disposed of her darling husband.

She straightened to her feet abruptly, a hard, cold, steeled expression on her face. "Go pack your things. We are leaving."

"But Mama!"

"Do as I say. When Detective Thomas arrives we will

go back to town with him. We are not staying here another instant. It isn't safe, don't you understand?"

"But Mama, Mona isn't dangerous—she's just different." An exaggerated pout consumed her small face. "She said grown-ups would act like this," and she crossed her arms in defiance.

"Mona may be nice, but her clan is ... is," she searched for the word. "Not right, not normal, and yes, dangerous. Now you go pack like I said or you'll be leaving here without any of your things!"

She turned to the neighbor girl, now pale with fright and trembling.

"Albino dwarves? I thought they were a myth."

"So did I, but with my husband and the others going missing and now this pale child Arabella sees at the creek, I'd rather get out of here before she goes missing, too. You should tell your parents so they can make an informed decision. Now, run on home."

The freckled girl nodded, quivering, and unable to speak. Then she did as she was told and ran home.

◊ ◊ ◊ ◊

Being Sunday, Quinton Thomas had a hard time convincing any other officers to accompany him and honestly he didn't try that hard. But young François was happy to tag along as his "man at arms" for a few coins. Quinn didn't think he would need assistance, but thought a witness may prove helpful. Being city dwellers, neither had a horse, so they set off walking out of town along Grunch Road. François was wise enough to advise Mr. Thomas to bring a skin of water along, which he did, and finished off long before arriving at the Hernandez home.

The heat affected the New Yorker more than locals,

but even locals would not have set out on a several mile hike at midday. The duo stopped frequently as Quinn would began to feel nauseous and need to sit in the shade. "How do you cope with this climate?" he asked his young companion.

"I's used to it, massa," he answered. "Mama says always wear a hat and drink lots o' water."

"Good advice." He tried to smile and wiped his face with his soaking handkerchief. "And why do you call every white man 'massa'? Your family is free."

"Mama says it's a show of respect. You wants white folks to like ya, so you shows 'em respect."

He nodded in understanding. "I think I can make another mile now," he said rising to his feet.

"Yessir, it's not far off now." François took the lead and Quinn, pistol tucked tightly into his belt, followed. "You should git yo'self a hat, Massa Thomas."

He allowed a little chuckle. "Yes, I should." The detective contemplated his wet shirt thinking aloud. "I suppose all this sweating makes you wet and the wetness helps to cool your body a bit. But it is so sticky and smelly. I must also use more Florida water."

As they rounded a curve in the worn path traveled by horse, wagon, and foot, Quinn spotted a medium sized farm and whitewashed house. He noted about 20 acres of tall sugar cane plants to the far side. Mrs. Hernandez sat in a rocker on the front porch fingering her rosary. The moment her eyes swept over them, she jumped to her feet rushing to meet them. "You came!" she exclaimed.

"Certainly, Madam. I am a man of my word. Now, if you could show me the area he was searching?"

Janette led them around back to the small fenced pasture, pointing out the dead goats. Flies whirled about the bloated carcasses and the strong smell of decomposition turned his stomach. "I left them for you to examine," she explained. "He had a lantern and a gun. I heard one shot. Also, we have two dogs and one of them is missing as well. I heard it yelp in pain and the other came running home. He must have followed whoever— whatever—it was into the swamp beyond that fence." She pointed toward the north side of the property where pasture gave way to thicket.

"Thank you, Mrs. Hernandez; I'll take it from here. Just in case there is still danger about, I'd like you to return to your home."

She hesitated, wanting to go with them. Then she nodded. "Mr. Thomas, when you return to town my daughter and I are going with you. I have learned disturbing things about the swamp people and do not wish to remain here."

Quinn paused, giving her a curious expression. "What things have you heard?" he inquired.

She paused, not knowing exactly what to say. "I now know that there *are* swamp people out there; they may not be friendly."

"I see. I will be on the lookout for them." As Janette made her way back to the house, Quinn considered her statement regarding 'swamp people' and wondered if she meant the albino dwarves.

Suddenly Quinn heard an unexpected rustle in the shrubs beyond the fence.

"François, I'm going to check the brush around this area. Maybe I'll find a body—hopefully a live one. You stay here and holler if you hear or see anything or anyone suspicious."

It wasn't until that moment that François became nervous about the outing. Whatever took Mr. Hernandez could be nearby. He rocked on his feet, his head snapping this way and that, trying to watch in all directions at the same time. "I's be fine," he said in feigned confidence. "No need ta worry 'bout François."

Quinn stepped delicately through the brush, not wanting to disturb the scene as he spied for signs of a struggle. As a sea of scrub and tall grass formed behind him and the swamp rose in front of him, he spotted blood. "Ah, ha!" he exclaimed aloud and took a closer look. "Signs of a struggle." There was blood on some leaves and on the ground with various scuff marks and boot prints in the dirt. And something else ... Quinn bent down to examine the strange foot print. It was the size of a large dog but had only 3 toes with deep toenail marks in front of the pad indentions. He pulled out his notepad and jotted down a sketch of the foot print. Pushing himself to his feet, he replaced the notepad and scrunched his nose. "What is that smell?" he asked himself. Then he shot a glance over his shoulder at the boy whose head he could barely see above the thicket. "François, do you smell something odd?" he shouted.

"Yessa, don't know what it is though." He continued his vigilant watch, nerves on edge.

Quinn removed his glasses to wipe away the sweat droplets which were making it impossible for him to see clearly. *Crunch.* Abruptly his head shot up and he began to scout with hearing as well as impaired sight. "Who's there?" No response. Slowly he withdrew the single shot pistol and held it at the ready. "This is Detective Thomas of the New Orleans Police Department. I am armed. Please identify yourself." The brush behind him crackled. Quinn spun around but saw nothing. An inexplicable uneasiness swept through his mind and body as all the words of Madame LaRoux flooded back through his consciousness. A strange animal she had told of ... it could be nearby. The air was so still and heavy Quinn found himself fighting for breath itself. *At least I'm in the shade*, he thought. Another sound, this one a vocalization, an animal cry of some bizarre variety he could not place. He spun around, firm grip on the pistol, trying to locate the creature. The crack of a twig snapping and he popped his head to the left. There it was, staring at him with red eyes. It was the size of the largest dog he'd ever seen, but it wasn't a dog at all. Grayish green skin covered its muscled frame which stood on all fours staring at him with those eerie red eyes. Slowly it rose up on its hind quarters to a height of almost five feet. The nearly cat-shaped face seemed to grin at him with a wide mouth containing two upper fangs and one in the center of its lower jaw. Along its back sprouted a row of spines poking up as protection from potential foes. But nature had not equipped this strange beast with protection from bullets—or at least that is what Quinn hoped as he steadied his aim with both hands and squeezed the trigger.

With a poof of smoke the pistol kicked back in his hands and the beast screeched, staggering back with blood streaming from its chest. It writhed and flailed and fell back into some ferns. Quinn warily stepped closer, wanting to study this new species, but he was cautious. It may not be alone. He scouted to the left and right and behind him, and then began to reload his weapon. "What's happenin'?" called François. "Was that you that shot?"

"Stay there!" he called. "It may not be safe."

The boy rocked back and forth on the balls of his feet, trying to be taller, straining to see what was going on. But he stayed in the middle of the open field. Unbeknownst to them both, more of the vicious monsters were hiding in the swamp, stealthily inching their way toward Quinton Thomas. Once his firearm was reloaded, he moved in to examine the peculiar being. From a yard away he watched it take its last breath. His eyes were fixed on its alien features, the three-clawed feet, the anomalous head, the hairless hide. Then all at once he was struck from behind, nearly throwing him off balance. A cry sounded loud in his ear as talons tore into his shin. He pointed the pistol over his shoulder and pulled the trigger, the report almost deafening him. A yelp sounded but the injured freak of nature held on and sunk its fangs into his soft flesh.

"HELP!" he cried out in agony and fear. Terror swept over his being like a dark, menacing shadow. There was no hope to reload his gun, so he used it to bash the creature about its head.

In pain itself, it let go, dropping to the ground like a discarded backpack. Quinn spun toward the farm house where he could see wide-eyed, panicked François, frozen in place, staring at the battle. He moved his mouth but no words uttered forth. Then he waved an arm frantically in warning. Quinn managed two hasty strides before a third grunch assailed him, and plunged its needle-like teeth into his neck. This time blood spurted out rapidly, gushing into the beast's mouth and down onto Quinn's shirt. Immediately he felt woozy and perceived it was a severe wound. He also struck this one in the head with the heel of his weapon, but the angle was bad and he was weakening. Try as he might, he could not dislodge his attacker.

Collapsing to his knees, he cried out to God in desperation to save him. The bloodied, injured grunch raised itself from the dirt and slowly circled in front of the detective. It seemed to be studying him with its glowing eyes as it swayed its head back in forth in a gentle rocking motion. Quinn could barely see as blood flowed freely from his wound and unconsciousness tried to claim him. With blurry eyes he watched helplessly as what appeared to be a grin widened across its face, eyes lighting with seeming delight. Suddenly it sprung forward, jaws open, at Quinn's face. He let out a blood curdling scream which resounded through the trees and swamp, down the road, and perhaps all the way back to the city as well. Birds and animals stopped, listened, and fled at the soul piercing anguish of the sound. And then there was silence.

A short time later three weary yet satisfied reptilian-canine creatures dragged a blood drained, motionless body into the camp of the mysterious albino dwarves. One albino was tall; one dwarf was peach colored. Many had grotesque, distorted features typical of inbreeding. One older squatty, bearded man who appeared to be the leader stepped forward inspecting the still warm corpse by torchlight. "Humph," he snorted in disapproval. "Scrawny, but he'll have ta do. Blaine, if you will do da filletin' and Maggie will do da berlin'." He pinched the man's lifeless arm. "At least da skinny mullet's tenduh." Several in the group laughed. Mona was not among them; the hour being late, she was tucked soundly into bed.

◊ ◊ ◊ ◊

François fled back to the police station and told Constable Charbonneau and everyone he met about what he had witnessed, but they were disinclined to believe the hysterical babblings of a black boy. Janette and her daughter moved away from Little Woods and for a while there were no more disappearances. But every so often down through the decades and centuries strange occurrences and creature sightings were reported on Grunch Road. When the Crescent City had consumed all dry land along the river bank, engineers began to build levees and canals and drain the swamp so the mammoth metropolis could continue its expanse. What once was the village of Little Woods became part of the Ninth Ward.

◊ ◊ ◊ ◊

Modern Day

Katrina was so tired of people comparing her to the hurricane that destroyed New Orleans she had simply changed her name to Trina. She wore cut-offs, a white tank top, and a passel of wine-red and black braided weaves in her hair. Her elbow hung out of the open window of her boyfriend Jarvis' white Ford pick-up. They turned off Haynes Boulevard just before sunset onto a gravel road which didn't appear to go anywhere. "Is this the spot that Latoya and James were telling us about?" she asked and then threw her chewed gum out the window.

"This is it; nice and private." An anticipatory grin crossed Jarvis' face. His dark eyes sparkled at Trina as he slowed the truck, pulling into a partly graveled, partly grassy area.

She looked around. "It is far enough off the main road, but is it safe?"

Jarvis put the truck in park and turned off the key, making a nonchalant gesture. "Well, we could go to your house where your Dad will be all up in our business all night or to my house with the pesky little brothers and sisters." Her countenance dropped at the thought of those alternatives. "Beside," he added with a wide, confident grin, "you have the rather large and strong center of the football team to protect you."

Trina smiled back at him, a twinkle in her brown eyes. "Well, that is true." They both leaned into a kiss. As Trina slid across the seat closer to her beau, she spotted something odd out of the windshield. "Look, Jarvis." She stopped moving, giving the curiosity her full attention.

Irritated at the interruption, he glanced in that direction. "A goat. Now what is a goat doing out here? Let's go see it."

Morning headlines: White Ford pick-up found abandoned off of Haynes Boulevard in the Ninth Ward; two teenagers missing.

Charon Coin Press

◊
Charon Coin Press
◊

AUTHOR BIOGRAPHIES

TERESA BERGEN

Teresa Bergen's first horror story was a tale of giant tarantulas taking over the world, written in fourth grade. Since then, her writing and interests have been wide-ranging. She regularly writes health, fitness and travel articles for many websites. Lately, she's obsessed with cobras. Her current fiction project is a trilogy about a teenage girl who unlocks her latent cobra powers. She's also working on a celebrity bio of Adhira, the famous leucistic cobra who rampaged through Thousand Oaks, California in 2014. Teresa's novels *Killing the President* and *Madame Tingley's Organ* are available on Amazon.

STUART CONOVER

Stuart Conover is a father, husband, blogger, published author, geek, entrepreneur, and horror fanatic. He lives in the Chicagoland area and when not delving into the land of horror, comics, and science fiction he spends his days working in IT and his nights with his family. Passionate about writing you can find his work in a variety of outlets and books. When does he sleep you may ask? No one is sure that he does!

http://www.StuartConover.com
https://www.facebook.com/StuartConoverAuthor
http://www.twitter.com/stuartconover
https://plus.google.com/+StuartConover

J. LAMM

Born in Baton Rouge, LA, in 1976, Jay Lamm began his foray into writing when he published his first essay, *The Dark Tunnels of the Bone Box: the Astonishing Story behind the Music of Mr. Doctor* in 2003. After receiving a BA in Criminal Justice and English from Southeastern Louisiana University in 1999 he pursued a life of music, releasing one solo album of planetarium/new age music and two studio albums with his mercurial metal band, Cea Serin. He has been a featured performer and touring musician with Cirque Dreams, and also provides session work as a bass player, keyboardist, and vocalist for other studio albums. Jay Lamm has also written and recorded original music for movies, television, web series, and planetariums. Lamm maintains a steady blog schedule on his personal website where he writes about music related topics and "how-to" instructionals— mostly geared toward bass guitar and live performance issues. Lamm currently serves as the Administrator for the Louisiana Art & Science Museum's planetarium/science blog where he frequently contributes articles relating to science, recent discoveries, and space exploration. Currently, Lamm is working on a third album with Cea Serin, a solo album, and his first novel.

J.M. LAWRENCE

Jamie Lawrence is a 28 year old journalist, currently editor of human resources publication *HRZone*. He is originally from the flat, straw-colored county of Suffolk on the east coast of England but now lives in historic Bristol on the west coast with his fiancée Sophie. Jamie has been writing for much of his life and has had several short stories published, as well as non-fiction that reached #2 on the New York Times Children's Bestseller List. Aside from writing he likes watching films, staying fit and healthy and traveling to new places around the world. Like many writers, he's currently working on his first novel, which will of course take the world by storm and win every prize under the sun. Of course.

EDWARD MOORE

Edward Moore is a Brooklyn transplant currently living and working in the San Francisco Bay area as an environmental professional. He enjoys music, movies, writing and experimental cooking, always trying new recipes and ideas from his imagination and food/culinary publications. In addition to having several stories published on the Internet, he has had fiction printed in *Futures Mysterious Anthology Magazine*, *Berkeley Fiction Review* and several anthologies.

JONATHAN S. PEMBROKE

Jonathan S. Pembroke is a lifelong fan of speculative fiction. He cut his teeth reading superhero comics and grew up on the works of Stephen King, Michael Moorcock, and Larry Niven. He has published a number of short stories in small venues over the last decade. His first novel, *Pilgrimage to Skara*, a low-fantasy/sci-fi story set far in Earth's future is ready for publication and is searching for a home. Jonathan has also started on the first book of an unrelated fantasy series, *Princess of the North*. He blogs and babbles about writing and multimedia speculative fiction at http://flinthatchet.wordpress.com , which is not safe to be read by anyone.

Jonathan graduated from a large midwestern university

and served in the military for twenty years. He now lives in the American Southwest with his wife Lisa and a horde of unruly dogs.

NATHAN PETTIGREW

Nathan Pettigrew was born and raised near New Orleans, and lives in the Tampa Bay area with his wife and two rabbits. His story "Dog Killer" was named among the Top 5 Winners and Finalists of the *Writer's Digest* eighth annual Popular Fiction awards for the Crime category. Publications featuring other stories include the award-winning pages of *Thuglit*, and *DarkMedia Original Fiction and Poetry*, where Nathan's story "Roland The Conqueror" was one of their "most popular pieces of original horror fiction to date" when it appeared in 2012. Visit Nathan at Solarcide.com or follow him on Twitter @NathanBorn2010.

HERIKA R. RAYMER

Herika R. Raymer grew up consuming books - first by eating them, later by reading them. Her mother taught her the value of focus and hard work while her father encouraged her of love literature and art; so she has been writing and doodling off and on for over 30 years. After much encouragement, Mrs. Raymer finally published a few short stories and has developed a taste for it. She continues to send submissions, sometimes with success, and currently has a collection of stories in the works. She was the Assistant Editor for a science fiction magazine and Lead Editor for a horror magazine, so has a healthy respect for proofing and editing. A participant of the voluntary writer/artist/musician cooperative known as Imagicopter,

Herika R. Raymer is married with two children and a dog in West Tennessee, USA.

MELODIE ROMEO

Melodie Romeo is a native of Vicksburg, Mississippi. She earned a bachelor's degree in Music Education from the University of Southern Mississippi and a master's degree in History from the University of West Florida. Ms. Romeo is a retired school teacher who currently travels the country as an over the road trucker with Prime, Inc. Her first book, *Vlad, a Novel*, was published in 2002. She has short stories published in anthologies by Seventh Star Press and Charon Coin Press. The mother of two, she resides in Utica, MS with her partner of 18 years.

You can find Ms. Romeo on Facebook on her personal page, her novel page and also a page for an anthology containing her story. Those links are:

www.facebook.com/melodie.romeo
www.facebook.com/VladANovel
www.facebook.com/pages/Southern-Haunts/417536915003428

ARMAND ROSAMILIA

Armand Rosamilia is a New Jersey boy currently living in sunny Florida, where he exacts revenge on his enemies and neighbors alike by writing them into his *Dying Days* zombie series. And not in good ways. He has over 120 releases to date, with more coming. He is also a radio and internet DJ and runs *Arm Cast: Dead Sexy Horror Podcast*, with interviews from the best authors, etc. in horror. He loves talking in third person. http://armandrosamilia.com and armandrosamilia@gmail.com if you want to chat.

B.A. Sans

B.A. Sans is a renaissance man, switching between author, musician, teacher, and parent among many other duties. His first published work was a children's story entitled *A Grand Dilemma* that appeared in a popular online children's magazine. From there, his attention turned to adult horror and suspense, having numerous short stories published in a plethora of magazines and anthologies. His first novel, a young adult paranormal romance entitled *From the Flames*, was published in 2010. His second novel, *Age of the Damned* began taking the world by storm a year later. In 2012, he came back to his roots and published his first children's book, *Damselfly in Distress*. Presently, B.A. Sans is performing around Las Vegas with his band Geezus Cryst & Free Beer and imagining the wild carpet ride of literature that will become his next piece of writing.

Ambrose Stolliker

Ambrose Stolliker lives in the Pacific Northwest with his wife and son. He is a former newspaper reporter and magazine writer and currently works in marketing at a global technology company. His work can be seen in *Ghostlight Magazine*, *Sex and Murder Magazine*, *Hungur Magazine*, *Sanitarium Magazine* and *The Tincture Journal*. His Civil War ghost story, *Reckoning in Spotsylvania,* will be published later this year in *Stupefying Stories*. Keep up to date with Mr. Stolliker's ramblings on writing, reading and all things Seattle sports by subscribing to his blog (https://ambrosestolliker.wordpress.com/) and following him on https://twitter.com/horrorwriter74.

ANTHONY WATSON

Anthony Watson is co-founder and co-editor of Dark Minds Press (http://www.darkmindspress.com/) with Ross Warren. Dark Minds Press has published two collections of dark fiction – *Dark Minds* and *Darker Minds* and are currently working on the third book in the series, *Darkest Minds* for publication in 2015. As well as this, he runs a horror review blog "Dark Musings" (found at: http://anthony-watson.blogspot.co.uk/) which has had over 28,000 visits.

He has been published in *State of Horror: Louisiana,* and in *Sanitarium* Magazine with his short story *Elder's End.* He also has a story, *Interstice* scheduled for inclusion in the next Spectral Press annual ghost story anthology. 2015 will see publication of his war/horror novella *Winter Storm* in a seven author collection.

Anthony lives on the Northumbrian coast amongst its rolling hills, ancient castles and unspoiled beaches with Judith and their dog Themba. He taught himself to play guitar ten years ago but still can't manage a barre chord.

ABOUT THE EDITOR

Jerry Benns started writing when he was quite young. However, he began seriously writing in 2010 by launching his blog, TripThroughMyMind.com. Since then, he has expanded the site to include interviews with authors, book reviews, and sections to encourage building the writing community. Jerry's deep-seated enjoyment of reading and writing now has him embarking on the exciting journey of publishing by launching Charon Coin Press.

In 2014, after becoming the editor for the State of Horror anthology series, Jerry pursued the opportunity to purchase the series, and others, in order to release them under his new publishing company, Charon Coin Press. Jerry brings his experience from his previous marketing/branding company, as well 15 years of experience as a networker and project manager to Charon Coin Press.

Jerry continues to write short stories and his blog, in addition to working on an urban fantasy series. He also looks for ways to share the love of reading and books with the next generation.

◊

Charon Coin Press

◊

◇

Charon Coin Press

◇

◊

Charon Coin Press

◊

◇

Charon Coin Press

◇